"Wow...w
from beginning ~~to end,~~ ~~this~~ ~~story~~
I could have even imagined..I mean I thought this was
gonna be good...but wow... Severance had me on a roller
coaster of thrill, romance, and mystery and wouldn't let
me off the ride till the very last page."
   -Haley, Ya-aholic

"Severance was an amazing second installment of the
Volition series! It was an official mind blower! If you enjoy
angels, romance, and action then this is the perfect series
for you!"
   -Cassandra, YA Reader Extraordinaire

"This book was just as great as the first book,
Volition, jam packed full with action, suspense, and
romance...This is definitely a must read and you go buy it
right now."
   -Books Ahoy

"Personally, I think I like this one better than the
first, now I loved the first, but this one definitely has more
action/suspense and I'm an action/suspense kind of girl. I
think Shawn Kirsten Maravel had it going on with
Severance."
   -Loves All Things Books

"If you enjoyed Volition, you will love Severance. Just
like the first book, twists and turns will keep you glued to
the pages. The story and characters are truly lovable."
   -Gabby, What's Beyond Forks
   ★★★★☆

Severance

Shawn Kirsten Maravel

Chapter

1

*S*harp pain was splintering through my body from every direction. Pain. Something I had only ever experienced through very diluted senses. My shoulder blades. They were throbbing and ached relentlessly. The tingling burning pain like needles in my skin was almost more than I could bear. From the flat of my back, I squinted against a light so bright I couldn't be sure that my eyes were even open at all.

Charlotte? Where was she? Had I saved her? As I propped myself up against my unrelenting affliction, I could feel a new pain coming from my chest and back. My hand rushed to the spot and I winced against it. Inch for inch, my body was frantic, trying to warn me of the injuries that it had taken onto itself.

I had jumped in front of Charlotte in the bank, unveiling myself as her guardian angel, knowing that I would be taking the bullet that had been meant for her. When I'd found out that the shooter was Matt, the bartender who'd drugged her the night I'd first made myself known to her, I knew that he wasn't simply trying to intimidate her. He was out for revenge. Armed with one chance to save her, I did what I had to.

I looked down and noticed that beneath my hand there was no sign of blood or even an indication that I'd been shot at all. I was dressed in the same clothes from that evening but when I lifted my shirt to investigate my injury there was only un-penetrated and even skin. I winced again as pain shot through the invisible wound that lay nestled between my ribs and clear through to the muscles in my back.

As I breathed in and out of my lungs, I could feel a very distinct and real sensation that I was drowning. My left lung was full of liquid. Full of blood. I coughed, noticing that I hadn't left any blood on my hand, and righted myself again. I couldn't focus on my pain as long as I knew that Charlotte could still be in danger.

Sitting up and breathing through suffocated lungs, I tried to grab hold of something that could take me back to her. Looking around, I noticed nothing. There was white, only white.

I'd been to this place before.

Limbo.

When I'd been created, it had been in this place that I'd waited for my assignment. I'd waited here for Charlotte. Rising to my feet in pure agony, I looked around in a panic. It wasn't often that I was uninformed. I'd come to this place the first time with all the knowledge I would need to welcome Charlotte into the world. I'd always known. But no matter how much I searched inside of myself, I could find nothing. There were no answers or instructions of any kind.

Feelings I couldn't understand began to flood my system. Fear. Panic. I'd never felt them before. Emotions that carried with them a distinct and tangible sting.

I threw back my head in desperation, "Why am I here?" I called out. "What's happening to me?" I coughed, my words equaling no more than a wasted effort.

There was no reply. I knew there wouldn't be.

Surged again with pain, I buckled under the weight of it. For a stay in limbo I was experiencing more pain than I might have expected.

Bracing myself on the ground in a crouched position, I closed my eyes. Trapped in a place out of reach and of no help to Charlotte, I felt my new emotions again; undiluted. My heart raced and I shook my head in defeat. I had told her that I would protect her. I needed to know—if this was the end— that I had.

I drew back in pain and found myself in the bank again. Matt was pointing a gun at Charlotte. I stiffened with determination. In the same instant that Alex pushed himself away from his desk and charged at the cloaked coward, I threw my body in front of hers and materialized just in time to absorb the blow. Then everything went black.

Gasping for air, I opened my eyes to the eternal white surrounding me. I was exhausted. Energy I had never needed in the past made itself known by draining from my muscles. My body craved something I had never needed before. Sleep. I wanted to give into it. To be taken by it and carried away to a place much simpler than the body I now found myself trapped in. Determined to fight the desire, I pushed myself up to rest in a kneeled position.

My only option was to wait. To hold onto what I could and wait. Closing my eyes, I tried to keep Charlotte close to me. With a weak smile, I could see her running through the hay field at her grandparent's house, her long dark hair dancing in the wind. She was only six at the time. The world was no more than a light breeze on the crop surrounding her. Like an ocean, she waded through it. Her smile was so big it could end a hundred wars; her bright green eyes were full of promise and hope for the future. Her fingertips brushed over the hay that was almost as tall as she was. She closed her eyes and continued to run, not afraid of anything. I stood mesmerized by her. I wanted to know the joy that she felt. But as I looked at her, I knew that the wish was wasted because I already did. Sprinkled with freckles from the Alabama summer spent with her grandparents, I knew right then that I loved her.

Eyes still closed, I began to hear the shaky melody of my harmonica seeping into the bleakness that surrounded me.

Emotion and distress were lethally wrapped around each note. Charlotte?

"Charlotte!" I shouted, standing up, forgetting the pain that took hold of my body. "Charlotte, are you there?"

I knew that she couldn't hear me if she was there. But the sound was enough to grab me, to hold me to hope, and with desperation that I'd never known before, I knew that I must find my way back to her.

Chapter

2

When the juror read Matt's sentence, I felt nothing. He was a man who'd targeted dozens of women, luring them in to take advantage of, and he'd gotten what he deserved. I sat motionless, crying internally, knowing that the bigger threat was still out there and pursuing me. Chris, a lawyer I'd come to respect and trust with my life, drove me home, allowing me to keep up a constant air of silence. He probably assumed that my reason for not talking was because Joel still hadn't woken up. And yes, that was a big part of it. But the real reason I couldn't form words or a smile about our small victory was because I wanted to scream at the top of my lungs that it wasn't over.

Alex, my old assistant manager, who I'd come to trust and had even considered something of a friend, was the real threat. Or at least real threat number two. Having Matt locked up was all well and good but convicting him had been easy. The guy had everything from unpaid parking tickets to attempted murder on his record. But Alex. Alex was the saint they'd forgotten to name a church after.

What he'd said to Joel's sleeping body echoed in my mind like a warning siren of what was to come.

"You have been screwing shit up from the very beginning. You had to show up at the club that night and take her from me. You couldn't just let me have her could you? I didn't let you die for one reason, and that was to cover my own ass. If you ever wake up, which you better pray that you never do, I am coming after you. And Charlotte will either be mine or dead."

And then he'd moved out of the chair beside Joel's bed, leaning in to inject his last hateful words into the air. *"You got that, angel boy?"*

I couldn't get over the fact that who I'd always thought Alex to be had been just a front. He'd always known exactly what to say and I had never detected even an inkling of anything else. But now I knew better. I couldn't be sure how serious he'd been but I had overheard him admit to something no friend would ever do. I needed answers and I needed to feel safe again. Without Joel, I wondered if either were within my reach.

* * *

It had been a week since Matt had been convicted. And a long and agonizing week since Joel had been shot. I couldn't even make myself cry about it anymore. My body had ceased its ability to do much more than breathe. I wasn't hungry or tired but I had no desire to be awake either.

I didn't walk out on my responsibilities and scare away the people around me with melodramatic tantrums. Giving in, curling up in a corner, and crying over Joel's shirt, soaked in his scent, wasn't an option. So I went to work and tried to ignore the failed attempt at lifting Joel's blood from the carpet beneath my chair, and the spackle covering the hole in the wall behind my station where the bullet had made its final resting place. I made polite efforts at making the new assistant manager, Linda, feel welcomed even though I knew that she could see right through my false smiles and fake laughs.

What I found myself doing more often than anything else was trying to work through the ways to prove that Alex was dangerous. Without hard evidence, there was not even a remote chance of removing him as a threat. Hell, most of the time, I had to convince myself that he was even capable of such a thing. It still felt so bizarre and unreal that Alex could really mean what he'd said. I even found myself wondering on occasion if I'd heard him right. Maybe I was going crazy. He'd always been a really great guy. His only motive had been a small crush that he'd never even acted upon in the past. It seemed unreal that he'd been the cause of all of this. That I'd been mistaking obsession for a mere infatuation for so long.

Had he been serious about killing Joel? About killing me? I certainly wasn't about to ask him. I had to believe that he had been serious. Would Matt remember him? If he did remember, would he tell me after I'd gotten him imprisoned for life? Probably not. Would Matt's word even hold up in court if he did tell me anything about that night involving Alex? If it did, would it be enough? With a tight knot in my stomach, I doubted it every time I ran the string of questions through my mind. The only solid answer I had was that I needed Joel back. He needed to wake up.

"Hey," I heard Heather say in a whisper as she peered into the break room. "How is he?"

Her dirty blond hair was pulled up into a ponytail and her pale skin was washed out by the florescent lights in the room. She smiled kindly and her modest beauty shined through as it always did. She slid into the seat opposite me and rested her hand over mine for a moment.

A genuine smile flooded my lips. The relief of having someone to talk to openly with was almost enough to bring tears to my eyes. Of course she still had no idea about Alex, but Heather knew what Joel was. While I wished that Alex hadn't been there to see Joel absorb the bullet that had been meant for me, I was happy that Heather had. She had always been a true confidante in my life and I felt relief in knowing that I wasn't alone. At some point I might need to tell her about what Alex had done. If Joel never woke up, something I was still very much in denial of being a possibility, I needed someone that I could turn to completely.

"I don't know," I said, my voice cracking. I cleared my throat and went on. "The doctors and nurses all give me this sympathetic look whenever I visit him, like they feel sorry for me. I hear them whispering about him. I know that while they say he's still stable they don't think it's going to last for much longer."

"I'm so sorry, Charlotte." Heather reached across the table and took my hand in hers again.

"I don't know what to do. Joel's not human. I don't know if my stubborn hope is reasonable or not." I hung my head and pushed my uneaten sandwich to the center of the table. "The doctors don't seem to think so."

"Well the doctors are stupid," Heather said, almost angry. "Joel is strong, he'll pull through. I just know it. I know that he would really appreciate that you spend every spare minute you have with him too." She smiled. "I bet he's up there in heaven preparing to come back down to you. He's getting his wings fluffed, abs greased..." She winked. "He's waiting for the right time to grace us with his presence. Men are like that you know? They need to make an entrance."

I smiled again, knowing that Heather was trying to bring me comfort where no one else could. Her guess was as good as mine but I doubted that he was greasing his abs. Still, my smile spread wider just picturing it. In the week that Joel had been in the hospital every condolence had been offered but the kind that I needed. None at all. Joel wasn't dead and I needed people to stop acting like he was.

"You know, Alex keeps calling and asking for you," Heather said, sitting back in her chair. "Don't you think one of these days you should answer? I've stalled him but I know he's worried. He did help—"

"I know. I know," I tried to sound more withdrawn than livid. Alex had done nothing but look out for his own best interest. "I just...I really can't talk about it right now."

Ignoring Alex's calls to my cell phone and at home had only led him to start calling my friends. I knew that I needed to answer one of these days if I wanted to keep up the façade that I didn't know what he'd done, but I needed to be able to talk to him without grinding my teeth first in order to do that.

"Yeah but Alex knows what—"

"Please," I begged, putting my head in my hands. "I just...I need time."

"I'm sorry," Heather said, putting her hand over mine again. "I can't imagine what you must be going through. Take your time. I'm here for you, okay?"

Heather rose from the table and made her way to the door.

"Hey," I called after her.

"Yeah?"

"Thank you. For everything."

"Don't mention it," she said with a smile and left me to sit and run through my internal monologue for what must have been the millionth time.

When I entered Joel's room at a quarter past seven everything looked as it had when I'd left. The rhythmic beeping from the machines to either side of him had begun to sound so natural that I didn't even notice them anymore.

With his eyes closed, I couldn't find comfort in his bright green eyes, though I saw him every time I looked at my own reflection. His dark brown hair was erratic as I'd always known it to be. Whenever the nurses had offered to comb it, I'd requested that they leave it be. His hands were heavy at his sides, unmoved, weighted by his inability to wake. His body was here but where was Joel?

I made my way over to the chair beside him and dropped my purse at its base. I pulled out the book I had been reading aloud to him. I figured that with limited topics to maintain a positive one-sided conversation, reading was the best way to stay connected with him. I had picked the book up the day after he'd been checked in along with a change of clothes for when he awoke. I needed to remain convinced that the day would eventually come. I curled up in the chair and smiled at the pillow and blanket that the nurses had brought me a few days into Joel's stay. This was home. Beside Joel was the only place I had any hope of finding peace.

Slipping my shoes off, I pulled my feet up to sit cross-legged and flipped through the book to find my place and began to read.

As I read to Joel, I allowed the world to slip away from us. Most of the time since he had been shot I was certain that I was becoming a bit unhinged. But beside him I could still find a faint sense of serenity…and more importantly, sanity. When I read to him we were connected. I could almost feel him smiling.

"Good afternoon, Ms. Rush," I heard a soft voice say in greeting from the doorway. "I could set my watch by your visits." Vicky, Joel's head nurse, had become my favorite staff member at the hospital.

Her long red hair was the most vivid color in the dreary white room and her freckles made her face friendly by default. Not that she needed them for the job. Vicky had not only read the book on bedside manner, she'd practically written it. She was the only person in the whole hospital that seemed to have any remaining hope that Joel would still pull through.

I watched as she checked Joel's monitors, chart, pulse, and changed his bandages. I marveled at the meticulous way that she handled him. When her eyes flashed up to his face and brushed the surface of it, I could tell that she was mesmerized. Every time she popped in to check on him I could see it. I couldn't blame her. Joel was more beautiful unconscious than Brad Pitt had been in his prime, fully awake.

"He's beautiful isn't he?" I asked.

Startled, Vicky turned to face me. I hoped that I was emitting the understanding and gratitude that I felt.

She smiled, her incandescent skin flushing immediately. "He is," she admitted, straightening up and crossing her arms. "I don't mean to stare..." she said, trailing off, almost ashamed. "The fact that he jumped in front of that bullet for you." She looked up and shook her head in bafflement. "A man that's willing to do that for a woman...that kind of beauty isn't just skin deep."

I was beginning to understand that Vicky was looking to Joel and his recovery as not only hope for him, not only for me, but for herself as well.

"I just need to know that all the decent guys out there aren't going to end up being sacrificed for the greater good. And the bad ones will just continue to infest the world like cockroaches," she added confirming my theory.

"You and me both," I said with a smile that didn't reach my eyes. I needed to know that more than anything else.

Making her way around the bed, Vicky eyed my arm. "How's it healing?" she asked, gesturing towards the bandage wrapped around where the bullet had grazed my skin.

Truth be told, I couldn't look at it. It was a reminder of too many painful memories that I already had a hard time keeping out of my dreams at night. A bullet that had gone through Joel's body had also nearly gone through mine. A very big reason for why I hadn't managed to get much sleep in the past week.

"It's fine," I said, trying my best to cover the bandage with my short sleeve. "Dr. Moore says it's healing well."

"That's good to hear," Vicky replied with a smile. "We don't need you getting checked in too because of an infection. You need to be right as rain for when Mr. Benedict wakes up."

I bowed my head in a smile then looked up through my lashes at her. Picking up my book again, I propped it open to where I'd clamped it down on my thumb when she'd entered.

Vicky made one last mark on Joel's chart then put it back at the foot of his bed and left the room with a goodbye smile. She and I had an understanding. While the rest of the hospital was taking bets on how long the coma patient would last, we were determined to believe that he would wake up.

Chapter

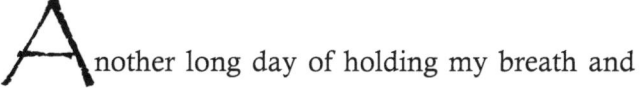

3

Another long day of holding my breath and glancing up at Joel's monitors had proven to be no more than a continued disappointment. As I paced the room with the new book I'd picked up at the library, I knew that this was no life. I was investing more and more of myself into an outcome I couldn't predict and would very likely be disappointed by. But for me there was no other option. So I placed my book down and cleared a section of food wrappers from the bedside table.

Visiting hours had come to an end far too quickly but I didn't want to be instructed to leave. I needed to be able to pull myself out of the room before anyone else did. I tucked my purse under my arm and went to Joel's side. He was peaceful as always but that fact gave me no peace at all. I bent down and kissed his cheek, letting a tear fall from the corner of my eye, landing where I'd left my kiss. After wiping the tear away with my thumb, I closed my eyes, took a deep breath, and left the room again. It was a delicate surgery to undergo but I'd been achieving it for some time now and so far I'd managed to survive it.

I took my time walking through the hallways that led outside. They were quiet and isolated with the occasional nurse passing by to make their rounds. The busy section of the hospital, the emergency room and all things linked to it, were kept away from the recovering patients. Though I imagined it was likely how most hospitals were setup, I'd never taken notice before. I appreciated it now.

The night air that escaped into the entryway from the automatic doors was cold on my face and smelled of a vengeful winter. The contrasting temperature of the hot and stuffy hospital and the cold unforgiving night made me hug myself automatically. I turned towards the cluster of chairs that made up the waiting area, knowing that I couldn't leave just yet. As I took a seat in the far corner, I could still feel a string of comfort keeping me up simply in knowing that Joel was in the same building.

I sat back in the chair, feeling weak and drained of energy. It was at night, when I had to leave Joel and I was forced to manage to get a few hours of sleep, that I was at my weakest. I was capable during most hours of the day to keep myself together and focused on other things. It was when the day came to a close and nothing more remained of it that the simple knowledge that Joel was still unconscious consumed me.

I let out a shaky breath and looked around the waiting area. A little boy and his sister were curled up in adjoining chairs, fast asleep. Their mother sat whispering into a cell phone in a quiet panic. She was likely keeping family and friends informed of the state of her husband or a parent, maybe even another child. But by the look on her face, like some of her strength was elsewhere, her fingers rotating the wedding band on her ring finger, I figure it was her husband. I looked away, unable to watch any longer. The only time she could afford to crumble and only to the slightest degree was when her children were asleep. She was the glue that was keeping the family together. It made me ashamed for my own ability to sink into a chair and just be sad for a while.

I continued to scan the room, noticing a group of people talking quietly to one another. There was a young man who looked to be only a few years younger than I was, sitting in a wheelchair. His arm was in a temporary sling and all in all he seemed to be okay. The people with him, probably family, smiled and laughed with only the subtle afterglow of shock and concern on their faces. He had likely injured his arm playing a sport, the wheelchair was just a precaution, and he would probably leave sometime that night with a cast and some Tylenol. The relief from his family was so strong that I couldn't help but feel it myself. At least someone in that forsaken hospital would have no more than a funny story to tell when their stay was over.

I pulled out my phone and checked the time. It was 8:15pm and I was already exhausted. Another painful side effect to the evenings was that my body reminded me in a big way how little sleep I'd been getting. My eyes began to water and they burned when I tried to keep them open. I yawned as if on cue and I could feel my limbs growing heavier by the second. My stomach growled reminding me that not only was my body starved of sleep but nutrients as well.

I eyed up the vending machine and considered spending my last dollar on a bag of stale chips, but my need for sleep was greater than my need for food. I sunk down in the chair and stretched my legs out in front of me, crossing my arms over my chest. I would sleep just long enough to ensure that I could drive home safely. A small nap and I would be on my way.

When I saw the robber walk through the bank doors, I panicked. My heart raced and I tried to think through my options as best as I could. No matter how many times I came back to this place, I always felt so helpless to stop it.

Joel sat at the desk closest to the door and he stood up immediately. His eyes darted to me, translating without words that he'd do whatever it took to protect me. The robber turned on a pivot and shot him in the chest without hesitation. I drew my hands up to my mouth and muffled a scream. Joel dropped to the ground and the robber turned to me. He removed his mask and pulled back his hood revealing his face.

Alex now pointed the gun at me and smiled menacingly. A knot that I'd become rather accustomed to feeling the presence of twisted inside of my stomach. A face that had once represented friendship, kindness, and understanding now depicted purely bad intentions.

As he made his way over to the counter, his form shifted and he began to take on the appearance of Joel. Though his eyes were still pitch black and I knew it wasn't really him. He continued to make his way over, a black set of wings unfolding out behind him.

"We can be happy together," he promised, Joel's soothing voice coming out of this imposter's body, his gun still pointed at my head.

Tears streamed down my cheeks but he didn't seem to notice. I couldn't speak. The words I wished to say were ripped out of me when I'd watched the real Joel's lifeless body drop for the countless time. I turned to run from behind the teller line and found myself planted firmly in the dark Joel's arms. He was shirtless now, the image of danger and evil mixed with the allure of a man I knew to be neither. He took my face in his hands, forcing me to meet his eyes.

"I will have you," he said, looking me over like a meal to be devoured.

I fought against happiness and contentment. He looked so much like my Joel. I wanted nothing more than to say, "You do have me." But I suffocated the words I wished to say and stared with deliberation, bound to silence.

His eyes were focused on mine when he shifted again to take on the form of Alex once more. Though his dark wings

*remained, he no longer embodied the man that I loved. He
looked me over and pushed me out in front of him, raising the
gun to me again. When he pulled the trigger, I closed my eyes
and at the sound of the gunshot I gasped and shot up from my
chair.*

"Are you okay, dear?" a small old woman asked
from across the row of chairs.

I shifted in my seat and sat up, still very much
afraid. "Yeah," I managed. "It was just a bad dream."

I rubbed my face and held back tears I wanted so
badly to release. Whenever I closed my eyes, whenever
I tried to regain even a small amount of energy, the
night of the bank robbery replayed in my head. It was
always different. Sometimes I was unable to move as if
stuck in quicksand. Other times it played in slow
motion and I felt helpless to stop it. Some nights the
shooter was Matt, other nights it was Alex. But this
was the first night where he'd shifted to Joel. The eerie
way he'd been manipulated into the man that I loved
was the worst part of the whole dream. I felt excited at
the idea of Joel holding my face in his hands again,
though I knew better than to believe it.

I held onto the hope of him waking up, it was the
only way I remained sane. But I needed to settle for no
less than the Joel that I knew. A Joel that I'd managed
to dream up, especially one who was *really* Alex, could
not be the one to bring me comfort in a time like this.

Now even less capable of leaving the hospital, I
made my way to the cafeteria. Though I still couldn't
picture myself eating anything, I knew that I had to try.
Once I got home my likelihood of putting anything
together for dinner was slim to none.

On my way back from the cafeteria, with a turkey
sandwich in hand, I noticed a sign pointing in the
direction of the atrium. I'd never been a fan of hospitals
and I rather appreciated the fact that, until recently, I
hadn't stepped foot in one since my allergy attack when

I was a kid. Though I'd heard great things about the facilities here, I had never intended on exploring them. But now, like a bad joke, my stomach turned at the thought of leaving. So with a big forced bite of my sandwich, I headed towards the atrium.

Walking down the steps to the lower floor, I found myself in awe, wondering how I'd missed seeing such a place in all the time I'd spent there. They'd somehow managed to fit a small park in the middle of the hospital. Absently taking another bite of my sandwich, I walked towards one of the benches along the path.

I closed my eyes and took in a deep breath, sat down on the bench, and let it out slowly, hoping that I would have the opportunity to show this place to Joel one day.

"Do you mind if I sit?" I heard a soft voice ask from a few feet away.

I opened my eyes and smiled when I recognized Vicky standing beside me. "Of course," I said with a smile, scooping up my purse from the spot beside me.

"I used to come here a lot when I first started working here," she said, sinking down onto the bench beside me. "It was my favorite part of the whole hospital."

"I can see why," I replied, looking around at the lush green that surrounded us and the well-kept brick walk below our feet.

"After a while I got more and more busy and I allowed myself less time to relax. As I got accustomed to the atmosphere of the hospital; the sadness, the fear, the guilt...I got used to it I guess. I needed this place less and less."

"I don't know if I'd be strong enough to get used to this place," I admitted.

"You're stronger than you give yourself credit for." Vicky sat forward and pulled her hair out of its bun, letting it fall around her shoulders. "I had to start coming back here when your boyfriend was admitted. I can't explain it but I guess your story, what he did, everything…it just got to me."

I placed a hand on her shoulder in an effort to comfort her. Though it was a strange practice to comfort a woman whose job it was to look after the ill and dying, something she must be used to by now, it made me feel at ease. Comforting her reminded me that while at times it felt less prominent, I still had all the confidence in the world that Joel would pull through.

"You know, when I first met Joel, I had to convince myself that he wasn't the bad guy. He had this way about him that was so pure and true that it felt fake almost. I've never in my entire life met anyone like him."

"How'd you meet?" she asked. "If you don't mind me asking."

"Oh, of course not." I laughed at the thought of our first meeting and the strange and nearly sound-barrier-breaking speed of our relationship.

Though I hadn't been able to fully grasp it at the time, given my sedentary approach towards relationships in the past, I knew now why I'd been so eager to become intimate with him. I'd known him forever.

"He rescued me after someone had drugged me at a club."

"You're kidding?" Vicky smiled in shock. "It sounds like he's been protecting you from the very start. Even as a complete stranger."

"You have no idea." I laughed. "I had an interesting time trying to decide if I could trust him or not. It's hard to rescue someone from a situation like that and not look suspicious yourself."

"Oh, I'm sure."

For a moment we both remained quiet. I sat looking back on all that Joel had done for me. It felt good to talk about him, about us. For a week now all anyone ever asked me about him was his recovery status. More commonly, however, people avoided him as a topic all together.

"It feels so good to talk about him," I said. "It's been awhile. Well, you know, apart from discussing his recovery, or lack thereof."

"It's not easy, what you're going through." Vicky sat back on the bench again and threw her hair back up in a neat bun. "I've worked at this hospital for five years now. I've seen things no person should ever have to see. I've experienced grief more times than I can count, and I've seen even the strongest people fold under the pressure of trauma."

"Why do you do it? I mean, it's such a humble job and God knows the world needs people like you...but, hospitals are so..."

"Depressing?" She laughed. "Yeah, I guess that's why they built this place. But you know, with all of the sadness and loss, there is something that keeps me coming back for more every day."

"What?" I asked, leaning over my knees, crumpling the plastic wrap from my sandwich in my hand.

"The miracles. They don't happen nearly often enough but they do occur. A woman whose been told she'll never walk again being able to feel her toes. A last minute transplant that saves a young boy's life. And I just know that Mr. Benedict will be one of those miracles." She looked at me and flashed a girlish smile. "If he's not, I quit."

I couldn't keep from laughing. "Thank you, Vicky."

"Anytime." Rising from her spot on the bench, Vicky bent down and gave me a hug before leaving the atrium.

I sat for only a minute or two longer, feeling more refreshed and hopeful than I had in a few days. It had been easy to expect the best early on but with the days adding up, I'd let my faith slip. As I pulled my tired frame from the bench, I registered for what felt like the first time how truly exhausted I was. Without a single glance back, I made my way to the parking lot and felt with confidence that I would sleep dreamlessly that night.

I parked Trigger out front and made my way towards the door, excited to fall into my bed.

I might not have noticed Alex's car at all had I not been on some level of alertness at all times. When I caught sight of his red Pontiac, my heart jumped from my chest to my throat. I should have expected for him to come by at some point. He'd been dating one of my roommates, Tara, for a few weeks now. And despite the fact that I had discovered that he'd drugged me at the club the night Joel had entered my life, they were still together, though I had no idea why. If he was interested in me, which he had made very clear was the case, why was he continuing to pursue a relationship with Tara?

I'd hardly maintained the energy to drive home but seeing Alex's car had ignited every ounce of fire left inside of me. I knew that he was already probably well aware that I'd arrived home. Trigger, my orange metallic Mustang, wasn't the kind of car one might choose for stealth operations. Lacking a brilliant and inconspicuous alibi to leave again, let alone the energy to do so, I sat down on the porch and put my head in my hands. The last thing I wanted to do was to go inside and play nice, having to make it look as convincing as possible for Tara's sake.

I heard the door open behind me a few minutes later and though my heartbeat quickened, I commanded my body to appear composed.

"It's pretty cold out here," Alex said, shutting the door behind him.

"I don't mind," I lied.

He lowered himself to sit beside me and I began to count the seconds that lapsed until he spoke next.

"I'm sorry about Joel," he said almost convincingly.

"There's nothing to be sorry about." I tried with great strain not to sound resentful towards him.

"This has all been very hard on you, I'm sure." Alex sounded like the same caring and sensitive guy I'd always known. But now his tone, his words, and the way his dark eyes scanned my face were all a noticeable false.

"Listen," he began with a slight undertone in his voice, digging his hands into his nearly black hair. "I understand that you're upset. I get that you're withdrawing from everyone a bit. But why cut me out? I'm the only one that knows..."

Alex had either forgotten that Heather was there to see Joel materialize in time it took to take a bullet for me as well, or he was talking about something else entirely.

I couldn't forget the fact that he had seemed unalarmed at the sight of Joel's wings that had quickly turned to ash after appearing. Shocked yes, but surprised...no. Another puzzle piece I would need to find a place for.

"Alex..."

I was exhausted in every sense of the word. It hurt in an almost physical way to sit and question every move that Alex made. The wall I'd built to keep him a safe distance from me was becoming increasingly difficult to uphold.

"You don't know what it's like to watch your world crumble right before your eyes. To have run so fast and so far from life to land yourself right in its arms...To realize that one person has the key to it all. Then to have them torn away from you, leaving so much pain in their wake that just breathing hurts..."

Why was I saying this to Alex? Why did a corner of my imploding sanity think that it mattered one way or another? Be it my lack of sleep or lack of known consequence, I'd said it. And there was nothing he could do to me for having said it that would be worse than what had already been done.

His hands began to clench into fists, relaxing before tightening completely. Maybe he even thought that I hadn't noticed it at all. But I knew that I'd struck a chord in him.

"Pain and the desire to be with someone forever are bound together. There isn't one without the other." Alex's voice was somber and he seemed almost remorseful.

As if we were addicted to the same drug, and though it would undoubtedly bring us both further suffering, wounds we inflicted on one another, in that moment, I knew that he was feeling as sorry for me as I was for him.

I looked up at the clear night sky. There was little to no light pollution and the stars shone bright in the sky, reminding me of nights spent with Joel looking up at those very stars.

"Desire and need are two very different things," I said, turning again to face him.

He glanced over at me, his face lit by the soft light that spilled out from the living room. "And do you know the difference?" he asked, challenging me to give him a reason to turn and walk away, never to look back.

I pushed myself up and headed for the front door. I looked back at him to meet his stalking eyes. "Do you?"

Chapter

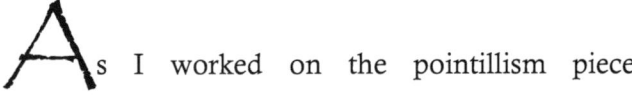

As I worked on the pointillism piece

Professor Norman had assigned the class, I could feel a few of my classmates' eyes on me. By that point, about half of the school had heard about what had happened. But I wanted nothing to do with the attention. Only a few months earlier, the girls in my art class had looked at me with jealous hate in their eyes as Joel posed nude for my class. Now they pitied me. I wanted no part of it.

I stippled away, trying to ignore the fact that the classroom was eerily quiet. Usually the room was full of whispered conversation and the occasional outburst of laughter. But in recent days I felt that if anything was passed between my classmates' lips, it was gossip about me. Then again, I could just as easily be overreacting and assuming the worst due to paranoia. Either way, all eyes were on me.

While Joel was hands down my favorite muse, art still provided an easy escape even when I wasn't using him as my model. I could think about mixing colors, adding detail, and bringing a scene to life instead of everything else that was going on. And like most tortured artists that had become famous for their insanity, it seemed my work had gotten better since Joel had entered into a coma. It wasn't exactly the tradeoff I'd hoped for.

As I continued working on my piece, I could feel the quiet approach of a fellow student. I immediately stiffened and turned my body just enough to provide myself with the excuse that I hadn't seen her. Maybe she was just passing by, on her way to throw out scrap paper or to pick up new brushes. Sure enough, despite my attempt at repelling her advance, Brenda, a girl who had done little more than look at me throughout the semester, slid onto the stool beside me, placing her half-finished piece on the table in front of her. I looked down and noticed that it was beginning to take on the shape of a butterfly and I wondered if she couldn't think of anything more profound to paint or if she just really liked butterflies.

"That's really good," she complimented, motioning toward my canvas.

Though it wasn't finished, it was coming together just how I'd pictured it. A couple dressed in blue walked along a path lit by street lights, snow falling down around them, carpeting the landscape. Off to one side, a frozen lake spread into the background while a line of trees covered in ice and snow formed a wall on the other.

"Thanks," I said. "Yours is really good too." It wasn't a lie; pointillism wasn't the easiest method of painting in the world, and for what it was worth, Brenda had managed to capture the butterfly rather well.

"Eh," she said, brushing the compliment off. "It's just a butterfly."

I waited in silence, dipping my brush back into the light blue paint, and waited for her to say something else, hoping that she wouldn't. A few minutes lapsed while we both dotted paint onto our canvases before she spoke again.

"I heard about your boyfriend," she said in a low voice. "The guy who modeled for us a few months ago, right?"

She knew who he was and that he was my boyfriend. She'd been one of the girls gathered around him after he'd come back out from getting dressed. But I appreciated her tone, no detectable bitterness, so I turned to her and smiled.

"Yeah."

"I'm so sorry," she added, placing a hand over the one I wasn't painting with. "I can't imagine."

I wanted to disappear. The look in her eyes forced a lump into my throat and I tried to choke it down. I didn't want to cry again, I'd been crying for days after it had happened. In fact I still cried about it. The last thing I wanted was to break-down in class in front a girl who didn't even know me.

I shook my head. "He's fine," I lied. "It's just a matter of time."

Her smile lacked hope but she flashed it for my sake anyway. I was the girl in denial of reality. And the longer I sat there with Brenda and her sympathy, the more I realized that I'd completely lost hold of it. Joel was not going to wake up.

After class, I made my way out to my car. Paint covered my hands, though I'd made an honest effort to scrub it off before leaving the classroom. As I approached Trigger, I noticed a folded up piece of paper tucked neatly under my windshield wiper.

I plucked the note from my windshield and slipped inside the car before opening it. After buckling myself in, I unfolded the note and read it.

Charlotte,

32

I'm sorry about the other night. I can't believe how insensitive I acted. Meet me for dinner at seven at La Paesana, so that I can apologize in person for how stupid I've been.
  Alex

A shiver ran over the surface of my skin as I tucked the note into my purse. Meet Alex for dinner? Tonight? This had wrong and stupid written all over it. But as much as I wanted to blow him off, I knew that it was a chance for me to get some answers. I could keep avoiding him or I could face the problem head-on. If there even was a problem at all. I had to keep in mind that he'd said a few things in the heat of the moment to Joel, not knowing that I'd overheard him. I wasn't going to be stupid about it by any means but I wasn't going to hang him for being jealous either. At least not until he gave me a real reason to.

When I arrived home from work that evening, Tara was sitting at the kitchen table with her homework fanned out in front of her. Her loose dark curls were pulled up into a bun, a look she rarely sported. It was always an indication that she had no intention of leaving the house for the remainder of the day.

"Hey," I said, making my way into the kitchen. "You're looking rather studious this evening," I added, noticing a pencil she'd probably forgotten about sticking out of her bun.

She smiled up and blew a loose curl out of her face. "Well, Alex ditched on our date tonight. I figured I might as well get something productive done."

I swallowed hard. Alex had broken off plans with Tara to wait in a restaurant that I might never show up at? I could feel guilt creeping up my spine. I didn't want to tell Tara that I was the reason she'd been blown off, that I was going to meet her boyfriend at an expensive Italian restaurant after she'd been left hanging.

"I'm sorry." I tried not to sound guilty when I said it.

"It's no big deal. I've got an exam coming up anyway." I could tell that she was still disappointed, though she dare not show it.

"You guys have been spending a lot of time together lately huh?" I inquired, grabbing one of her pens to fiddle with, keeping my hands busy.

"Yeah," Tara replied dreamily. Oh boy.

"You like him," I pointed out.

"It's hard not to," she admitted. "He does seem a bit distracted though recently. I'm trying to tell myself that he's just stressed about getting a new job, but part of me feels like he's not even trying. He's talking about finding work at the hospital but it seems like he's just saying those things to keep me off his back about it." Tara put her pencil down and sat back in her chair. "I mean, when we make out it's like he's not even there. Like he doesn't feel anything when he kisses me."

I swallowed hard. I really didn't want to be having this conversation with Tara. There was a fine line between supporting my friend and feeding her to the wolves, and frankly I had no idea where it was.

Realizing that I had yet to repl, I cleared my throat and clicked the pen in my hand. "He's probably just stressed, that's all."

"Yeah, that's what I keep telling myself." She looked a little relieved, now under the impression that I thought it was nothing too.

I had no idea what else to say to her. It was taking all of my energy not to blurt out that Alex was all wrong for her but despite all that he'd done—might have and probably had done—I was still meeting him for dinner. A dinner date he'd written on his calendar. Right over his and Tara's previous plans. I put the pen down and let out a long sigh.

"So what are your plans for tonight?" Tara asked, picking up her pencil again and flipping to the next page in her text book.

"I uh," I stammered. "I'm meeting my parents for dinner." The lie had unfolded before I could even prevent my lips from telling it.

"Cool," she said like it was a normal plan to have. And it was, had it been true. "Tell them I said hi."

"I will," I said, trying to keep my voice even.

This already felt wrong. With Joel still in the hospital and Tara under the impression that Alex was a stand-up guy, I began questioning my easy acceptance of the invitation.

As I got ready in my room, slipping into dark washed jeans and a tight-fit black button-up, I wondered who I thought I was kidding. What could I say to Alex that would change his mind? Did he even really care about Tara? All I could hope for was to keep the conversation light and pleasant. He didn't know about my fear of him or why I had it in the first place. All he knew was that the past week had been hard for me.

I can do this, I thought to myself. *This is my last chance at crafting an easy way out of this terrible mess.*

The restaurant had a warm romantic feel to it. I cringed at the light yellow haze that washed over the room, cast by candles on each table. Romantic wasn't exactly the setting I'd wanted for this dinner. The last thing I needed was for Alex to get the wrong idea. I'd accepted his invitation out of defense, not because I was actually looking forward to it.

The man that stood at the podium in the entryway was dressed in a fine suit and I started questioning my own outfit choice. I hadn't exactly wanted to dress up on Alex's behalf but it was my first time at this restaurant and I didn't want to leave that night having made a bad impression.

"Can I help you?" the maitre d' asked, scanning me with judging eyes.

"I'm meeting someone here," I replied nervously, pulling down on the hem of my shirt.

"Ms. Rush?" he asked to confirm.

"Yes, that's me."

The man stretched out a hand and guided me to a table near the back. At the sight of me, Alex pushed his seat back and stood up. He wore a dark grey sweater and dark jeans, making me feel a little better.

"Thank you," I said to the maitre d' as he pushed my seat in behind me.

"Bon appétit," he replied.

I pulled my chair up to the table and Alex sat down, following suit, unable to guard a smile from breaking onto his lips. He was handsome; I had to give him that. His hair was perfectly gelled and his face was smooth and free of stubble. I could even detect the scent of cologne, something I knew him to rarely wear.

"I didn't expect you to show up," he admitted.

"Then why'd you invite me?" I hoped that I hadn't sounded rude.

He chuckled and tucked his napkin into his lap. I did the same. "I guess I'm just a glutton for punishment."

There was a long and quiet moment where Alex watched me in silence and I pretended not to notice. His eyes fell heavily over the surface of my face but I managed to keep mine angled down. I didn't want to meet his eyes, certainly not in a moment of silence accented by candle light. I grabbed my menu from the table, looking for an excuse to focus my attention elsewhere. He followed my lead and opened up the menu in front of him.

We both skimmed our menus and he ordered a bottle of red wine when the waiter came by our table. I took into account that he had sprung for one of the most expensive bottles they had, which considering the prices that started at twenty-five dollars, was highly unreasonable.

"Order whatever you'd like," he prompted, taking a sip of his wine.

"You couldn't have settled for four stars?" I asked, looking down at the pricey menu. Even the chicken finger platter had a two-digit number in front of it.

"You've been through a lot," he said in earnest. "And I haven't exactly been understanding."

I pressed my lips together and looked back to the menu. He was making it so hard to hate him. To use the words he'd said in Joel's hospital room against him. It took a large amount of my concentration to remind myself that he'd betrayed me. That the only thing his eyes, the color of a starless sky, were capable of holding was selfish lust.

"So tell me," he said with a voice, thick with sex appeal. "When was the last time you really enjoyed yourself?"

"I—" I took my glass of wine and put it to my lips, trying to find an answer that involved Joel. I needed to say his name. Too much time had gone by since I had said it last. But the memories of Joel only made my heart ache more. I wanted to preserve what we had. I didn't want to share those few precious moments with Alex. "I don't know," I finally said.

"That's a shame," he replied, his smile up to no good. "You should join me for some fun. Get your mind off things a bit. I know a great band that plays locally. They perform a lot of cover music but they do a great job. It's like the real thing. It's always a good time."

"I don't need to get my mind off of anything," I insisted.

The waiter stepped in to take our orders and I breathed in relief as he broke into a conversation that was headed to no place good.

When the waiter left Alex took another generous sip of his wine. "It would be fun, I promise," he said, picking up where we'd left off.

"What about Tara?"

"What about her?"

"I'm pretty sure she'd have a problem with you and me going to a concert together. This dinner even, does she know that you're out with me?"

"No," he said quickly. He wasn't defensive, hell, he didn't even seem worried about it, but his tone had changed slightly. "What is there to tell her? We're two friends having dinner together. You've been through a lot these past few months. We used to see each other every day at work, I haven't had a chance to talk to you recently, that's all."

I tilted my head in challenge. Did he really think that excuse was going to hold any water? Either way, he knew he was safe. I'd come to dinner knowing full well that Tara hadn't been informed about it, in fact, she'd been ditched so that we could meet tonight. I was just as unlikely to tell Tara about the dinner as he was. I instantly hated myself. I could have been spending the night at Joel's side but instead I was out on a date with Alex, like everything about it wasn't wrong.

"How are you and Tara doing, anyway?" I asked, hoping to corner Alex in a lie. If he wanted to keep up his front, he would have to validate their relationship at least for a little while until he no longer needed her for his plan, if that's all she was to him.

Part of me kept second guessing all of my accusations. Without Joel around, my head was a mess of unorganized thought and lack of rationality. Alex could just as easily have genuine feelings for Tara. Though, I doubted it.

"We're doing great," he said easily. "We're celebrating our one month anniversary soon." He almost sounded like he gave a shit.

"Has she taken you to meet her parents yet?" I egged on. "They're very sweet."

"I haven't met them yet, no." He was uncomfortable.

It was evident that he didn't want to talk about Tara or the dozens of other things he had pretended to care about. He wanted to start building something between us. I could sense it by the way he looked at me.

"Do you love her?" I asked, mimicking intrigue, propping my chin up on my hands, encouraging him to answer.

He looked down at his glass. "It's too soon for that I think, Charlotte." He looked up and flashed a false smile. "But I think I'm beginning to," he said unconvincingly.

There was a long pause before either of us spoke again.

"I don't want to talk about Tara and me," he said regretfully. "I don't want to make it harder on you. Since Joel's..." he trailed off.

I felt my expression fall flat. Alex had saved himself. He'd given himself a reason to cut Tara out of the conversation while simultaneously destroying my ability to push him further for answers. Not to mention the sound of Joel's name. It was enough to make me abandon my plan to question him into admitting the truth about that night at the club.

My breath caught in my throat but I pushed past it. "Really, its fine," I insisted.

"Charlotte, I can't hurt you like that." He took my hand in his and I froze.

My heart raced and the cold touch of his skin rendered me powerless. The sensation he gave was no match for Joel's but I still found myself fumbling for something to say. Anything.

I looked down at our hands and slid mine slowly out from under his. "I'm sorry," I said, wiping a tear from my cheek.

He pulled his own hand from the table and bowed his head. "I understand," he said with force.

The rest of our dinner remained mostly silent. I had nothing to say to Alex. Anything I wanted to say was nearly impossible to get out without getting choked up. I didn't have the strength to challenge him. Nor did I have the strength to pretend like nothing was going on.

I avoided the way that he looked at me over the table, like this was a scene he wished to play over and over in his mind. I tried to ignore the fact that I'd actually given him something that he wanted. I had given him time that I would have spent with Joel otherwise.

Almost two hours later we were standing outside of the restaurant, my keys already in hand, and I silently prayed for a swift good-bye. "So, thanks for dinner," I said with a tight smile.

"It was my pleasure," his voice a little too smooth for comfort. "Let me walk you to your car," he offered.

"Oh no, I'm okay," I insisted, attempting to end the night there.

"I insist," he said. Of course he did.

With no polite way of bypassing his offer, I relented and let him walk me to my car. "This is me," I said, stopping in front of the Mustang.

Alex raised a gentle hand up to my back and pulled me closer to him and I swallowed my nerves in an effort to keep myself steady.

"Good night," I said, trying to ignore that he was bringing me closer.

"Charlotte," he cooed into my ear. "You seem so lonely, it makes me sad." His voice wasn't full of remorse, but poison. He grazed my ear with his lips and waited a moment for me to respond. But my body was paralyzed.

I was frozen in place again by his disarming advance and by guilt that bubbled up inside of me. "Alex, please don't," I begged.

My body grew flimsy and swayed slightly. I wondered if I might pass out. But Alex didn't pull away and his touch, the touch of a man, something I had longed for since Joel had been brought to the hospital, spiked my veins with life.

I winced and hoped that he would turn and walk away but he didn't. Instead, he brought his lips down and pressed them tenderly to mine, parting them and urging me to participate in a kiss. I couldn't make my body resist him. I couldn't command myself enough to stop him. He took my face in his hands and kissed me harder, and I could taste supremacy on his lips.

I managed to press my hands to his chest and ease him away from me. "What do you think you're doing?" I exhaled.

"You didn't seem to mind," he argued.

"Well I did."

He took my face in his hand and smiled cunningly. He may have caught me off guard and vulnerable once but I was sure to never let it happen again.

"Don't touch me," I said, pulling my face from his hand. I walked around the car and opened the door. "How could you do that to Tara? How could you do it to me?" Tears were streaming down my face and I felt guilt burning a hole into my heart.

How could he? *How could I?*

I had to see Joel before I let the day come to a close. I couldn't let the feel of Alex's lips on mine be the last thing I felt. Visiting hours were over but I had to see him.

I slipped past the desk attendant who remained pre-occupied with one of the nurses and walked quietly over to the open door that lead to the hallway where Joel's room was located. I walked lightly and checked behind me every few feet. I needed only a few moments with him, but I couldn't lose them, I couldn't be forced to leave.

I found myself standing outside of Joel's room in a quiet panic. I couldn't imagine having to face him and what I'd let happen. What would he think of me once he found out? I stifled an onset of sobs. *If he found out.*

I pushed the door open, against my high anxieties, and let myself in. The room was dark, lit only by the moonlight that came in through the window and the small lights from the machines beside his bed. I crossed my arms over my chest to try and tame my quickly beating heart.

He was beautifully peaceful. His cheek rested on the pillow and his hands lay where I'd left them. His face was lit by the moon, making him appear that much more at peace.

I walked quietly to his side and sat down in the chair beside his bed and took his hand in mine. Warm and rough to the touch, they were hands that had always been there for me. Hands that had held me up and caught me as I fell. They were the hands of a man who'd sacrificed everything for me, and I'd betrayed him.

Tears streamed down my face and I swiped them away. "Joel," I murmured. "Please come back to me."

I pushed up from the chair and curled up next to him, no longer able to keep the distance between us. Deserving of it or not, I needed to feel him beside me. Why I hadn't been more stern in resisting Alex hardly mattered. It had nothing to do with Joel or my love for him. I was a medical diagnosis away from depression and a slew of other mental and emotional problems that could quite easily earn me a stay in an institution. What I'd done, or more accurately, what I hadn't done, was meaningless.

I nestled into Joel's side and ran my finger gently over his lips, watching them draw back reflexively after my finger left them. I drew my hands over his face as if in a trance. It was his lips that I'd wanted so badly to kiss. I wanted him then more than ever before. I wanted him to hold me and to tell me that everything would be okay. I felt fragile and helpless without him.

I raised myself up in bed and sat over him for a moment, my hair cascading down around his face, before leaving a gentle kiss on his lips. His skin was warm, his lips moist and full of life. Even with the absence of his consciousness, Joel had managed to deliver a kiss that in some small way had put me back together again.

When I left the hospital, I felt relief, though I still couldn't forgive myself for not pushing Alex away, having known full-well what he'd planned to do. He had been gentle and kind which I honestly hadn't expected, and maybe that was why I hadn't resisted him. I shook my head in an effort to force the thoughts from my mind. I couldn't keep thinking about it, it would only give him what he wanted.

I got home at around eleven o'clock and I'd managed to sneak past Tara and Emily's rooms undetected. I didn't want to have to face either of them, especially Tara. I'd lied enough for one day. On top of everything I'd already done, I didn't want to lie to Tara for the second time to round out the night.

I just wanted to go to bed and forget that any of that night had ever happened. Had I really let Alex get to me? I couldn't think about it anymore. I'd been betrayed again by my inability to judge his bad intentions and I was angry for it. I'd allowed for myself to fall, even if only for an instant, into his trap. I lay in bed, eyes closed, hoping that when I woke up it would be no more than another bad dream.

Chapter

5

*T*ime had been immeasurable since I found myself

in the place between somewhere and nowhere. Had an hour gone by? A day? A week? A year? I didn't know. I sat utterly defeated at the idea of it. My pain had subsided some but it came back in jolts and spurts. The hot and cold way that my body had been acting was making me sick. I forced myself endlessly to push past the wavering hold that I had on the world around me. Though it seemed more of a lack of world, I knew that I needed to grip it tightly. I was tired but sleeping wasn't an option. Falling asleep in such a place could only mean one thing. And it was already the beginning of the end, no need to embrace it.

I held onto memories of Charlotte and leaned on them heavily for support. They kept me pushing through the time that elapsed. I'd recalled and revisited probably over two hundred memories already. Her high school graduation. The look on her face when she received her acceptance letter to the university. I remembered how tediously she'd saved up money from every paycheck for her car, skipping lunch towards the end of a pay period because she had put most of the money into the bank already. I remembered the year she trained and ran a half marathon with her mother and how proud her father was when they'd crossed the finish line. I smiled knowing that she could never pass a homeless person without offering whatever money she could to help them out.

She had a kind heart and sometime in the quietest moments of silence that surrounded me, I could feel its beat against my own chest. It was a gift I'd never pictured receiving in all my time of watching over Charlotte. I'd entered into the position of being her guardian knowing full well that she would never know me. That we were on two sides of a fence they stretched on up to heaven.

I had been newly created and it was rare for an angel of my age to receive such a prestigious position especially at conception. Customarily, angels were assigned at birth, there was no need for them to be assigned any sooner but I'd been sent down early. Be it because I'd never done it before or that Charlotte and I were special, I'd been with her through her mother's entire pregnancy.

I hardly knew what I was doing at first, but it only took the sight of her and her sweet eyes in the hospital room the day of her birth to know that I would do whatever was required of me to protect her.

In the vast amount of nothing, I heard her sometimes and it brought tears to my eyes. The muffled sound of her voice through the static. My holding cell. Whenever my weakening body threatened to drag me down through to the gates of hell and on to heaven, I heard her. In those moments, I found myself holding onto the mere suggestion of her so tightly that it hurt. Like breathing air through a plastic bag, I struggled against it.

Time had no meaning. I grew more and more restless with every passing second...or day. Whatever time was to me in that place, it meant only one thing. I wasn't with Charlotte. I began to yearn for her in ways I'd never felt lacking before. The time apart had corrupted my body it seemed, making me weak and altering my need to protect her, morphing it into a desire to just be near to her.

I knelt down in defeat and forced myself to find calm. As I remained in a form of meditation, I began to hear her laughter as clear as day. Excited and anxious to finally awake, I looked up to find an image painting in midair like a movie in front of me. Charlotte was seventeen.

I stood up in awe of her. Her hair was cropped at shoulder length with wispy bangs that she often pinned up to keep out of her eyes. She was walking home from school, where she usually spent an hour or so after classes let out to talk and study with her friends.

She was accompanied by her best friend at the time, Rachael. I remembered the scene as vividly as any other moment in her life but the perspective was strangely different than that of the one I'd actually experienced it from. The angle rotated until I could see the unmistakable figure of Alex knelt down and out of sight. He looked exactly the same. He was watching her as a wolf would stalk its pray.

My stomach tightened and I felt powerless as I watched. It was evident that he'd known her far longer than Charlotte or even I had been aware of. Though I had never been given any reason to question him in the past, I knew that something was terribly wrong. Why else would I be seeing such a scene play out?

As the view faded and my surroundings were nothing but bleach white again, I felt a fire being lit inside of me. An anger and a need to break free from this place.

I shook myself. I needed to get back and tell Charlotte about what I had seen. Whatever else there was to it, I knew without a doubt that Alex was a danger to her.

I couldn't sit in solitude any longer, not with Charlotte still in danger. In an instant of certainty, I made the decision to leave the place I was being detained. I closed my eyes and took in a deep breath deciding once and for all that enough was enough. I needed to break free. Standing still, bracing myself against the unknown, everything went black.

With much effort, I began pushing my eyelids open. Slowly at first against an invisible weight that made the task nearly impossible. I hunched forward gasping for air. When I finally managed to prop my eyes open at full-length, I was startled by the equally shocked expression of a petite redhead at the foot of the bed I was laying in. With her eyes and mouth agape, she held a clipboard in her hands that were shaking feverishly.

I backed up into the bed as far as I could and found that words were not yet at my disposal. My eyes shifted, darting around the room, taking in my predicament. I was in a hospital. Was Charlotte here too? Had something happened to her?

"Charlotte," I croaked, with a voice that sounded un-used and raspy. I turned in a sudden panic to face the empty bed beside me. Her name being the only word that seemed fluid enough to leave my dry mouth. "Charlotte," I said again with panic.

The woman with the clipboard rushed to my side when her sudden brush with paralysis had fled her. She tossed the clipboard onto the foot of the bed, pressed a button above my head, and put her fingers to my wrist.

I jerked my hand away slightly when her finger tips made contact with my skin. Her skinny fingers rested gently on my pulse and the feeling was stranger than anything I'd ever felt before. It sent a surge through my veins that shook any rest that my body might have still been holding onto. At the slight hesitation, she smiled kindly and reduced the amount of pressure that she applied by a degree. She was a harmless little thing but her touch, the physical contact of another, I'd never experienced it in that way before. Strange.

I pushed myself up in an effort to sit more upright and almost choked on the pain that it caused. I couldn't decide what hurt more, my shoulder blades or the hole that made its presence known right through me.

"Oh, honey, try not to move," the little woman with fire colored hair instructed. She poked and prodded me as she urged me not to move, checking this, adjusting that.

"Charlotte," I said again in question. My vocabulary and ability to speak on par with that of a Neanderthal.

A smile fanned across her face knowingly. "She's fine. I'll have her informed immediately that you are awake."

I scanned the room again, registering a degree more of what was around me than I had previously. A blanket and pillow lay ruffled and used on the chair beside me, soda cans and snack wrappers littered the night stand, and the woman rustling up the tubes on my arm's name tag read, "Vicky".

I placed my hand over hers. She was frantically working away at the checklist that I imagined flashed across her mind. She looked up with a start then looked down at our hands, mine engulfing her own.

"Thank you," I said as sincerely as I could past the ache in my side.

Her eyes flashed with a rainbow of emotions but she brushed them all off. "No, thank you," she replied, pulling her hand tenderly from beneath mine. She turned and smiled one last time then exited the room with an air of victory about her.

* * *

Professor Williams collected our tests and my hope at passing it blew off the page right along with my eraser shavings. It had been nearly two weeks since Joel had been checked into the hospital. And five days since Alex had kissed me. Following suit, it seemed that everything else in my life was withering away. I'd been under two hundred dollars in my drawer at work a few days earlier and I broke down crying whenever I called home. My mom's voice was soft and understanding, my dad could hardly stand to hear me cry, she had taken most of my calls. It was getting painfully obvious that I needed to pull myself together and get a grip on the inevitable.

With no "known relatives" the plug would be pulled on Joel's life support at the end of the month. He would be gone forever and I would never get the chance to apologize for accepting Alex's advances, or for not having done enough to try and save him. I was full of regret and remorse, and full even more with guilt. At this rate, I might find myself with a few dozen cats one day, hacking and choking on my allergies, the crazy allergic cat lady...but at least it was a life, right? I had to work something out.

I'd ignored all of Alex's calls since the night at the restaurant and he hadn't called in the past few days, though I knew it wasn't the end of his efforts, especially with Joel still conveniently out of the picture.

I had the rest of the class period and the rest of my day to consider all of these things again at least a few dozen times. Getting a grip was priority number one but it didn't mean much that the task was on a list. Its likelihood of happening was still very low.

I had been looking forward to visiting Joel since the moment I'd woken up. Despite the circumstances, he remained the highlight of my day.

As I flipped open my textbook to join the rest of my class in reading the assignment for the day, or more accurately, to simulate their participation in class, I felt the persistent hum and vibration of my phone. Usually the considerate student, I ignored my phone but everyone that might normally be calling me was at work or in class themselves. So I dug deep into my pocket and retrieved my phone, opened it, and put it to my ear.

"Hello?" I whispered, shielding the phone and my voice with my hand.

"Ms. Rush?" a small voice said from the other end.

"Yes," I replied.

"Mr. Benedict has woken up."

I flipped my phone shut, shaking and smiling like an idiot, collected my things from my desk like it was on fire, and stood up to leave the classroom.

"Ms. Rush, where do you think you're going?" Professor Williams asked, almost stunned.

"I-I..." Suddenly words were hard to come by. "I need to go," I said in a hurry. "To the hospital," I added, hoping the short reply would suffice.

I could read hesitation on his face but with an entire classroom to observe my urgent need to flee the room, he waved me on with no more interrogation.

"Thank you," I said, not able to stop myself from sprinting from the room.

Irrational tears streamed down my face as students and teachers alike looked on with curiosity while I ran as fast as my feet would take me back to Trigger. My hands were shaking so feverishly that it took me five tries to jam the key into the ignition. It would be a miracle if I made it there without incident. Lucky for me, if anything went wrong on my way, at least that's where the ambulance would wind up.

I ran through the halls of the hospital with disregard, catching a few smiles from faces that had become familiar in the last two weeks. Slowing down as I approached Joel's room, I felt the nerves that I'd managed to suppress bubbling up inside of me. I had no idea what to expect.

As I breached the doorway, I walked in on what looked to be business as usual in the busy hospital room. Nurses and doctors were bustling around Joel's bed as he sat still, waiting for the next question or the next adjustment. Everyone flowed smoothly around him and there seemed to be a very distinct order about them. But when Joel caught sight of me in the doorway, the staff was put to the test. He jerked and he jostled to get free from his bed and the tubes that bound him to it. He yanked out his IV and plucked off the other sensors that were attached to his body in strategic places. When the doctors stopped trying to force him back onto the bed, we met halfway and landed in each other's arms with such purpose that the rest of the world seemed to shake with it. He lifted me in his arms past pain I knew he was feeling by the groan that he let escape.

He squeezed me so tightly that it might have hurt had it not been exactly what I'd needed. I could feel the desperation he shared with me to prove that everything was okay...and that the embrace was real.

"Charlotte," he moaned into my hair.

"Shhh..." I replied with a laugh.

For almost two weeks now I'd been so distraught and so fragile. The moment I saw that fear in his eyes and its accompanying relief, I knew that it was vital that I reassure Joel. My biggest concern was gone. He was awake. Now my sole responsibility was to ensure that he was really okay. I had no idea what he'd been through, if anything at all. But the big questions could wait.

"Mr. Benedict," the husky voice of Dr. Moore called from beside the abandoned hospital bed.

We hugged one another more tightly then loosened our grips to turn our joint attention to the doctor. If it was possible, the man looked more amused than he looked frustrated.

"If you wouldn't mind?" he gestured towards the ruffled covers of the bed.

Joel turned his attention first to me. With a giggle, I nodded. He made his way back with my hand in his. The doctors and nurses, Vicky included, smiled and stepped aside so that we could make our way back. I slid my hand from Joel's and stood beside the bed as he climbed back in.

"Where were we?" Dr. Moore asked as he grabbed the rejected IV.

Joel's eyes remained permanently fixed on me. He watched me intently, as if looking away would risk losing me again. I brushed my hand through his hair gently and a look of strain washed over his face. When I pulled my hand away, he took it firmly in his hand and kissed it, insisting that I not stop.

Once everything that had been ripped off was re-attached, the crowd of nurses and doctors left the room, making marks on their charts and whispering in astonishment amongst themselves as they did so.

"You're causing a big fuss," I said, realizing how strange it was to finally have him back again. To be alone with him again.

His eyes searched my face, soaking it in, rediscovering it. "I've missed you," he said firmly. "I've missed you so much."

I'd never seen so much vulnerability in his eyes before. It was almost too much to bear. "I've missed you too," I croaked past a lump in my throat. Tears began forming in my eyes and through the haze, I saw Joel raise his arm to welcome me onto the bed.

I slipped in beside him and nuzzled up against his firm chest. He tensed in a way I'd never experienced before. It was almost like he was surprised by something. During his time spent mentally abroad, the likelihood of a few wires being crossed was very possible. As an angel, I had no clue what such an ordeal could have done to him.

Past his hesitation, he pulled me into his side with determination. He brought his other hand around, resting it on my arm and stroked it softly.

"What's this?" I heard him say as he pulled up the sleeve of my shirt.

"Oh, it's nothing," I said unconvincingly, tugging my sleeve back down.

"It's not nothing." He propped himself up and angled himself to observe my bandage.

"The bullet grazed my shoulder, that's all."

I tried not to be frustrated but as Joel's expression hardened I couldn't help it. He had been shot in the chest, puncturing a lung, and had been in a coma for weeks, and he just couldn't resist worrying more about me and my little scratch.

His eyes rose to meet mine. I raised my eyebrows as if to say *what are you going to freak out now?* But he didn't. His eyes scanned the rest of my face and he traced a finger over my bottom lip inquisitively. My temper simmered immediately as I watched his innocence absorb me.

"I'm sorry I worry so much," he said, pulling his eyes up to meet mine again.

I swallowed hard and was angry with myself for finding his concern frustrating for even a second.

"No, don't be sorry," I said, resting my head back on his chest. "It's your job."

Joel didn't reply, he simply stroked my hair and kissed my forehead, making me ache inside. I'd woken up in the morning fighting the desire to stay in bed and never get up again. I had no remaining hope that he would ever come back to me. But there he was, awake and holding me against all odds.

As I breathed in and sent a small prayer of thanks to heaven, I realized how sore and heavy my eyelids were. My body was finally able to find comfort in bed as I wrapped my leg delicately around Joel's. Without any more resistance, the tension I'd been carrying for weeks had faltered and I fell into the deepest sleep I'd ever experienced before.

"...to change the bandage," I heard Vicky say through a fog of sleep.

"Hmmm?" I managed as I rubbed my eyes and shifted on the bed. Joel was wincing past what seemed to be excruciating pain. "Are you okay?" I asked worriedly, pushing myself up.

He smiled halfheartedly and adjusted on the bed. "I'm fine," he lied.

"I've come to check on your wound and change the bandage," Vicky repeated patiently. "Does it hurt?" she asked as she approached the side of the bed that I wasn't taking up.

I pulled myself from the bed and plopped down in the chair beside it, still groggy from sleep.

"My shoulder blades," Joel explained through gasping breaths.

"Can you sit up?" Vicky asked kindly.

Shifting his weight, careful not to enrage the bullet wound, Joel sat up in bed. I gasped immediately, standing straight up with my hand to my mouth. Blood soaked the pillow beneath his shoulders and his hospital gown.

"Oh my," Vicky exclaimed. She placed a hand on his shoulder and peeled his gown away gently with her other hand. "You got these tattoos right before you were shit?" she asked inquisitively. "They might be infected. They don't look irritated but they seem to be the source of the blood, and probably the pain," she added.

I leaned in with astonishment. Joel had large intricate wings tattooed on the length of his back starting at his shoulder blades and they were crusted with blood. "I don't believe...."

Vicky looked up at me with a guilty smile and back to Joel, "Did you not know about them?" she asked worried she'd ratted him out.

"I-I...." I stuttered. I was pretty sure Joel hadn't known he'd gotten them either by the look on his face. "No..." I finally added. "I didn't know."

"Here, if you could take that gown off, I'd be happy to fetch you a new one," Vicky said reaching out her hands to receive it.

Joel immediately stiffened. "I um…" his eyes shifted to me and back to Vicky. Was he? Embarrassed?

My eyes widened and with weak knees, I sank down into the chair again. Something was very wrong.

Chapter

6

Whenever Charlotte touched me it was enough to set me on fire. I'd treasured her touch before. It had been a step up from having observed her from afar. But the warmth of her skin had been nearly undetectable in the past. Her fingertips had never been capable of standing the hair on my arms up with a simple graze. Not even with a meaningful caress. But now even without physical contact, Charlotte evoked an urge in every muscle of my body to be closer to her. To feel her in my arms.

What I felt now, it was an entirely different animal. She gave me feelings and sensations that I felt ashamed of. Feelings I didn't even have names for. We'd had sex in the past but I was coming to realize that whatever she'd felt at the time had been far greater than what I had felt.

Since awakening, the conversion of my feelings had intensified, becoming almost more than I could stand. The more it seemed I repelled them, the more they pushed back. The touch of her hand through my hair alone had been enough to give me a seizure.

Then there was the pesky fact that being nearly naked in front of a strange woman I'd only just met made me feel...humiliated. A feeling I knew of by definition but not by personal experience. It was becoming painfully obvious that something had changed in me.

Emotions, fierce and raw, made themselves painfully obvious. I didn't know how to handle them, where to even begin with understanding them. Feelings aside, I had new tattoos bleeding on my back, and they hurt like hell.

"Joel," Charlotte said hesitantly after the nurse had left.

She was still sitting in the chair beside me as if I might morph into a storybook creature. It wasn't out of the question. I was no more informed than she was.

"What happened while you were...gone?" she asked.

I wish I knew.

I shook my head and placed it in my hands. My sheets and gown were clean, and new bandages had replaced the old ones on my bullet wounds, with the addition of gauze that had been taped to the entire length of my back to cover the tattoos. They'd been cleaned and moisturized before the gauze had been put on over them. On top of my pain, I was beginning to take on many levels of discomfort.

"I was...between worlds," I began, trying to word my answer in a way that Charlotte could understand. "Nothing really happened. Mostly I just felt pain," I said, turning my head in my hands to face her. Her expression was understanding but worried still. "And I heard you sometimes. Very faintly."

An endearing smile spread across her face and she seemed pleased with my answer.

Slowly her expression changed into a question. "Are you...you know?" she asked almost shyly. "Still an angel?" she added in a whisper.

I didn't know the answer to that. I felt different that was for sure. My body was purging something but I couldn't tell what. It was very possible that I wasn't. In fact, the likelihood that I still had my wings at all was small.

"I honestly don't think so," I said truthfully. "I haven't made a single effort to mask anything and my wings aren't exposed. I couldn't possibly with all of this medication inside of me. And the tattoos...that's a pretty clear indication—"

"Your wings," Charlotte said with a shadow in her bright green eyes. "They turned to ash." She began to cry with what I assumed to be the memory of the day I'd lost consciousness.

Suddenly I felt very foolish. Through her brave efforts to stay in one piece, I was sure that Charlotte had endured a lot in the time that I had been in between worlds. The more I considered it, the more obvious it became. Her beautiful full lips were chewed almost raw, dark circles made a home under her eyes, and her hair was messily thrown up into a ponytail. I couldn't imagine what horrible thoughts must have crossed her mind. Had it been me. I shuttered, not wanting to think about the pain it would have caused to see Charlotte unmoving for nearly two weeks.

"I'm so sorry," I said, reaching my hand out to touch hers, hoping that I was still able to sooth her in some small way. "I can't imagine—"

"I'm fine," she said, shaking her head bravely.

She looked as if my being gone had been the least of her problems. After I'd woken up, she should have seemed more relieved had that been the only thing worrying her. But in the way that she now avoided my eyes and tried to be stronger than she needed to be on her own, I knew that there was something else.

I sat up straighter in bed, watching her face, searching for the truth. I was missing a very large piece of the puzzle and I should have noticed it earlier.

Charlotte had looked drained of life and hope. My newfound emotions had created a wall between myself and my job. A job that I would never stop doing no matter what I was becoming. I needed to protect her at all costs.

"There's something you're not telling me," I said firmly. I took her face in my hand and willed her to meet my eyes. The look she gave me was more than unsettling. She was terrified.

"Joel, I'm fine," she lied blatantly. I could see it now as clear as day.

"Don't lie to me, Charlotte," I breathed.

I'd never...ever been angry at Charlotte. Her stubbornness had just been part of her. But now it was becoming a part of her that angered me. She was putting herself at risk by withholding information from me.

"Damn it, Charlotte," I said, louder than I'd meant to. I seemed incapable of maintaining any control over my quickly escalating temper. "Talk to me. I need to be able to trust that you are telling me everything. Otherwise I can't help you."

"Gosh," she said defensively.

I could tell that she still viewed me as a patient above all else. Bless her heart. She was trying not to reciprocate my agitation. I blinked hard in an effort to banish my frustration but it still lingered dangerously at the back of my throat and in the tips of my fingers.

"Listen," she said, asserting herself. "We have *no clue* what's going on with you right now. Your wings are gone. You have *huge* new tattoos that, oh, I don't know, *bleed* every now and then. I think that your recovery should be top priority and you're being irrational to think otherwise."

I turned fiercely to face her and drew back instantly against my frustration and the angry pain from my wounds that seemed endless. I pounded my fist so hard into the bed that I felt the springs fight back with vengeance. New pain now surged through my knuckles.

I was losing control of myself. What was happening to me? I hunched over and dug my hands into my hair.

"Please," I begged. "Please, just tell me what happened."

When I faced Charlotte again, she looked startled, and I felt ashamed for being the cause of it. What did I think I was doing? Was I thinking at all? It didn't seem to be the case. I adjusted myself on the bed to pull her into my arms and against the pleasure that reached places I would rather not acknowledge, I held her tightly.

"I'm sorry," I moaned into her hair, unable to fully suppress the ecstasy that I felt when I smelled her. Her hair emitted the aroma of eucalyptus and a light autumn breeze.

Startled by another uncontrollable emotion, I eased her out of my arms. Hopefully I had calmed her some. I'd once been able to do so, so efficiently. Now I seemed more likely to frighten her.

Nervously brushing a strand of loose hair behind her ear, Charlotte relented. "I'm not sure how serious he is about it," she began. "But Alex said something...the night you were taken in. He was the one who'd paid Matt to drug me."

I grew almost nauseous with anger. A rage that I'd never imagined myself capable of. Again, I was plagued with it so pure I couldn't get a grip on myself. What I'd seen while I was between worlds had been real. She must have seen my expression change because she was immediately by my side on the bed again.

"Right now you need to get better," she urged.

I shook my head, disappointed in myself. How had I not seen Alex as a threat in the past? Or at the very least suspected him as one? The guy had made no real efforts towards hiding his feelings for her. Even without knowing that he'd been watching her for years, I should have seen it. He had always been so obviously infatuated with her. From the day she walked through the door for her first day at work I saw it on his face. But I'd seen that look on countless faces. Had I brought each one in for questioning, I would have needed to rent out a concert hall to detain them all.

Charlotte was more stunning than she would ever give herself credit for. Her personality alone was magnetic, but lucky for me and my paranoia, her personality wasn't her only alluring asset. Her hair was long, nearing the small of her back. Her eyes were the most captivating shade of green. And her body...at the thought of her humble curves, my own body jerked. With a sigh of exhaustion, I realized that with my new status as a...fill in the blank, there were a handful of new hurdles I would have to get over.

Redirecting myself, I gritted my teeth and spat my next words, "Right now...You need to tell me exactly what he said to you."

Leaning back Charlotte looked at me with indifference. I could see the spark of brass that she got in her eyes when she felt as if she were being treated like a child. Something I stubbornly found myself doing often.

"He didn't say anything to *me*," she said, crossing her arms over her chest, holding the information she possessed for ransom until I gave her more credit.

I smiled unconsciously and rubbed my face. I knew every tilt of her perfect face, every shift of her eyes, the way she slid her tongue over her teeth in an effort to stop sour words before they slipped out. Over the years, I'd been able to study her so intricately that while she didn't know it, she was already communicating with more clarity than any words could. Not that it mattered much, Charlotte was perfectly happy to say exactly what was on her mind, and frankly, I was stunned that she hadn't let me have it already.

"Let's start over," I said with apology. "If you could, I'd appreciate being filled in on what happened while I was...while I was away."

* * *

My blood was still hot in my veins nearly an hour after Charlotte had told me what had happened that first night in the hospital. The mere idea of it nearly set me into a blind rage. I'd convinced her that I was okay long enough to send her down to the cafeteria for some food. While I didn't like the idea that she and I would have to walk on eggshells for a while, it was a fact I had to accept. Her wellbeing and my hot and cold mood swings needed tending to first. I couldn't possibly be of any help to her if I continued to act so impulsively. It would be no favor to Charlotte for me to put her in more danger than Alex was putting her in already.

My knuckles were white as my hands remained clenched tightly into fists. I needed to find a way to control myself. Forcing my fingers to fan out, I paced around my hospital room. When Charlotte had been younger her father would make her list off the good things in her life when she was angry. It seemed to help her quite a bit.

When Mikey Anderson had pushed her off of the jungle gym at recess, the little punk, Charlotte had come home spitting nails and making up all kinds of *mean words* as she made her way up the stairs to her room. I had followed her calmly through the house, aware of only one thing, she wasn't hurt. Just a degree cooler than the surface of the sun. But without missing a beat, her father had gently taken her by the arm, turned her around, wiped the tears from her eyes, and pulled her in for a hug. I remember having wished that I'd been able to do the same for her.

He knelt down in front of her, took hold of her arms and said, "Now, Charlotte," he said, his voice calm and nurturing "what happened?"

Her lip instinctively began to quiver and she took in a deep breath to let him have the whole story, in one long breath if she could manage. But he put his finger to her lips before she could let a single word escape.

"Take it slow, honey," he prompted.

She let out the lungful of air she'd taken in, rolled her eyes, tapped her foot, and waited for her temper to simmer. When she'd finally pulled herself together, she told him what Mikey had done and while her father wasn't happy about the bully's action, he never got angry. He'd even smiled when she added that she'd given him a bloody nose in return. He then looked her in the eye, took her chin in his hand, and kissed her forehead.

"Now tell me about the happy things in your life," he said.

Charlotte had learned early on that she would not be able to leave unless she listed off at least three things. So with only a little hesitation, she pulled up her delicate little hand and counted off on her fingers.

"Mommy said that I can get a kitten, I got cool new shoes with sparkles on them, I got an A in music class today, and Gram and Gramp are coming to visit this weekend." She looked up angelically, already forgetting about her angry tears and the reason she'd shed them in the first place. "Can I go now, Daddy?"

"Yes, you can go," he said, because she really was calmer.

I could see it in her eyes sometimes, even now, as she mentally listed off the good things in her life to find peace. While I had never fully understood why she'd needed to do it in the past, I understood it now.

Charlotte entered the room sipping generously at the coffee in her hands. When she made her way over, I took her in my arms firmly. My anger was still so solid that any emotions her touch might trigger had been stopped before they'd started.

"You're in my arms and healthy," I began, resting my chin on her head and closing my eyes. "I have some pretty cool new tattoos to add to my collection." I heard her giggle and it encouraged me to continue. "The hospital food isn't as bad as I thought it would be. And I could actually consider this somewhat of a vacation."

I held Charlotte out in front of me and smiled down at her, feeling calmer and more refreshed already. Knowingly, she let me hold her in silence for a while longer. By the time my nurse, Vicky, came back in to check on me again, I'd almost forgotten what had made me so upset in the first place. Almost.

"I've got good news and I've got bad news," Vicky began. "Which do you want first?"

"The bad," Charlotte and I said in unison.

Smiling, Vicky thumbed through her chart. "Well, you're going to have to stay here tonight for observation. You've seemed to come out of the coma rather unscathed which is great, but for legal reasons of course, we have to charge you the extra day and probe you a bit more before we let you leave."

"The news could be worse," I admitted, though I wasn't really eager to stay in a hospital bed overnight. I'd been blessed to have spent my time thus far in the hospital without knowledge of it. My time left would undoubtedly be the longest day of my life.

"And the good news?" Charlotte asked.

"I've convinced the staff to let you stay with Mr. Benedict tonight. It wasn't easy, but given the circumstances, they were willing to make an exception."

"Thank you," I said, extending a hand in gratitude.

Once we were alone again, Charlotte made her way over to the bed wordlessly. I watched her tuck herself beneath the covers and felt a sense of peace take over. I joined her in bed and we both sat up in silence for a while. It was still inexplicably torturous to be so close to her. There was a constant flow of electricity running through me that made relaxation nearly impossible. Like pins and needles, I could feel my body coming to life for the first time. But nothing could keep me from holding her.

"I need to tell you something," Charlotte said, her voice shaking uneasily.

"Anything," I said, rubbing her shoulder.

"I don't know how you'll react, especially now." She couldn't meet my eye. She looked guilty, which I hadn't expected.

"What is it?" I asked, pulling her face up to look at me.

Her eyes were big and her lip immediately gave way under the pressure of something I couldn't read. "I kissed Alex," she breathed. "Well, he kissed me, but I didn't stop him." She looked away and a tear fell from her eye. "I didn't want to. I just...I couldn't pull away."

I turned my attention to look straight ahead, anything I might have said caught in my throat. Something unexpected tugged at my heart and my stomach turned. I felt dizzy and I became convinced that my body was actually beginning to shut down. I couldn't speak for a long moment. Fire pumped through me and my vision was blurred by anger I hadn't expected. I was jealous. I was angry and hurt and a slew of other things I couldn't grab a hold of.

"Oh, Joel," she said tucking herself into my side. "I'm so sorry." She cried freely and I knew that she was sincere. Charlotte was a faithful and strong woman and I didn't doubt that it had all been Alex's doing. A well crafted plan to take her from me in my weakest moment. The important thing was that he hadn't succeeded. No matter what my body was compelled to feel, I had to keep things in perspective.

I turned to face her but couldn't force myself to give a reassuring smile. "Do you want to be with him?" I could still feel a knot of doubt in my throat.

"No, of course not!" Charlotte sat up to look in my eyes and took my face in her hands, resting her forehead against mine. "I want to be with you, I *need* to be with you. I was so afraid. I wasn't sure if you'd ever come back to me. I was paralyzed by it, Joel."

I took my hands and cupped them over hers and felt all of the pain and agony drain from my body. "I know," I said. "I know."

"They were going to turn the machines off...they were going to let you die..."

Her voice was controlled again and I knew that she was making every effort not to cry. I couldn't imagine how long the weeks must have been as she awaited my return to the land of the living. Though I knew some of her pain, based on the new feelings I was experiencing since waking up, what I'd been through had only been a fraction of what she'd had to withstand.

"I guess it's a good thing I woke up when I did then." I pulled her into my arms and clenched my teeth against the electricity that it sent through me.

I was home.

Chapter

7

"I think this is a lot bigger than just a crush that got out of hand," Joel said as we walked the path of the atrium. "He's obsessed with you. He knew you before working at the bank."

"Where is this all coming from?" I asked. The tone of his voice didn't indicate unwarranted concern. "How can you be sure? I mean, how could he have possibly known me before?"

The idea of it was absolutely terrifying. If what Joel was suggesting was in fact true, then our Alex problem had just doubled in size.

"When I was...away, I re-visited a memory of you. You were seventeen, walking home from school. I was observing the scene from afar which I found strange, considering I was usually right beside you, and then I saw Alex. He was watching you. When I saw it, I didn't know how much of a threat Alex was, though I knew that there was one based on the flashback, but when you told me about what he'd said and that he'd kissed you...you validated it. I don't know why or even how but Alex knows you better than we'd originally assumed, and there is likely even more to it than that."

"I guess I shouldn't be surprised," I said sarcastically. "But honestly, neither of us saw this coming. How can I not be?"

"I'm ashamed that I never saw the signs before. He hid it so well I—"

"Joel, don't." I shook my head. I knew that he would immediately blame himself but I wouldn't have any of it. Alex had fooled both of us. "We can't blame ourselves for not having known about Alex being around for all of these years. We need to concern ourselves with how he managed to stay under our radar instead of being upset with the fact that we never saw it before."

As we rounded the corner on the path for the countless time, we made our way out of the small park towards the staircase, knowing that we'd walked off as much as we could in one day. I could tell that Joel was still weak, though he tried very hard to mask it. He'd held his breath as the pain from his wounds threatened to break him. But I hadn't been able to keep him in his room so we'd met halfway and spent the last hour in the atrium. He was trying to rebuild himself and while he said nothing of it, I knew that he was attempting to suffocate his pain away.

"You're right." Joel shook his head and clenched his teeth past another bout of pain. "But before we try and sort anything out, I've got a lot of adjusting to do since waking up. Something's drastically different." By the tone of his voice, I could tell that it wasn't something he was happy to admit.

I could tell that he was right about being different. Not only was he capable of feeling much greater amounts of pain, unable to heal as quickly as he had in the past, it would also seem that even the simple things were much harder on him. He looked at me as if he were ashamed of something he saw when his eyes met mine. But it wasn't what he was seeing; it was how he was seeing it.

"I wish God didn't give us so much credit sometimes," I joked, leaning into him.

We made our way back up to Joel's room, feeling anything but refreshed. The journey ahead of us was arguably going to put to shame any mayhem we'd already been through together and there was nothing we could do to stop it.

* * *

Charlotte had called out of work to spend the remainder of my stay at the hospital with me. Though I feared that she was pushing the limits of her resources, I hadn't been able to suggest that she go to work and leave me. I enjoyed her company far too much to consider any consequences of it.

When she came back into the room, I felt dangerously alive. Her hair was neatly brushed and the circles under her eyes had lightened to a mere suggestion of exhaustion. Her walk was bubbly once more. Something that I loved most about Charlotte was that she could separate stress so easily from the moments where she decided to allow herself joy. It was a fact I'd never really appreciated until that moment, when I could feed off of it and find peace simply by observing hers.

"Vicky just told me that you are being released tonight," she said, so full of excitement I could hardly detect any other emotion she might be feeling. "Your vitals and all that other medical mumbo jumbo seem to be stable and in check. She said it's like you were just sleeping and not in a coma."

I was grateful for the news to say the least. There were too many supernatural events taking place in my body to be able to hide for too much longer, and Alex was still out there.

Charlotte kissed my lips tenderly and a surge of delight shocked my system. With most of my anger extinguished from the day before, her touch was once again lethally enjoyable. Resisting the urge to jump back, I waited for her to casually stroll around the room, picking up wrappers and cans as she went. She was clearly as ready as I was to be gone.

"I bought you a change of clothes for when you woke up the day after you got here," she said as she let the garbage tumble from her arms into the wastebasket beside the door.

"Always the optimist," I said lightheartedly. Charlotte was a determined woman. She packed enough punch and determination to shun any doubts that might be piled up against her.

She turned around and gave me the stink-eye, indicating that losing hope had never been an option for her.

"They're over there," she said, pointing to a paper shopping bag. "I didn't know your measurements so I had to pester a few guys in the store that looked to be about your size. I hope you don't mind American Eagle."

I walked over to the bag, remembering how unclothed I still was. The blue hospital gown, my boxer briefs, and white socks left little to the imagination, leaving me to feel a tinge of humiliation again. As I stood embarrassed by my scantily clad body, I wondered how I'd ever managed to pose nude.

Human nature, I mused. As an angel I hadn't possessed the ability to be ashamed of my own skin. I had shown up in Charlotte's art class in order to plant myself further into her life and to maintain a close eye on her. Taking on the role as the model for her class had seemed like the easiest way in. It was something I hadn't thought much about. When she'd asked me how I'd been able to model, considering the human nature of being uncomfortable in your own skin, I had replied by saying that I didn't have any. At the time it had been true, but now I thought maybe human nature was something I'd begun to experience firsthand.

Turning around as I took hold of the bag, I faced Charlotte apprehensively. "Charlotte," I said with question in my voice. The mere thought of what I was considering was unsettling.

"Yes?" she said, looking up from the blanket she was folding.

"I think...." The words caught in my throat like peanut butter. "I think I might be human."

Chapter

8

Human. Wow. It was something that, oddly enough, had remained off my radar. I had never considered that being an angel and being human were on the same wavelength. I had never flirted with the idea that it was something Joel could become.

But now. Now that I'd witnessed what I had. His wings turning to ash. His unyielding and uncontrolled emotions. His lack of calm that had always been part of who he was. His new tattoos. It was just as believable as finding out that he'd been an angel in the first place. The moment I felt like I understood what was going on, it seemed the earth shifted and he was something else. Maybe when he was shot next, heaven forbid, he'd turn into a werewolf or maybe a wizard even. It was pretty farfetched of course but it seemed the whole purpose of his morphing was to throw me off of reality's scent.

"Charlotte?" I jerked at the sound of Joel's voice beside me. Trigger was still idling as we sat in the car parked in front of my house.

"I'm sorry," I said, shaking my head from the craziness that was swirling around inside of it.

I took the key from the ignition and opened my door. Joel watched me closely before opening his own. Turning to watch him exit the vehicle, I felt my first genuine sensation of joy since the shooting. Joel was human? Could I be so lucky? Were we getting our answer, our validation that we could actually be together? It had been the one unbreakable barrier between us and now it was gone. So it seemed at least.

"Are you coming?" he asked, ducking his head back inside of the car.

"Yeah," I said, lifting from my seat and shutting the door behind me.

I took Joel's hand in mine and we headed up the walk towards the house. It felt so good to have him out of that hospital. Just being in the unsettling atmosphere had left me feeling ill at ease. Being home didn't mean that we were in the clear yet but I preferred to be home with my thoughts, Joel at my side, then in a stuffy and cramped recovery room.

As we walked through the door Emily and Tara were making their way into the living room, both clutching their purses.

It was evident by the way they were dressed that they were we headed out. Emily wore her short platinum hair down and was dressed in jeans and a long tunic shirt with her black puffy jacket pulled over top. Tara's dark hair was down as well and she wore a skirt, tall boots, a graphic t-shirt, and her pea coat.

"Oh my gosh." Emily exclaimed. "Joel." She threw herself into his arms and squeezed him tightly. "*It's so good to see you.*"

Joel let his small bag of personal belongings drop to the floor and wrapped grateful arms around her. "It's nice to see you too, Emily," he said into her hair.

Tara quickly took Emily's place in his arms and hugged him speechlessly for a few moments. "We were so worried about you," she said, wiping a runaway tear from her cheek.

The girls scanned Joel's body but with the black and white plaid flannel shirt I'd picked out, his bandages were hidden. Apart from a six o'clock shadow I hadn't noticed before, he looked like his regular self.

"You look like a lumberjack," Emily joked, crossing her arms over her chest.

Joel glared down at me, confirming the hesitation he'd expressed in the hospital toward my selection of clothes. Yes...the artfully tattered jeans and flannel button up hadn't exactly screamed *Joel*, but I had a soft spot for the working-class-man look. I snubbed his look of distain and stuck my chin high up in the air. I was more than content with my choices.

"Well we were just on our way out to Applebee's to meet up with Alex and a few of his friends," Tara said rustling through her purse to locate her keys.

I could tell from my peripheral that Joel was making an equal attempt at stifling any signs of hatred towards Alex.

"I know you guys probably want to hang out here for the night, but you're welcome to join us," she added.

"Thank you for the invitation," I said with a strained smile, "but I think we're going to stay in tonight."

"Yeah, I figured," she replied.

"Well, enjoy the house to yourselves you two." Emily winked. "I'm sure you have a lot of catching up to do."

Joel shifted nervously beside me and I realized that it was probably best that we not *take advantage* of the alone time. It seemed there was still had a lot that he needed to get used to.

When Emily and Tara left, the house was instantly filled with the longest few minutes of silence I'd ever experienced. Like two teenagers, we were both palatably nervous with the possibilities of what might happen when given so much freedom. I could already tell that the intimacy that we'd shared in the past might as well have been wiped off the board. We were starting from scratch now. Lucky for me, there was so much other crap going on that I didn't even have it in me to feel insulted. We would ease back into things when he was good and ready to do so.

Joel rubbed his neck and looked to the stairs. "I should probably shower."

"And shave that sandpaper off your face," I added. "I never knew you were the scruffy type. I kind of like it."

He shrugged, avoiding the truth of the matter. He'd never once had to shave before today. This look was new. Something else he'd adopted since waking up. And with the addition of every new element tied to his apparent humanity, we both became a bit more unnerved.

I took his bag from the floor and headed into the kitchen. "Hit the showers."

After grabbing a yogurt from the fridge and tidying up the kitchen a bit, I made my way up stairs. As I passed by the bathroom, I could hear the shower going and I knew that it probably felt pretty incredible to take a shower after such a long absence from the world. Joel was sure to feel rejuvenated and hopefully a bit more like his old self when he was done.

Scraping the last of my yogurt from the bottom of the cup, I began a hurried attempt at organizing my room. I had let the space get rather grotesque in the time that Joel had been in the hospital. My hamper was overflowing and my school books were scattered all over the room. I made my bed for the first time in who knows how long and I dusted my dresser with a quick pass of my hand.

When I leaned back in my desk chair to relax, I heard Joel cry out in a raw and bloodcurdling roar of pain from the bathroom. The sounds of chaos accompanied his scream, headed by a very large thud. Immediately, I shot up from the chair and bolted out of my room, tearing open the bathroom door.

With the shower curtain pulled down and gripped tightly in his fist, Joel grunted through clenched teeth, kneeling down at the base of the tub. His huge white wings were slowly, and as it would seem, painfully, retracting into his shoulder blades. Covered in blood that trickled down his back with the running water, he tensed and hunched over to try and absorb the pain as best he could.

I felt helpless. There wasn't a thing in the world I could do for him. With my hands pressed to my mouth, shaking with fear, I watched as Joel's wings disappeared into his back, leaving the bloody tattoos in their wake.

When he breathed out in relief, I darted over and jumped into the tub with him. With the shower still going, I was instantly drenched but I hardly noticed.

"Joel, oh Joel," I said, resting my head on his shoulder. He let his head tilt to the side and rested it against mine.

"It's not over," he said breathlessly. "I'm still making some kind of transition."

Blood pooled around our feet and snaked its way to the drain, thinning as the water washed the remainder of it from his shoulders. There didn't seem to be any gashes or incisions on his back. The blood had stopped flowing when the wings had retracted completely. Like a floodgate being opened and closed. I shook my head with grief and turned the water off as an afterthought.

"Let's get you into bed." I said, standing up, trailing my hands through his hair.

"So I can stain your bedding with another onset of whatever that was?" He stood up slowly, bracing himself on the lip of the tub. "No."

"Joel," I said weakly. "You're going through a lot right now. Be it a change or—"

"Change?" he laughed without humor. "I'm teetering on the edge of an electric fence, Charlotte."

Biting my tongue, I swallowed the venom in Joel's words and exited the bathtub without another word. I walked through the door and made my way into my room, still soaked to the bone.

From my bedroom, I could hear Joel struggling angrily with the shower curtain rod which I'd noticed had been compromised in the heat of the moment, ripped from the wall entirely. The grand finale of his efforts ended with one final hard crash, confirming that he had accepted its un-reparable status.

I took my time getting dressed in dry sweats and a fresh t-shirt. It seemed that a little alone time might be the remedy that we both needed in order to pick ourselves up from discovering this new piece of the puzzle. Joel was shifting uncontrollably. It weakened our game plan. We both knew it. However, until Joel learned to harness and more importantly, holster his newly developing emotions, it was my job to keep calm.

Figuring that he was about as cooled off as a newly emotional half-angel half-man could be, I strolled back to the bathroom and rested heavily against the doorframe.

Joel sat utterly defeated on the side of the tub with a towel wrapped around his waist and his head in his hands. I pulled one of his hands gently from his head and held it so that his palm faced up. Without words, I took his harmonica from my sweatpants' pocket and placed it in his receiving hand, folding his fingers around it.

He looked up at me with gratitude as if he'd been reunited with an old friend. Kissing me softly on the forehead, he stood up and walked over to the sink. Tucking the harmonica into his towel, he placed his hands on the countertop and looked into the mirror. His face exuded a look that was purely male. He picked up one hand and ran it over the surface of one stubble-clad cheek.

I walked over to the shower and plucked my razor from its place on the soap dish. Grabbing a can of shaving foam, I put them both beside Joel. He looked through the mirror at me then shifted his gaze to the razor that lay next to his hand.

"You're not serious?" he said coolly.

"Don't you want to shave?" I asked, confused. He didn't seem too pleased with his new look.

"Yes."

"Then what's the problem?" I said, raising my eyebrows.

"Charlotte," he began, turning to face me, "I've been with you every moment of your life. *Always by your side.*"

"And?"

He took the razor between two wary fingers as if it were contaminated with the plague. "I know where this has been," he added with a playful smile.

With blush filling my cheeks, I yanked the razor from his fingers. "For goodness sakes." I popped the used razor head off, opened my drawer, and clipped on a new one. I waved it in the air in front of his face. "Happy?"

With a smile, he took the razor from my hand and nodded his head sweetly. "Yes, thank you."

Looking up at his reflection again, I could tell that Joel was apprehensive. He had the body of a twenty-five-year-old and the life experience of a young child. He'd never had to shave, shower, or even brush his teeth before. Showering, I'd imagined, had been an easy one to figure out. But now he held a sharp blade to his face and I knew that he was considerably less confident in tackling the strange new task.

His eyes darted back to me. "Are you going to watch?" he asked, trying not to sound embarrassed.

"Guess not," I said, backing out of the room with a smile.

Leaving a crack in the door, I walked across the hall and slid down to sit opposite the bathroom door to wait patiently for him to finish. If something else paranormal happened I didn't know what I would do.

"I know you're out there," he called from behind the door.

"I'm not watching," I rebutted.

After the water ran for a short while and I heard the rhythmic tapping of the razor against the edge of the sink, I was finally able to relax. Being the held-together one was wiping me out.

Through the crack in the door, I heard Joel bring a sharp breath of pain through his teeth and I immediately pushed myself from the wall and entered the bathroom. He was tending to a nasty cut on his cheek, mumbling it seemed at the razor in question.

"A used blade doesn't tend to cut as much," I said bravely. Joel's eyes dialed in on my face and I could tell that he was biting his tongue. I put my hands up in mocked surrender. "I'm just saying."

Taking the razor in my hand, I slid up onto the counter and crossed my legs beneath me. I took his nicked up face in one hand and ran the razor under the faucet with the other. Realizing my intention, Joel jerked away.

"Uh, uh, soldier, I'm helping you and you're just going to have to grin and bear it."

He stared at me, pride, concern, and doubt all wrapped up in one expression. I could tell that he didn't want this change to occur. No matter what it meant for us, it also meant that he would be faced with challenges he'd never faced before. And I knew that in his mind he'd lost a part of who he was. Maybe he was even afraid that I viewed him differently now. But Joel was no different in my eyes than he'd always been. He was strong and gentle at the same time, vulnerable in his heart but strong in his mind. And if it took a lifetime to prove that to him, I wouldn't hesitate for even a second.

With great care, I took the razor and ran it gently down his cheek. When it got caked with hair and shaving cream, I cleaned it off under the running water and went back again. Joel's eyes darted over the surface of my face, watching me intently. Without words, we both put our guns down and signed a silent peace treaty. I knew that he was going through a hard time, but he seemed to be under the constant impression that he was going at it alone.

As I cleared the foam and hair, Joel's former smooth face slowly began to make an appearance. His eyes softened and closed on occasion against something I couldn't begin to understand. He was going through hell.

"I don't want to be angry anymore," he said with a heavy heart.

"Then don't be."

I knew that it wasn't nearly that simple, but he didn't need my well-worded advice. There was no doubt in my mind that he was already on his way back up. The way his hand rested on my knee, rubbing it tenderly. That was the Joel I knew. And while this new side of him was different, he was no less himself, and it seemed that that was his biggest concern. If I knew Joel at all, protecting me was still priority number one, and he would only view his mood swings as a hindrance.

"Okay, all done," I said, putting the razor down on the counter. "Good as new."

I slid down and stood at his side as he looked at his smooth faced reflection. "I wish it was that simple," he said, bringing a hand up and resting in on the small of my back.

"You know, Alex is going to find out tonight that you're back. We'll need to form some kind of strategy," I said, picking up my brush and running it through my hair.

"As much as I hate to admit it, for now we're just going to have to play ignorant while keeping a *very* close eye on him." I could tell by the tone of his voice that he didn't like the idea any more than I did.

"Agreed."

"If we give him any indication that we know what he did, who knows what could happen. He may have been saying those things in the heat of the moment to a guy that couldn't hear him anyway. Maybe he's serious. We don't know. The only thing I know is that I'm not going to leave your side until we find out."

I put the brush down and examined my exhausted face. While we still had the time to re-energize that's what we needed to do. I hadn't slept a solid eight hours let alone four since the day Joel had been shot. He, on the other hand, had slept for a good while longer than eight hours but it hadn't seemed to be a very restful experience.

"What do you say to getting some shuteye?" I asked, kissing his cheek softly.

Joel yawned in reply and I couldn't help but laugh.

We made our way to the bedroom somberly, the past couple of weeks draining the last of our energy as we entered my room. I let myself fall back on to the bed dramatically and moaned softly at how good it felt. Joel stood stiffly beside the bed, watching me curl up and un-tuck the corners of the newly made bed.

"Are you going to sleep standing up?" I asked, shimmying out of my sweatpants and tucking myself under the covers.

He watched me tentatively and I could see a craving in his eyes that I hadn't noticed before.

Suddenly it became very clear to me that my effect on him physically in the past had probably been just as diluted as his anger had. The way he looked at me now, with a gentle curiosity in his eyes and the fierceness in which he tried to stop it, brought me excitement. I could tell that he was trying to tame his primal male desires.

Unmoving, I tried not to stir up any additional tension. Whatever Joel wanted to do or not to do, I had to let him do it on his own. He closed his eyes and took in a breath of what seemed to be an attempt to cool the fire in his veins.

Making his way over to the bed, he took his harmonica from his towel, placed it on the nightstand, and let the towel hit the floor. He pulled up the covers and slid in beside me. With the fire now burning brightly in his eyes he lowered himself on top of me. Feeling his weight on me again was intoxicating. Slowly and tenderly, he covered my mouth with a kiss as he dug his hands into my hair. As our tongues explored together, I could hear and feel his heart beat growing faster. He pressed himself against me with a need I'd never felt before.

Running his hands down my ribcage, he moved with more urgency. His touch became rougher and more lustful. I laced my arms around him, running my hands over his new tattoos. As my fingers smoothed over the intricate wings on his back, he pursued me more fiercely.

"Charlotte," he groaned into my ear. "I can't..." he brushed his abs against me. "I can't control it. I can't stop."

His words had surprised me. Usually when Joel said he couldn't, he meant that he had to resist doing something. That being with me was something he would refuse to do in order to protect me. But now it meant something drastically different. It meant that he couldn't stop his primitive instincts from gaining control over him.

"Then don't," I said, kissing his lips and encouraging him to let himself go.

I could feel the exact instant that Joel allowed everything else fall to the floor. I'd never realized how strong he was until he had me pinned so mercilessly against the bed. I was surprised by his force. His emotions were taking control of him and the untamed beast inside of him was intent on ravishing me. Kissing me simultaneously, he cradled me in his body. I had assumed that Joel's desire for intimacy might be less after what had happened.

It hadn't been my first miscalculation.

Later, as I rested my head on his chest, Joel traced his finger over my back. He kissed my hair tenderly and the contrast of his intimacy made me smile into his skin. He could be so raw in one moment and so docile the next.

With an agreement of abstinence between us now, until we had a better hold of what was going on with Alex, my body felt that much more deprived of him, though we'd only just been together. While I was sure that he would manage to harness his lust just as much as I was sure he'd harness his rage, this wasn't a side of Joel that I would easily give up.

Chapter

9

It had been nearly a week since Joel's wings had ripped through his skin, leaving the wing tattoos to bleed in their wake. While I figured it wasn't wise to get too optimistic about it, it had been a good sign nonetheless.

Since he hadn't been able to join me at work and school, Joel spent most of his time in my room trying to rein in his emotions. I'd asked him once what he did to do so and he mostly avoided providing me with an answer. It seemed to me, however, that he came just short of torturing himself. But I couldn't argue with the results. Every day he seemed more and more like his old self.

With a lazy Thursday afternoon stretched out before us, I decided that it would be a good idea to breathe some life into his wardrobe. Before being shot, Joel had been able to simply show up in a new set of clothes. Inevitably, he'd lost that ability as well in his transition.

"I'm really okay with what I have," Joel argued as I finished up getting ready in my room. "Two outfits are more than enough."

"I would hardly consider *that* an outfit," I argued, jerking my finger in the direction of Joel's alternate choice. "Its blood stained and has a bullet hole clear through it."

"I never leave the house. Why do I need you spending your money on clothes for my sake?" he argued.

"Because at one point I'd like for you to leave the house, hence us going to the mall. And it's fun for me," I answered with a smile. "Besides, you need a coat, new shoes, maybe some more underwear, and socks. We're going to get reported to an environmentalist group at the rate we've been washing clothes around here."

Like most men I knew, Joel wasn't too fond of being looked after. He viewed that as *his* job. But the fact was, he had no money, he had no way of getting money, and I had made a habit of saving up for rainy days that never came anyway. I wasn't about to let him convince me otherwise, and by the look on his face, he knew it was best just to give in.

With only a moment or two more of hesitation, he surrendered and we made our way downstairs. I hadn't been able to enjoy a single normal, non-work or school related thing for what seemed like years. I was actually beginning to look forward to doing a real date-like activity. We might even catch a bite to eat on our way back. The possibilities of normalcy were endless.

"Hey," Emily called from the couch, muting the television. "Where are you two off to?"

"The mall. Joel needs some new clothes," I replied, slipping into my jacket.

"While you're there do you think you could pick me up another bottle of my perfume? I'll give you the money for it."

"Sure, no problem."

Emily made her way to the kitchen table to grab some money out of her purse and I turned to grab hold of Joel's hand, but when I turned to face him, he was gone. I hadn't even heard him move from my side. Then, before my very eyes, like a flickering light bulb he appeared for a split second hunched over with exhaustion.

Oh shit. Oh shit.

"Where'd Joel go?" Emily asked, making her way over from the kitchen.

I whipped around in a panic. Ah hell. "Um, he left his wallet upstairs."

"Oh, okay. Well, here's the cash for the perfume, you know the kind I get right?"

"Yup," I said nervously. Joel seemed to lack control of his disappearing act. He would undoubtedly flicker back any second now. If at all.

"Man, I'm glad I got up, I really had to pee," Emily said, walking briskly towards the stairs. "Have fun!" she called back.

Once her back was turned, Joel flickered back into view, still hunched over, for a second longer than before and he was gone again. I stood perfectly still, trying to stop the nervous pattering of my heart. Once Emily was all the way upstairs and out of earshot I turned to face where he'd just been.

"Joel, oh my gosh, what's happening to you?" I said in a whisper, just loud enough for him to hear.

Appearing again, he seemed to grab hold and managed to stay visible. He turned his head and looked up at me, clearly exhausted. "Charlotte," he said quietly, trying to remain calm. "I'm going to need to stay here."

"I'll stay with you," I insisted, rubbing my hand over his back.

"No, I won't be the reason you're trapped. Go, enjoy yourself. I need to figure out what this is all about. If it'll happen again."

"Joel," I argued.

"Please." He propped himself up and took my hand tenderly in his. "I'll be fine…as long as you don't try and dress me up like a lumberjack anymore."

I couldn't help but smile. Looking him over I *still* couldn't see a single thing wrong with his outfit. "Any requests?"

There was no use in freaking out over another supernatural addition to Joel's ever growing collection of setbacks. While I wanted to freak out and ask a million questions too many, none of which he would be able to answer, I knew it was best to try and stay calm.

"Try and stick to plain shirts and jeans *without* holes in them," he said, sticking a finger through the hole in the knee of his pants.

"You're no fun at all."

"Fun wasn't in the job description."

"Well," I said, waving my hand around in his general direction. "It seems to me that you've been fired, might not hurt to pick up some new skills."

Shaking his head with a smile, he kissed me lightly on the forehead and made his way back up the stairs. "No plaid!" he called down at me.

"No fun!" I called back.

I had once thought that shopping for myself was probably my biggest vice, but looking through the racks of clothes in the men's section of Express, Abercrombie, and Bon-Ton proved to be an even bigger addiction. Hell, picking out boxer briefs in American Eagle had nearly made my life. Joel might have favored the Simon Cowell look when it came to his clothes, but there was no reason he had to continue the trend with his underwear.

Fanning through the sales rack, I tried to find shirts I knew that Joel would find suitable. Nothing too flashy. I picked up a long sleeve baseball style tee, navy blue and white. It was plain but it wasn't boring either. And for six bucks it couldn't be beat. I tossed it over my arm that carried a handful of other shirts and jeans and dove back into the rack for more.

"Hey," I heard from behind me. When I turned around and saw Alex I couldn't stop myself from jumping with surprise...or more appropriately, anxiety.

"Oh, hi," I said, trying to fake a smile. My luck had been doomed once I'd woken up as it would seem. "What are you doing here?" I hoped that he'd gotten the hint after I'd refused to answer his calls that what had happened between us had been a mistake. One I wished to pretend hadn't happened.

He didn't have any bags and Tara was nowhere to be seen. Though I would have been more surprised if Tara *had* been there. But it didn't exactly make him a stalker either. It was a public mall after all. Pity.

"I'm here to pick up some scrubs, actually." His voice was fluid and smooth. "I got a job at the hospital a few days ago."

"That's great." Great. Just great.

He leaned against the clothing rack, dangerously close. "So how's Joel doing? You two must be busy. I figured I'd hear from you after he woke up. I've been calling," he added, as if I didn't already know.

After the stunt he'd pulled at the restaurant, I couldn't help but wonder why on earth he thought I would call him or answer any of his calls. He was clearly taking the pretend-like-nothing-happened approach.

"Uh, yeah. It's been pretty crazy." I adjusted the pile of clothes on my arm. "You know, everything's just a bit different with him now."

"I'd imagine. How did that effect his...well, you know? What he is."

"Oh, just a few hiccups along the way but he's as good as new." Giving Alex detailed information would have been like giving a burglar the key to my house. He didn't need to know the weaknesses that would help aid in his mission.

He pushed himself off of the clothing rack and put up his hands in mimicked shock. "Is he here right now, watching us?" He laughed but I could tell that he really did want to know if I was safe to be around, if we really were alone.

"I don't know where he is actually. Maybe he is," I laughed, trying to leave it an open ended answer.

Was it safer for Alex to think that Joel was still an angel? Or was it safer for him to think that he was human? Probably something Joel and I should have discussed. Either way it could backfire.

"So I guess you two are free to have your relationship now." His smile was hollow. "That's great, huh?"

I moved around the rack of clothes to dilute my restlessness. "Yeah, it is."

"About that kiss the other night," he began.

"Oh, forget about it," I said, trying to act nonchalant. "I know it didn't mean anything. Heat of the moment and all," I added flippantly.

Alex's face grew hardened. It had clearly meant something to him. "Yeah, sure it was." He made no effort at convincing me that he really agreed.

He stared into my eyes and searched them for a grain of feelings that I might have for him. I wished him luck, it was something he was sure never to find. I pulled my eyes away and looked down to the rack of clothes again and tried to ignore the static in the air around us as he drew closer.

"So, do you two..." he walked around the other side of the rack to meet me in the middle and rested his hand on the rod right in front of me "have sex?"

"That's a little personal don't you think?" Not that I pegged Alex as the type to respect those kinds of boundaries.

"Maybe," he said, plucking a shirt from the rack, still hovering closely over me. "Angel's probably can't get enjoyment out of a physical relationship anyway," he said mockingly.

Lifting my brow in challenge, I ran my tongue neatly over my teeth to tame my escalating temper. "He seems *more* than capable of pleasure," I said sharply, letting the suggestion fall where it may.

Alex's expression hardened with jealousy so thick it was a mask on his face. His fist tightened around the shirt in his hand as he watched me, placing it back on the rack.

"Do you and Tara?" I asked, hoping I wasn't pushing the wrong button. "You two have gotten pretty close." I said it, pretending that he hadn't already made it very clear that his feelings for Tara were a false.

"I'm saving myself," he answered in a deep voice that made my skin crawl. It was sexy, a voice sexy enough to be totally terrifying.

"Saving yourself for marriage is admirable, not many people do it these days." I was trying desperately to keep my head above water in a conversation that threatened to drown me.

"I'm not saving myself for marriage," he corrected, taking my face in his hand. "I'm saving myself for you."

Swallowing hard, I fantasized about running out of the store so vividly I nearly managed to convince myself that I actually had. I backed away, realizing that since I was still there, it was probably vital that I say or do something. Anything.

"Ummm..." Brilliant.

Alex let his hand fall to his side and made his way out of the store, clearly pleased with himself. "It was nice seeing you again, Charlotte."

Just like that, he'd sunk his hooks in me again, like he thought he had any right. I wanted to call after him and challenge him to a death match. Something. *Anything* more profound than the stammering attempt I'd made at defending my ability to choose. But no. There I was, clutching Joel's new wardrobe in a tight death grip instead.

Why had Alex decided, after all this time, to make a move? He'd had *years* to do it before. He might have even stood a chance in the past. But now, now he had abandoned any decorum. Dating my best friend and going after me, knowing that I was currently involved with a man unmatched as far as my heart was concerned.

Driving home I was paranoid. I hadn't seen Alex since the night at the restaurant and he hadn't stopped by the house since I'd run into him on the porch. Be it my blatant avoidance or desperation that had driven him to say what he had, he was clearly moving right along to plan B. Joel hadn't died, so he would have to be replaced. As it would seem, normalcy was still very much out of reach.

When I walked through my bedroom door, I plopped half-a-dozen bags down on the floor and fell face first onto my bed.

"I think that the saying 'shop till you drop' is a pretty accurate description of your experience at the mall today," I heard Joel observe from my desk chair.

I turned my head to look at him. He was shirtless and coated in a thin sheath of sweat. "I think it's more like 'shop till your luck runs out'," I said, draping my hand off the side of the bed. "Do you think you could bring Emily her change and perfume for me? Then I need to tell you something."

"Sure." He got up from the chair apprehensively but didn't question me. He simply looked at the array of bags with amusement.

"Don't worry, you can try everything on soon. The perfume is in there," I said, pointing to the American Eagle bag. "And here's her change." I reached out my hand and placed the money into his.

With concern apparent on his face, Joel wasted no time on the errand. Telling him about what had happened at the mall was the last thing I wanted to do. It was something In fact, it was something I wanted to pretend hadn't happened at all. But stupidity wasn't a habit I cared to practice willingly. He and I needed to remain on the same page.

When he returned, Joel took a seat beside me on the bed. I'd sat up since he'd left and was cradling my head in my hands, trying to sort things out. Could I have stopped any of this from happening had I acted differently before? The what if's swirled around in my head but I knew that it was a waste of time. He placed a hand on my shoulder and with a knowing air about him, he waited patiently as I pulled myself back together.

"I ran into Alex at the mall today," I finally said. Though I saw a twitch of agitation flash across his face, he remained calm and waited quietly for me to continue. "He made it *very* clear that he means to have me. And I have a feeling that today was just a glimpse of what's to come."

Closing his eyes and taking in a breath, Joel centered himself before he spoke. "Well we knew this day would come. It was only a matter of time."

"We need to start finding out what we can about that night at the club. See if we can legally tie Alex to it in any way. I really think that we should try and talk to Matt—"

"*What?* Are you—" He paused and took a breath before continuing. "Charlotte," he began calmly. "That man tried to *kill* you."

"Well, lucky for me, he may not be the only one with that goal," I said sharply. "Right now he's the only one that might be able to help us, as strange as that sounds. We have a chance of building a case against Alex if we can prove that he had been involved that night and go from there. We have nothing else to work with."

Joel massaged his neck quietly and seemed to be searching for an argument. Neither of us wanted it to come to asking Matt for help.

He sighed. "I hate to admit it, but you might be right."

The very last thing I wanted to do was to spend even a second more in court trying to protect myself. Going up against Alex was even further down on my to-do list. But what were my options? He'd clearly grown impatient, ready now to do whatever it took to get his point across. Though I knew deep down that it would be far from that simple.

"I was thinking we could go Saturday after I get out of work. I really don't want to wait much longer. Alex was very...determined. I don't need to see what he'll do next."

"Hopefully I can get my disappearing act in check by then. I feel like exercise could be the answer. The stronger my human body becomes, the easier it is for me to take hold of it. Hopefully that's the answer. I have a pretty good feeling that it is. The throbbing from my shoulder blades has gone down in just the hour or so that I spent working out while you were gone."

"That's good news." I said with a smile. I would need plenty of good news to work with until Joel and I could get some answers.

With a knock on my door, Joel and I turned to see Tara peeking in. She hesitated at the sight of his bare chest and looked over to me for assurance that she hadn't walked in on anything.

"Hey, Tara, what's up?" I said, rising from the bed and grabbing the shopping bags from the floor.

"I just got off of the phone with Alex," she said, focusing her attention on me while Joel dug through a bag and slid a plain grey t-shirt on over his head, tag still dangling from the sleeve. "He thought it would be fun to go snowboarding at Crystal Mountain on Sunday. We'd love it if you guys could come. We haven't hung out in forever. Emily's already on board."

Excavating the clothes from their bags and piling them onto the bed, I stalled for time. It wasn't as if Joel and I could just skip out. I would undoubtedly hurt Tara's feelings while simultaneously letting Alex know that I was afraid of him. And maybe part of me was, but Joel and I needed to be able to find out what we could and that was going to be pretty hard while staying out of the picture.

"Yeah, sure, we'd love to," I answered, avoiding Joel's eyes.

"Great." she replied. "I'll leave you two be then, we're going to have so much fun."

I smiled warmly until Tara left the room. The silence that followed her exit was enough to make me nauseous. I finally gave in and looked up at Joel as I piled the shirts together. His expression was blank. It was unsettling how calm he was.

"Are you suicidal?" he asked, allowing a tone of frustration to coat his words.

"Listen, Joel, Alex isn't going to do anything in front of Tara unless he wants to lose his manhood. Besides, if he's stepping up his game, we need to step up ours."

Chapter

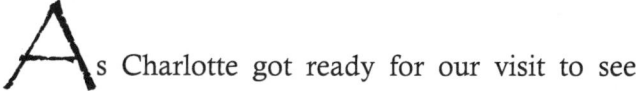

s Charlotte got ready for our visit to see

Matt, I realized a major flaw in my attempts at getting a hold of my new emotions. They were no match for her. She padded around her room in nothing more than her bra and panties. A sight I'd seen millions of times before. I'd become very accustomed to seeing her in much less in fact. It was a hard thing to avoid as a guardian angel. I was just there. But the thing about being a guardian was that I hadn't felt anything. Or at least, that might as well have been the case.

Leaning against her dresser, I tried to remember a single time before my transformation that just looking at Charlotte made me crazy with desire. In the few short weeks that I'd been human, her plump lips alone made me ache with longing. It was enough to drive me insane.

My body had always been capable before, but the sensations she gave me before had been subdued so much that I'd been numb to her. Like a well oiled machine, my body worked timely but gained no feeling or pleasure from it. But now. Now, I ached for her in a way I hadn't known before. My body was weak at the sight of her, the touch, the scent of her. Making love to her had been so intensely enjoyable that my body threatened to do nothing else. My focus was quickly shifting.

Loving her had always been easy. Protecting her had been unquestionable. But my physical cravings for her posed a threat unmatched by any other. It was a distraction, one that could put her in even more danger. And that angered me more than anything.

"What about this one?" Charlotte asked, holding up a small white blouse that plunged just enough to give me chills that felt so good they hurt.

"No," I said, clenching my jaw.

"No? Well that's harsh. I love this shirt."

"Pick a different one."

Charlotte wrinkled her nose at me in protest and I looked away with exhaustion. If every facial expression, shift of her delicate body, and pout of her lips was going to send me through the roof, I was going to need as much help as I could get.

I walked over to her closet and searched in vain. She didn't own a burka so I'd have to settle for a long sleeve sweater.

"Wear this," I said, stretching it out to her.

Her expression exuded two things. Insult and disgust.

"Listen, I know that this is coming off as an insult." I breathed in and closed my eyes. She was still dangerously underdressed. "But trust me. It's a compliment. Please..." I said with anguish in my voice.

Glaring at me again, she took the sweater off of the hanger and shielded my eyes from her naked skin as she pulled it over her head.

It was a start.

"Should I wear snow pants too? Maybe a scarf around my face?" She wasn't mocking me but she was obviously hurt on some level.

I took my spot beside the dresser again and waited impatiently as she pulled on a pair of jeans that, on any other set of legs would have been harmless. But on Charlotte, they were lethal. Maybe it was best that we were seeing Matt.

I needed the distraction as much as I needed my next breath.

* * *

The visitation room was on the other side of the prison. Charlotte and I had to walk through a long hallway of hooting, hollering, and horny criminals kept in the temporary holding cells. She did her best to ignore them, giving only the slightest indication of discomfort by gripping my hand firmly.

My human body left me defenseless and it was enough to drive me crazy. I couldn't rush her through the space of time it took to get to the end of the hall. I couldn't calm her to the level of drowning out their vulgar suggestions and name calling. I was the hollow man that walked beside her, wanting to punch them all square in the mouth. I could feel the anger, the burn at the back of my throat, and the tightening of every muscle in my body. But acting on that senseless rage would only hurt the situation, I knew that, but my body had clearly not gotten the memo.

As a guardian, I'd been equipped with purely useful tools with zero distractions. Had I chosen to, I could have ignored my feelings for Charlotte and been done with it. What I'd felt had been unnatural but it was in no way unavoidable. However, I'd loved her so flawlessly from day one that I had allowed it for myself. But even then it had never gotten in the way of anything before. As a human, it seemed that just about everything that came naturally to me was a weapon of self destruction. And worse...it threatened Charlotte's safety.

Reaching the end of the hallway, we stopped in front of a door that read, *Visitation Room*. I pulled open the door and we walked down a smaller hallway to a guard that sat behind a desk full of paperwork.

"May I help you?" he asked, closing the file that he held in his hands.

"We have an appointment to meet with Matt Cooper at two o'clock," Charlotte explained.

The guard looked up to the clock lazily. It was a quarter till. "We try and run a tight schedule around here. It keeps the inmates in line and it doesn't give them any extra time out of their cells. We're running a prison not a daycare."

Frankly, neither Charlotte or I cared. Though the guard seemed more than willing to offer his opinion. "That's fine, we'll wait," I said motioning for Charlotte to take a seat in the single chair that sat up against the wall across from the guard's desk.

"I'm feeling lightheaded," she groaned as she sat down.

"We really don't have to do this." In fact, I preferred that we didn't.

"Yes we do," she protested, looking up at me. "I am sick and tired of being walked all over and being forced into submission. Maybe we won't get the answers we're looking for. It's actually pretty likely that we won't, but I'm not going to let Matt scare me away. And I won't let Alex either." She was still holding her head in her hands, her cheeks bleached white.

I could see it in her eyes and the way she tried not to be scared. Charlotte needed this. "I know, you're right."

"You can head on in now," the guard said, pushing himself away from his desk. He waved a card in front of the sensor beside the door and opened ushered us in. "You have twenty minutes," he informed.

"Thank you," Charlotte replied.

"After you," I said, placing my hand on her lower back. As much as I wanted to lead the way, there was no need for my testosterone to dominate the situation. I had room enough to be polite.

"I'd like to go in by myself," she said baffling me. "I think it might be hard to get any real answers if you're there. He might actually open up if—"

I took a firm hold of her arm and directed her eyes to meet mine. "Charlotte." I was baffled by how trusting she was despite her obvious fear. "*This guy tried to kill you.*"

"I'll be perfectly safe," she argued, jerking to free her arm from my grasp, but I held her tightly and her attempts were lost. "We're separated by bulletproof glass for goodness sakes," she added with a sigh.

"He took a gun..." I said through clenched teeth "aimed it at your chest...and pulled the trigger."

Her eyes betrayed the guard that she'd put up and I could tell that she was registering for the first time that she had almost died. Bless her heart, she'd been so worried about me that she'd completely forgotten about her own safety. But I hadn't. It was my curse to be constantly aware of the danger that surrounded her. From attempted murderers to bald tires on her car, any threat to her life was something I made a conscious effort to prevent from endangering her.

"Fine," she said belatedly. "But you have to promise me one thing."

"I'm not *promising* anything with that man in a room with you."

She sighed and rolled her eyes. "Can you make an honest effort to do something for me then?"

"Yes."

"*I* want to be the one to talk to him. Okay?"

"Fine," I allowed. Any questions that might prove to be useful Charlotte would ask and I really had no desire to communicate with the man as it was.

She shot me a look of challenge as I finally let her have her arm back and breached the doorway at long last. I followed promptly behind her. The guard shut the door behind us and Charlotte took a seat at the booth while I grabbed a chair to pull up beside her.

For a few drawn out and eerily silent minutes, we sat and waited. Charlotte exuded nerves while I was sure that I exuded pure rage. It seemed that keeping quiet might end up being more of a challenge than I'd originally thought. As a man, my head was filled with counterproductive arguments. I wanted to ask him questions and accuse him of things that would get us nowhere. I would be more than happy to respect her wishes and keep the nonsense from escaping my head. She could control her words much better than I could at this point.

When the door on the other side of the thick glass opened, my muscles tightened involuntarily. Matt walked in wearing an expression of boredom and discontentment. The only reason he'd probably accepted our request to meet at all was likely to mix up the predictable monotony that was now his life sentence.

He sat down in the chair and looked blankly through the glass at us. Looking from Charlotte to me, he remained expressionless. I placed my elbows on the table and leveraged my body to favor one side. Never breaking my gaze, I leaned in slightly to ensure that he knew how capable my anger made me to break the glass barricade that separated us if he pushed me far enough.

Charlotte picked up the phone that connected them and waited quietly for him to do the same. Her heart beat was so fast and loud that I could nearly hear it over my own.

Matt lazily picked up the other phone and put it to his ear. He had suffered some…memory loss from the day of the bank robbery. The few seconds before being knocked out by Alex's impact had been blurred. Where I came from, we called that a clean sweep. It happened a lot like the security cameras cutting out during the robbery. Information had been snipped that might lead a person to believe that I had simply appeared out of thin air. Which, of course, would have been impossible. For Heather and Alex the reveal had been unavoidable, but all other edges of the incident had been cleaned up. Matt had been informed later that the bullet he'd intended for Charlotte had impaled me instead.

His eyes shifted and he looked me up and down. "Glad to see you're doing better," he said with distain.

The longer I sat in the room, the more skilled I became at getting a hold on my anger. Matt's words were meaningless garbage and there was no need to dignify him with a reaction to them.

The glass was thick but not thick enough to keep the conversation's privacy between the two of them. And where the penetration of sound left off, my ability to read his lips would pick up.

"Thanks for meeting with us," Charlotte said politely.

Matt surveyed her as he had done to me and said nothing, still resting the phone against his ear with indifference. He turned his head and cracked his neck in an effort to intimidate her. I smiled inside, knowing that it took much more to throw Charlotte. She simply leaned forward and let formalities go.

"There was a man that paid you to drug me," she began. "Why didn't you say that during the trial?"

Matt leaned in and a stoic grimace crept onto his lips. "What the hell difference does it make?" he said defensively. "Do you really think that I keep track of that kind of thing? Guys come in all the time wanting my *help*. How am I supposed to remember who paid me to drug who?"

Charlotte sunk slightly in her chair. It was more-or-less the answer she'd expected, but not the one that she deserved.

"How is it in there?" she asked sourly. "Making any new friends?"

He didn't answer but he had tightened his grip on the phone, indicted that her words had gotten to him.

"Helping us would probably earn you a few privileges in there. Maybe even a shorter sentence." She sat back with confidence and continued. "My uncle used to be a cop, and trust me when I say this, if they haven't found out that you're a convicted rapist in there, they will. And even criminals look down on rapists. The way they see it, an eye for an eye."

Matt glared through the glass and leaned in closer. "Fuck you, you little—"

I stood up immediately and shifted his attention to me. "One more word you no good piece of—"

"Joel," Charlotte hissed with warning in her voice.

Glaring one last time through the glass, I sat back heavily in my seat. Crossing my arms over my chest, I remained focused on Matt as Charlotte picked up where she'd left off.

"If you have no information, it makes no difference to me. You'll be the one who suffers for it, not me."

Matt's eyes glazed briefly with fear. It seemed from where I sat that he'd managed to remain under the radar since arriving at prison. It wasn't likely to last long, however, and I could tell in that moment he wished he could round up information useful enough to make a trade with. But as his silence lengthened, I could tell that he truly didn't remember.

I turned to face Charlotte and whispered in her ear. "He doesn't know anything." Part of me...the part that hadn't been shot, actually had pity for the guy.

"I know," she whispered, hanging up the phone.

Matt followed us out of the room with his eyes. A defeated man who'd sentenced himself to a life behind bars, watching freedom disappear as the door shut tightly behind us.

Chapter

11

We woke up at o-dark-thirty to head out to the mountain with Alex and the girls. Joel still lay groggy in my bed, marking yet another difference between angelic Joel and human Joel. As an angel, he hadn't slept. Not ever. Now he needed it as much as any human did, if not more.

"Mmmm," he groaned into a pillow.

"Get up," I whined from my dresser.

I tossed a pair of jeans and a long sleeve shirt his way and rustled around for some clothes myself. He had clearly wanted me to cover up for Matt the previous day and I would be covered in enough snow gear to make me sweat once we were there, I wanted to wear something a little cuter underneath if I could help it. Yes, Alex would be around, in fact, he was already downstairs waiting. But I doubted an outfit choice would drive him in one direction or another, especially with Tara around.

Joel shifted in bed at long last and looked over at me as I pulled my shirt over my head. He took a hand and swept it over his face, rubbing hard.

"Every morning," he moaned.

"What?" I asked, confused by the statement.

"This," he said lifting the sheets up and looking at the guilty party. "Every morning I'm ready and hurting for you. It's torture." He sounded legitimately distraught.

I curled my lips in and smiled through them. As much as he repelled the nature of being a man, it seemed to push back that much harder. Sometimes more literally than others.

"I'm going to finish up in the bathroom," I offered, reaching for the door.

"Is Alex here yet?" he asked, pushing himself up in bed.

"Yes."

"Then no you will not."

"I have to brush my teeth," I protested, putting my hands on my hips.

"Can you wait five minutes?"

"Maybe..."

Joel was already pulling his shirt on and pushing the covers away, revealing white boxer briefs with navy blue eagles all over them. I giggled at the sight of them.

"Is that why you got me these?" he asked, only slightly amused. "For your own sick entertainment?"

"Hey," I said defensively. "They're cute."

"I have birds on my crotch..." he rebutted.

"At least they're not pink."

"I'll consider myself lucky."

Joel sat in the front passenger seat of Alex's Pontiac while Tara, Emily, and I took the back. We all rustled around in our snow pants and heavy winter jackets as we situated ourselves. The sun wasn't up yet and a four and a half hour drive lay ahead of us. It was bound to be an interesting experience to say the least. I had a feeling that my mediocre skills on the slopes were going to be the least of my problems.

"Thanks for lending me a pair of snow pants," Joel directed at Alex as we pulled out onto the road. "I've never been snowboarding before." He could fake friendly with a skill I admired and would attempt to study.

"I'm sure you haven't," Alex said, sounding cocky to probably only Joel's and my ears. "Racing down a mountain with the wind in your face, it's the closest thing to flying in my opinion." The jackass was trying to sound like he knew anything about what Joel was.

"I can imagine," Joel replied effortlessly.

Alex turned the radio on to act as background noise and the five of us filled the remaining air with conversation. I hoped that the girls, especially Tara, didn't noticed my efforts in avoiding talking directly with Alex. It was just not a weapon in my arsenal to be cordial to a man that ultimately wanted the man I loved dead.

There was no explanation as to why Alex was still pursuing me. Why he had it out for Joel or why he'd paid to have me drugged in the first place. Who did he think he was? Since those questions were all that remained in my head and all that I could think of saying to him, I kept my attention to the girls. Joel was nice enough to keep Alex's attention with casual conversation.

When we finally arrived at the mountain, the snow was glistening beneath the morning sun. The lodge was spectacular and I immediately assessed the drive as well worth the trip. I'd never been on a more pristine slope.

As we all sorted through the trunk and pulled on the rest of our gear, I examined Joel longingly. I had seen him nude model, sprout magnificent wings, risk his life to save my own, but I'd never once seen him do something...*fun*. The idea of him actually kicking back and relaxing intrigued me. It excited me even. He tucked the lips of his gloves into the sleeves of his winter jacket and looked up to catch my gaze.

"What?" he asked, turning around immediately to look behind him, on high alert.

I couldn't help but laugh as I made my way over to him. When he turned around, he looked down, eyes darting over the surface of my face.

"You're amazing," I said, tucking myself into his arms.

With his guard lowered, he raised his arms to hug me in confusion. A man that didn't know why he was amazing was that and so much more. I pulled away and planted a warm kiss on his lips.

"Hey, love birds," Alex greeted, wrapping a friendly arm around us both. His tone was forced and his eyes avoided the sight of us together but all in all he was faking his *cool* pretty well. "Here are your passes for the day," he said, tucking our lift cards into Joel's outer jacket pocket.

He gave our arms a light squeeze then turned around and swooped in on Tara. My skin crawled at the sight of it. "We ready to head up to the top? You don't need to try your legs at the bunny slope first do you, Joel?" he asked with masculine challenge laced through his words. "You look like you can handle yourself." I could tell that he was holding his breath for the opposite.

"Yeah, let's head up," Joel answered, glaring back with equal challenge.

I looked up at him and when his piercing stare broke from Alex to meet my eyes I said, "Is that really smart with all of your *injuries*? You may want to get a feel for it first."

Without reply, Joel followed Alex and the girls up to the lift. Swallowing a lump in my throat, I grabbed my board and ran to catch up. I had a feeling that Joel was capable of turning even fun into work.

Emily, Tara, and Alex packed into a lift chair and Joel and I took the next one. The worst part for me had always been the transition from lift to powder, one foot strapped helplessly to my board. Joel put an arm around me and kissed my forehead and while the instant sensation of soothing he usually gave me was gone, I did feel much better.

"I'm sorry," he said, swinging his board slightly above the mountainside below. "This is supposed to be fun. I'm being kind of macho aren't I?"

"If pounding your chest and chewing on nails falls under that category..." I joked. "Listen, I get it. I totally understand. Alex is a loose cannon at this point. You're just trying to beat him at his own game. *But*, we could also try and look at this as a date. We haven't actually had one of those yet."

"What are you talking about?" he asked, shifting me in his arms to look me in the eye. "We went to McDonalds, we had coffee together a few times, we went sleuthing...I'm the best boyfriend in the whole world."

"Did Mr. Serious just make a joke?" I asked with a smile.

"Are you implying that I'm not the best boyfriend ever?" he replied, putting a hand defensively over his chest.

"I feel like *boyfriend* doesn't even begin to describe what you are to me. You've always been so much more than that."

He pulled me in and rubbed his gloved hand over my arm to fight off the chill. Words quickly fell short of expressing the rest of what we had to say. The ability to hold one another. The promise for a fun experience together. It all spoke so clearly for itself.

When the lift reached the top Emily, Tara, and Alex took turns gliding down the small incline at the top of the slope. They latched their free feet in and waited off to the side for us to reach them.

My balance was shaky but I managed not to fall, a monumental accomplishment in my book. Turning to my side, I noticed that Joel had remained upright as well. I closed my eyes in gratitude. While he was constantly honed in on my safety, I had managed to take up the role of his guardian as well somewhere along the way.

We joined Alex and the girls and latched our free feet in; both managing to do so without taking a seat in the snow. I was already impressed by Joel's rookie abilities. When I'd learned to snowboard it had taken me about five days of practice to manage staying up while securing my feet.

"Good start," Alex said, smiling with his lips but not his eyes. "Whatta say we tackle this little hill?"

I looked out at the expansive mountain below and concluded that calling it a hill had been a sizable understatement.

Joel and Alex's eyes locked in challenge and before I knew it they were both flying down the *hill*. How Joel had managed to learn the sport in under a second was beyond my comprehension. But the way he raced down the sleek white snow caused me to light up with excitement.

His board cut into the mountain like a butter knife. Leaning on his front and back edge like he'd been doing it for years, a skill that I'd learned after a few tantrums, a handful of face plants, and cursing out the mountain and the sport multiple times.

"Whoa, look at them go." Emily exclaimed. "I didn't know that Joel was such a sports buff." Neither did I.

"At least us girls can take our time conquering the mountain while the boys play nice," Tara added.

Nice wasn't a likely outcome of their spending time together.

"Shall we?" I asked, gliding my board over the packed snow towards the drop off.

The three of us cruised at a humble speed, riding our front or back edge when one fell behind, through the dips and bends of the mountain. We cut three clean paths as we went and wove in and out of one another in a steady rhythm we'd practiced to perfection on previous trips to resorts much closer to home.

When we made our way to the bottom of the mountain, Joel and Alex were both bent over, panting heavily.

"Who won?" Tara asked coyly.

"Beginner's luck," Alex said, looking up through his windblown hair. His eyes shifted to me and his expression bled with determination. Not only did he intend to break the mountain, he intended to break me as well.

Joel came over to me and kissed my forehead, smiling into my hair. He was pleased with himself, and dare I think it, he was actually having fun.

"Best out of three?" Alex asked from Tara's side.

"You're on," Joel called back, winking at me before we all made our way back to the lift.

Halfway through the day Tara, Emily, and I decided to break for hot chocolate at the lodge.

Emily sighed into her cup of hot cocoa. "We should have spent the whole day in here. Let the guys have all the frostbitten fun."

"I won't lie, it's tempting to wait out the rest of the day in here," I agreed, taking as generous of a sip as the temperature of the hot cocoa would allow.

"You two and your men are so cute together," Emily sighed, placing her drink on the table. "I wish I had a boyfriend."

"It'll be worth it when you find the right one," Tara said, resting her chin longingly on top of her interlocked hands. "Alex is incredible isn't he?"

Rock and a hard place. Did I want to encourage Tara to marry the guy? No. But was it very smart to rat out his indiscretions either? Hardly. I took another sip of my cocoa and breathed a sigh of relief when Emily picked the conversation up effortlessly.

"He's great." she gushed. "He's charming *and* funny."

"Definitely charming," I added, figuring it was safer to add an opinion before having one extracted.

"Charlotte, you worked with him. Tell me everything you know about him." Tara leaned in and waited with bated breath.

So much for avoiding extraction.

"Well..." I began. "He always seemed kind of, you know, possessive." I knew I was walking a thin line, but I had to make an attempt. "Does he seem like that to you at all? I've never known him to have a girlfriend so I can't say for certain. It just seems to be part of his personality."

"No, I haven't noticed that," Tara said, sounding disappointed with my answer. "You said he's always been like a brother to you. He probably just acts that way because you're like a sister to him too." In Arkansas maybe.

"Yeah, probably," I answered, cringing against the look on Tara's face. She wanted to hear positive things. If I told her that he killed kittens as a hobby, she'd have defended it. A heart that had chosen its path couldn't be led in any other direction. "When I worked with him he was always a great friend to me."

In fact, he'd easily become everything that I would normally want in a man. He never pressed me for answers, he was understanding, he asked about school, and cared about my lifelong dreams. It was like he had some kind of check list in his head. Everything I was typically attracted to, he was. He was an acting career short of a role on *Grey's Anatomy* for goodness sakes. Yet strangely, I'd never seen him as more than just a good looking and sweet guy. I might have looked back and thought how crazy I'd been not to pursue him. But the crazy part wasn't that I hadn't accepted his advances, it was that I'd ever trusted him in the first place. He had a massively important screw missing.

Looking back now, he'd seemed almost predatory. Like he'd hunted me, studying my every move.

"Yeah, you always had such sweet stories about him from work," Tara beamed, newly excited again. "He's almost as perfect as Joel," she said, winking over the rim of her cup. Not even close.

I laughed into my mug, hoping that it masked the flimsiness of it.

"He jumped in front of a bullet for you..." Emily mused. "I get chills just thinking about it. I mean, that stuff only happens in movies."

"You must be so relieved that he's recovering," Tara added.

"You have no idea."

"What do you say we head back out there? I'm sure the guys miss us *so* much," Tara said sarcastically. "We could have probably stayed home and they wouldn't have noticed."

Yeah, and one of them would end up dead. Not my idea of a fun time.

* * *

"So, Guardian angel turned professional snowboarder? Gotta have a fallback plan right?" Alex's words were dry but I could tell that he was deeply curious.

"Yeah, I guess I pick things up quickly."

"Guess so."

As we got closer to the peak of the mountain, I looked around at the beautiful scenery. Anything to avoid my close proximity to a man who had nothing but bad intentions for the woman I loved and had vowed to protect.

"How's that whole guardian angel gig going for you anyway? It seems like your jobs basically done, right?"

"Pushy aren't we?" I said, smirking at his obvious desire to wipe me from the picture.

"Hey," he said, putting his hands up in mocked defense. "I'm just saying. I would think that angels don't really get a vacation."

"They don't." I found myself running my tongue over my teeth, realizing that it helped some in soothing my agitation.

"What's the story then?"

"I've done my job. Now it's time for fate to run its course."

"Fate?" Alex laughed, sounding equally bitter and humored. "I have given everything...*everything*, to be with Charlotte. But she looks right past me. You have no *idea* what I've been through to try and become the man in her life. And all this time, I never realized it was because I've been up against fate all along." He laughed incredulously.

"Selfish lust is not hard work. It's easy. Effortless. But loving someone...that is what you're missing. That is the greatest sacrifice."

"You know *nothing* about sacrifice, my friend," camaraderie was nowhere to be detected in his words. Bitterness and hatred were masked minimally by determination.

"You know what? We could be friends," I offered graciously. In the end, the last thing I wanted was trouble.

"Keep your friends close and your enemies closer, right?" he said, looking off towards the range of cliffs ahead.

I followed his wistful gaze to a small cottage nestled neatly near a cliff, overlooking the winter wonderland below. It looked as if no one had lived there for year, due probably to its isolated location.

"It looks like a great place to escape from the world," I pointed out, hoping we'd moved past our standoff for the day.

Charlotte was clearly desperate for something she could store away as a fond memory. A day spent out with friends without disaster tacked on at the end. I wasn't in the position to change the world in a day, so I would make my humblest effort at granting her just one day.

"Perfect," he answered thoughtfully.

* * *

The guys had raced down the mountain countless times. I'd even caught them laughing together, and not a single aspect of their companionship came off as fake. I wanted to believe that Alex had moved on, come to respect Joel, and had accepted a role as friend in recovery in my life. But every time my hopes were up and I was enjoying the time with my friends, he'd look at me just long enough, hard enough, to give me chills. His deep onyx colored eyes would dig so deep into my core that detaching myself from his stare seemed nearly impossible.

As we made our way to the ski lodge to call it a day, Joel tugged on my arm. "Would you like to do that before we leave?" he asked, pointing to a sign that advertised a horse drawn sleigh ride.

My face was numb with cold and my body ached all over, not to mention the mental damage that had been inflicted from a day spent with a walking time bomb, but the idea was still strangely appealing. Nothing had happened to deter a day that had truly been amazing and a horse drawn sleigh ride was seemingly the perfect end to a shockingly perfect day.

"I'd love to." I exclaimed, jumping into his arms.

"Okay." He smiled and kissed me softly. "What do you guys think? Want to sneak in a sleigh ride before we head back?"

"Oh my gosh, yes." Emily beamed.

"How romantic." Tara added, looking over at Alex and giving him a suggestive smile.

"Let's do it," Alex said, notably less thrilled than the girls of the group.

As we walked over to the station that read "Winter Wonderland Sleigh Rides", I marveled at the big black horses that stood at the front of the sleigh. Their hooves were covered in long white fur, contrasting the coal black of their coats. Each had a nearly identical patch of white at the top of their nose.

When we reached the loading station for the sleigh ride, a middle-aged man escorted us onto the sleigh as the guys rustled around for money to pay for our ride.

"You folks are lucky, this is my last ride of the day," the man said. His voice was warm and welcoming, though I figured he'd probably greeted dozens of groups all day, as he fought off the bitter cold with a smile. "My name's Peter and I'll be your tour guide for this evening."

We all loaded into the sleigh and draped the thick wool blankets that were placed neatly on each bench over our laps. After a short wait for any other possible passengers, Peter gently nudged the big black horses to life. They began a slow and steady walk through the snow, snorting into the air as they went and we all jostled at the sudden movement of the hitched sleigh.

Peter lead the sleigh down a snow covered road that I imagined during the summer months was made of dirt. Forest stretched out to either side, the trees covered thick with snow. A natural bluish hue washed over the scenery. Branches bowed their heavy, snow laden branches, kissing the freshly fallen powder below.

Resting my head on Joel's shoulder, tucking my hands around his arm to fight the cold, I allowed my eyes to close and to feel my body slowly decompress. Apart from the gentle pull of the cart and the occasional whinny that came from the horses, there was beautiful and undisturbed silence.

"I will have you," I heard seep eerily through the crisp air. My eyes shot open, startled by the sensual tone in Alex's voice. Looking around, no one else seemed put-off by it. Joel's eyes were closed against the setting sun, Emily was looking around and taking pictures of the beautiful scenery, and Alex was nuzzling into the crook of Tara's neck provocatively.

He must have been talking to her. Clearly I was the only one that found it peculiar. Leaning into Joel once more, I kept my eyes open for sanity's sake. He kissed my forehead and rubbed my shoulder for more warmth.

"Charlotte..." Instinctively, I jumped at Alex's voice in my ear again. *"I can make you scream with pleasure, if you'll let me."*

"What is it?" Joel whispered, looking down at me with worried eyes.

"And if you won't let me..." his voice carried through the air like a well kept secret. His lips unmoving, apart from the nibbling he was partaking in on Tara's ear. *"No one will."*

"Nothing." I shuttered. "I'm fine." Holding back painful tears, I forced myself to breath. Something was colossally wrong, beyond the point it had already reached.

Chapter

12

Charlotte sat across from me in the café, looking more helpless than I'd seen her since I'd woken up. We'd already been through so much; it seemed unfair that it only continued to pile up.

When she'd informed me of what had happened during the sleigh ride that night, I had been in utter shock. If Alex could really speak to Charlotte's thoughts, then the threat had escalated to a dangerous level. It could mean only one thing; he wasn't from this world. And that wasn't a threat that I was well equipped to handle.

I tried to run the possibilities through my mind. Any scenarios that I tried to imagine didn't match up. Alex was just some guy that had worked at the branch Charlotte had been assigned to. He'd known her long before her job at the bank, but that fact alone didn't mean that he was something more powerful than human. Something capable of entering her mind. He harbored some crazy mind games that was for sure, but did that mean anything past the fact that he was cunning? I couldn't be sure. And the last thing I wanted to do was jump to a bold conclusion that might upset Charlotte further.

Rubbing my face, I couldn't think of anything reassuring to say to her. How could I protect her efficiently? As a man, I wasn't able to follow her around like a shadow. She spent most of her time away from me, unprotected. And I spent my time harnessing emotions like it did me any good, and pushing my muscles to their limits in preparation for the final battle, like there would ever be one.

We were sitting ducks.

"What are we going to do?" Charlotte asked, stirring her coffee aimlessly. "Bonding hasn't working. Trying to act like it doesn't faze us hasn't worked. It's like *having* me is his whole purpose. He can't be deflected."

Her words were heavy on my shoulders. She was right. It was becoming increasingly obvious that Alex had his sights set and there was nothing we could do to stop him. A man who acted as if he had nothing to lose was the most dangerous kind. If he was *more* than a man, if his strengths surpassed that of human, then dangerous didn't even begin to explain it.

It enraged me to think that Alex's entire goal was to tear down my life's meaning. It made me wonder what kind of person it took to be so heartless. What kind of man pursued a woman so intently, as if getting her was the only thing that mattered, even if it came at the cost of her life? It was a concept I couldn't grasp a firm hold of.

"I think we need to figure out why you could hear him yesterday. There could be a dangerously vital element that we aren't aware of. Best to start there. We need to narrow down the possibilities and determine if he's something...*more*. But we should probably wait to discuss this when we're somewhere more private."

While I still wanted to ensure that Charlotte remained under as little stress as possible, I figured that in the end it was in her best interest to lay out as many scenarios as I could. Being that she would be alone for at least part of every day. I felt safer in knowing that she would have any and all information if she found herself up against Alex on her own again. I could only hope that it wouldn't push her past her breaking point. She had remained so strong in the past few weeks, since the night at the club in fact. I found myself worrying more and more in recent days that she might be reaching her limitations.

She was a lot more worn-out in recent days, going to sleep earlier, waking up later on weekends. I'd noticed all of her slight changes on instinct. The way she had to steady herself at times, like the room was spinning around her.

"How can we find out what he is, if not human?"Her voice was firm and had little trace of distress.

"I'm not sure," I breathed, bringing my drink to my lips.

We sat silently for a moment, running circles around the same thoughts. I imagined that it was just as exhausting for her as it was for me.

"Hey," I heard Charlotte say. "You never told me the story behind that."

I looked up and noticed that she was pointing to my bracelet. She'd asked me about it in the past but I'd brushed it off before. At the time, she hadn't known what I really was. The Celtic wing charms and the simple leather strap held more meaning than anything else in the entire world. It was the only possession that I had and I treasured it greatly.

"You gave it to me," I said, reaching my wrist out to let her observe it.

"I did?"

"Yes. You knew that pretty soon you'd stop seeing me. You were almost four at the time. You'd seen it at a flea market and asked your mom if she could buy it for you."

Charlotte smiled as she turned the charms between her fingers. "Really?"

"You said you wanted me to know that no matter what happened, you'd always love me and would never forget me." My heart was instantly warm as I welcomed the memory. In my human form my memories were not as clear as they'd once been. But that moment in time had remained strong in my heart.

"And look at us now," she said, taking my hand in her own. "Together again."

"All these years…" Suddenly the reality of the last few months together came rushing in on me. Charlotte finally knew me, *really* knew me. "I was the silent and ever present figure in your life…but you." I kissed the back of her hand softly and closed my eyes. "You've always been the meaning of mine."

She took my hand in hers, studying it, turning my palm over and watching the charmed bracelet she'd given me so many years before graze the table as my wrist turned. When she took her eyes from my hand and met mine, she pierced my soul with a look so pure it was nearly heart stopping.

"Thank you," she said, shaking her head in bewilderment. "Thank you for the last twenty-three years of being you." She closed her eyes against something I couldn't read. "You have been by my side through everything…"

A tear fell delicately down her cheek and I immediately wanted to prevent more from falling but I resisted. It was Charlotte's turn to soak in what I'd had a lifetime to absorb.

"You've seen men break my heart. Friends stab me in the back without regard for my feelings. You've watched me fall and trip through life. You've seen me in my darkest hours." She met my eyes again. "For so long I thought that men were all snakes, that people

120

were selfish and egotistical without exception. But in the years that I've spent forming those opinions, you've spent proving them all wrong."

My heart raced, her words formed a circuit of energy through my entire body. The soft pout of her lips as she watched me watching her. The gratitude in her eyes. It all made me love her tenfold in a matter of seconds.

I took hold of her face with both hands and leaned in so close that we were only inches apart. "I may not be a guardian of God anymore, but I will protect you as a man more fiercely than I ever have before. And this time, being together at the end of this is not an option."

Leaning in further and stealing a kiss from my lips, Charlotte took my body captive. Mercilessly, she demanded its immediate reaction. Pulling her lips seductively to my ear, she whispered bewitchingly, paralyzing my ability to resist her.

"I can skip class," she said, nibbling at the end of my earlobe. I shivered with pleasure and my heart raced out of my chest. "If you're willing to cheat a little on your abstinence..." she trailed sensual kisses down my neck and back up again. "I want you to make love to me."

My body was screaming yes as I grudgingly tried to maintain control over my senses. I knew that my focus needed to remain on the danger that lurked so closely around the next corner. The threat of what Alex was, if something other than just a man with an obsession. One false step, one missed sign, and I could be endangering Charlotte further. However, she seemed to be in imminent danger regardless. I was in danger. There were so many things to keep an eye out for that we had yet to refuel our energy. Still, was indulging myself in pleasure the right move?

"I can't," I whispered unconvincingly, able once again to form words. I ran my fingers through her hair and held her head delicately. "I need to stay focused."

Sitting opposite me, the soft rise and fall of her breasts called out to me. Her smooth and flawless skin peeking out of her work blouse. It was just enough exposure to melt my refusal.

She leaned in and pressed her lips to mine. "Please?" she said in a whisper through my lips.

I took her hand in mine, leading her out of the café, no longer able to formulate a reason to say no. No longer able to wait even a second longer to be wrapped sensually in her arms.

We nearly sprinted to the car, where I took the driver's seat and she slipped easily in beside me. With her hand resting threateningly on my lap, I drove back to her house, making an honest effort not to speed.

Bursting through the front door, I shut it behind us as we stumbled through the entryway, kissing one another desperately. I took her face in my hands and explored her mouth with intensity. She hopped up gracefully from the ground and looped her legs around my waist, wrapping her arms delicately around my neck.

The thirst we shared for one another made it clear that the distraction would only come from deprivation. Charlotte was always on my mind. In my dreams, her name balancing fatally on my lips at all times. The scent of her drove me on through my everyday tasks. It was in denying myself of her soft skin and intoxicating presence that I truly began to lose my focus.

I hoisted her up into my arms before making my way to the couch. There was no time and no need to climb the endless steps that separated us from her welcoming bed. I placed her gently on the sofa and mounted her petite and able frame. Caressing her still, I succumbed to my bodies fervent needs. Like rain in the driest desert, she brought life back to my worn body. I felt easily rejuvenated at simply having her lie beneath me.

I ran my hands up her ribcage, drawing back her shirt. Lifting it over her head, she pressed her chest against me and made me ache with pleasure. She then began to loosen the buttons on my shirt and I shrugged it off. Lowering myself onto her, I kissed her neck, enjoying the salty and sweet taste of her skin.

"Joel," she said in a whisper.

"Yes?" I replied, moving my hand down to take hold of her waist.

"Nothing," she smiled into my cheek. "I just like to say your name."

A shudder coursed through me and I was sure that there was no place in the world I'd rather be. Our exposed skin radiated heat that stirred around us. Charlotte's expression exuded pure ecstasy. Her lips were pink and swollen and her eyes were glazed with yearning. Kissing her softly on the forehead, I wanted nothing more than to absorb her slowly, taking in every last inch of her.

From behind me, I heard the door open then slam furiously and I instinctively shot up from the couch; shielding Charlotte out of habit. Alex stood in the entryway, his gaze fixed on Charlotte from over my shoulder. My chest rose and fell with anger as he stood unmoving then shifted his eyes to me. He took in my naked chest and her equally disrobed body, covered minimally by her bra and jeans.

"Get out," I demanded in a deep and assertive voice. Clenching my fists, I prepared myself to force him out if that's what it had to come to. "Go upstairs, Charlotte," I added, no time for pleasantries.

With only slight hesitation, Charlotte took our shirts in her hands and covered her exposed skin as best she could, making her way hastily up the stairs.

"Get. Out," I repeated.

Alex shifted his weight in challenge and raised an eyebrow before speaking. "You have no idea who you're messing with, angel boy." Turning to leave, making an effort to suggest that it was by choice, he turned around once more as he took hold of the doorknob. "No more mister nice guy," he said and slammed the door behind him.

I walked heavily over to the door and locked it. Rubbing my face and looking out the window, I knew that he wasn't making a threat, but a promise.

I quickly made my way up to Charlotte's room, mounting the stairs two at a time. When I opened the door, I found her huddled at the foot of her bed, shaking and pressing her face into the shirts she clenched in both hands. I walked over to her in silence, unsure of what to say. I tried to find the right words to sooth her but found myself at a loss. All I could do was bring her into my arms and hold her as she breathed heavily into my chest. There was no doubt in my mind that Alex meant what he'd said.

"I'm scared," she whisper into my chest.

"Shhh," I cooed.

She shook in my arms and for the first time since my waking up, she finally gave in to all that she'd been through. She pressed off of my chest. "I'm going to be sick."

I was instantly on my feet and helped Charlotte up from the floor. She walked quickly to the bathroom and threw the toilet seat up. She choked and she gagged but in the end it had been a false alarm. I knelt beside her, holding her hair and rubbed her back.

With a whimper, she bowed her head and cried.

We stayed in the bathroom for what must have been twenty minutes in silence as I waited for Charlotte to find hope once more. I hated that she couldn't even seek refuge in her own home. There were major gaps in my ability to protect her now and it was that fact that I regretted most.

She wept out the remainder of her fear and we made our way back to her room. She crawled onto her bed and I took the place beside her. She lay still in my arms with only the knowledge that our fight for safety was far from over. She curled up into my side and I pulled her quilt over us. Running my hand through her hair, I waited for her to speak. I knew that she wanted so desperately to, but her words were tangled in a web of despair.

"Tell me a story," she said, just above a whisper. "Tell me a story about us."

"Charlotte, it's hardly the time…"

"Joel," she said firmly. "I need to hear something good. Something happy."

"We need to figure out—"

"Figure out what?" she demanded, cutting me off. "All we've done for months now is try and figure things out. So far it's led to my house being robbed and you taking a bullet. Right now…I need to escape for a little while." For the first time Charlotte actually sounded angry about the situation she'd been put in. And rightfully so.

I couldn't really argue her point though. Evaluation and plotting had seemed rather worthless in the past. Alex would do what he intended, we both knew it. In the time we might spend preparing for one outcome, he could be coming from an entirely different direction. And if Charlotte wanted to escape, then I would grant her that one wish, it was the least I could do.

I closed my eyes and easily ran through my many memories of Charlotte. Some of the greatest moments I'd experienced hadn't been in the few short years that she'd known of my existence. It was the times that Charlotte stood firmly in her own light that I found the most compelling.

"A few years after your grandfather died, you were sixteen at the time, you visited his and your grandmother's graves. It was a beautiful spring day, the trees in the cemetery were in full bloom, pink and white blossoms catching on the wind and dancing through the breeze to the grass below. After leaving flowers and a short letter to both of your grandparents, you walked delicately through the rows of graves. You read the names off of a dozen headstones." I brushed my fingers through Charlotte's hair as she rested her cheek on my chest.

"You whispered prayers for each person and those they'd left behind, being sure to indicate specifics based on what their headstone read. If there wasn't much more than a date, you'd close your eyes, trying to imagine what that person must have been like. Imagining what each of the dashes stood for. The time between the dates, the lifetime of accomplishment and struggle that wouldn't fit on a headstone. Then you made your way to sit beneath one of the nearby dogwoods, the grass beneath it carpeted with pink petals.

"You were picturesque under that tree. You had no bias about the graveyard. To you it was a place of beauty. A place full of love left behind for those on the other side to reach out and touch. I was sitting beside you. Even though you didn't know of my presence in your life at the time, in that moment, I felt like you could have. You've always been so accepting and open. There were times where I could swear you were looking right at me even. As you lay in the grass and I bent over you in observation it was as if our eyes met even if only for a second."

"Did you play your harmonica that day?" she asked, running her fingers over my tattooed ribs.

"Yes," I answered with a smile.

"I think I heard you," she said without alarm. Squeezing me tighter she nestled closer into my body and closed her eyes.

I closed my eyes too, picturing us lying together beneath the dogwood tree. Her hair splayed out over the petals, shadows of the tree branches cast by the midday sun over her face. And when she opened her eyes this time, she was actually seeing me, and we were safely tucked away in a place that love was not taken but given without moderation.

* * *

It hadn't taken long after closing my eyes, tucked into Joel's arm, for me to fall asleep.

When I entered my dream this time, the image was much clearer than my dreams usually were. In fact, it hardly felt like a dream at all. I looked down at myself, dressed in my "sexy wolf" costume from my freshman year at the University of Michigan.

Though the air felt strangely cold and very real, I reminded myself that it was nowhere near October.

Looking up into a fog littered yard, I recognized the scene rather vividly. I was at a Halloween party that a friend of Tara's had thrown freshman year. It had been held at one of the frat houses on Greek row.

I looked down, curious now, and pressed my hands to my costume. It was soaked and reeked of beer as I'd suspected.

At the party, nearly four years ago, someone had spilled an entire cup of beer on me. This dream was strangely accurate and I had to fight off the chills that threatened to unnerve me. At the party, I had gone outside for some air and…here I was. Was I revisiting a memory? I shook my head. Impossible. I had never in my entire life experienced something like that before.

Curious, I walked toward the house. Music blared out of every window. Cars were parked in a bumper-to-bumper pile up. Cups, cans, bottles, and who knows what other disgusting party paraphernalia littered the yard. A girl, I recognized her as Sophia from my chemistry class that year, was bent over a bush, relieving her stomach of the alcohol she'd clearly had way too much of. I covered my own mouth, just sick with the idea of it and turned away.

I looked down the street both ways, strangely deserted. I could remember how the rest of that night had panned out. I had taken my station wagon back to our house and showered in the hopes that I could wash the memories of my first and last college party from my mind. I had been groped by two wasted morons, offered about ten drinks that I politely declined, and watched one too many rounds of beer pong; concluding that it was probably the most idiotic pastime I'd ever had the misfortune of witnessing. I hadn't fit in at all, and I hardly regretted it.

As I stood, shivering now from the cold, I rubbed my shoulders, walking down the street toward where I'd parked my car. The fog was thick and eerie, a perfect accent to set the scene for a blowout Halloween party. I pulled the fake fur hood that came attached to my costume up over my head and quickened my pace. The darkness and fog seemed to swallow the world whole.

I approached the spot I remembered my car being parked and felt a lump form in my throat. It had been right there, I thought, looking at the empty parking space between two poorly parked rice-rockets.

I looked up, searching both sides of the street for any sign of my car. Then, like a ghost through the mist that crept slowly over the paved road, the silhouette of a man appeared. Instinctively, my heart beat faster and I started to back away. But like any other dream, it seemed that what I feared most didn't get further away, but closer. The man walked slowly toward me but with the space growing dangerously intimate between us, I refused to wait until he was right in front of me. I turned around and ran as fast as I could in the other direction, pushing through the fog, hoping that it only felt like I was running in place.

Before I could turn around to see if I'd managed to get away, a hand reached out and grabbed me. It pulled me back with little to no effort and I was whirled around to face Alex, holding me tightly in his arms. I gasped and he clapped a hand over my mouth before I could scream.

I moved back and my foot caught on the lip of a cliff that hadn't been there before. My heart raced and I blinked hard. When I opened my eyes again Alex took his hand from my mouth, kissed me hard, and threw me back over the edge of the mysteriously materialized cliff.

I shot up in bed, my throat dry and sore as if I'd just been screaming. I gasped and breathed out heavily. Sweat glistened on the surface of my skin.

"Are you okay?" Joel asked. He sat at the end of the bed with his harmonica gripped in one hand.

I dropped my head into my hands and wanted so badly to cry, or vomit, or both. "Ask me that when this is all over," I said, wishing the day could just be over already.

Chapter

13

With intimacy no longer in the cards for the day, I figured it was best to go back to school and attend my last class for the day. Sitting in my room with Joel and the knowledge that Alex was progressively more pissed off wasn't doing me any good.

While Joel had insisted that I stay home, I had managed to leave the house with the argument that I needed to do something normal. A concept it seemed I'd taken very much for granted up until the recent months.

I wanted to stay with Joel, it was a given, but I *needed* to go about my day as normal. I needed to show Alex that I wouldn't just sit cowering in my house, waiting for the next incident to take place. Alex was somehow capable of getting to me in a crowd of people. He walked right into my house without so much as a knock. Had he seen my car parked on the side or not? Either way, I wasn't about to allow him to prey on me as I huddled in a corner somewhere. I wouldn't simply hand over my freedom on top of everything he'd already managed to take from me.

Sitting in class, I felt relieved. Professor Sanders had been one of the few teachers who hadn't had the pleasure of meeting Joel. In that room, I was just a student. She paced around the front of the room reciting a poem as the class jotted down notes. Happily, I joined them, trying to pay close attention to detail.

Part of me hated the fact that Joel's absence actually felt like a break. For the first time, I could almost pretend that nothing in my life had changed. Maybe my previous life had been boring and predictable, but at least no one had tried to take it away from me. I'd gotten to the point of realizing what effect a man could have on me. I'd let men into my life and my heart only to have them trample it. Joel had done no such thing, yet somehow, a price had come attached to him as well.

Sitting in my chair, trying to put a great deal of my effort into my poem evaluation, I began to question the details I'd missed before. Since Joel's arrival and more specifically, since Alex had discovered who Joel really was, there had been a very distinct change in Alex's approach. While his drugging me had been the cause of Joel's appearance in the first place, it hadn't been obvious. The only way I'd known to link it to him at all was because I'd overheard him admit to doing it.

I stopped writing and massaged the bridge of my nose. Carefully, I extracted the facts. A switch had undoubtedly been flipped when he'd found out about Joel. But why would that have been the final straw? The concept was unreal to begin with, though Alex seemed to believe it without a single doubt.

Had any other man discovered that a girl he was pursuing had fallen in love with her guardian angel, he would have bowed out honorably. No sane man would think that he had any place fighting an angel for a girl's affections. Nor did he pose any chance at all of winning. But not Alex. Joel's divine title wasn't something he honored or feared but something he challenged.

To add to that, in the mall he'd claimed to have gotten a job at the hospital, though I was almost certain that he'd been lying about that. He wasn't working the hours of a newbie doctor, in fact, he seemed to have nothing but time on his hands.

On top of all of that, somehow he'd concluded that Joel couldn't feel. A fact that I hadn't known about when it was true, and a fact that wasn't true now that he had become human. Why on earth would Alex think to make such a bold assumption?

"Charlotte," I heard professor Sanders say with irritation.

"I'm sorry," I said, shooting my eyes up to the front of the room.

She stood at her podium waiting for me to answer a question I hadn't heard her ask. It had clearly been a mistake to imagine that I could separate myself from my own life for even the hour it took to sit in class.

Like middle schoolers, my fellow classmates giggled as the professor turned her attention to a different, more studious classmate. I let out a breath and tried to pay attention for the remainder of the class period. I would tell Joel about my concerns when I got home, not that I knew what to make of them.

Making my way to the car, I could feel winter's last bleak attempt at revenge against the warmer air in recent days. I closed the collar of my jacket around my neck and wondered if it would snow one last time before life was breathed back into the scenery. I hoped not.

As I reached for my door handle two hands took a firm anchor on either side of my body. I turned around with fear, knowing who they belonged to. Alex leaned venomously into me, pressing his firm chest into mine.

"Expecting someone else?" he said, looking me up and down as if to survey his prey. "The chosen one, perhaps?" His smile warned of trouble but I knew that to anyone else, his gaze would be deemed as deeply attractive. Smoldering even.

His jacket pulled against his muscles and his hard body allowed not even an inch of movement. To any onlookers a struggle wouldn't have been detectable. He took care to make it appear as such.

"You disgust me," I spoke sharply through my teeth. "You were my friend, you coward."

I worked against his body in hopes of breaking free and found quickly that it was a wasted effort. "Mmmm," he moaned into my ear. "So you like it rough?"

My skin crawled and I felt nauseous instantly. Even in the short time that had passed since our kiss at the restaurant, and more recently, his strange trickery at the ski lodge, Alex's demeanor had morphed into something so sinister it scared me. I figured that walking in on us had something to do with that.

"Get off of me," I demanded through clenched teeth.

"You will be mine," he insisted, pinning my body harder. Searching my eyes, he wore a century-long stare that translated desperation. A hunger it seemed unmatched by even the most ravenous creature.

"What are you?" I managed boldly.

With a thrill in his eyes, he pursued a fierce kiss, forcing my lips into his. I struggled against him, wishing against reality to disappear. His body was stiff and unresponsive but it was dead set on making a point.

"I can't believe you," I heard Tara say from the sidewalk in a shaky voice.

Alex released me slowly, paying no mind to Tara. He kept his eyes on me as I watched her walk off as fast as she could, maintaining as much pride as possible.

His kiss had been different than the one we'd shared at the restaurant. It was a message, a weapon, a tool. He'd planned his timing perfectly as it would seem, making a spectacle of us in front of Tara.

"Tara!" I called after her. She didn't even flinch. "You animal!" I screamed into Alex's chest, trying my best to fight him off again. "Let go of me!"

He looked me in the eye, taking my face in his hand to demand that our eyes connected. *"You can't escape the inevitable,"* I heard him say through un-parted lips.

I was certain that I'd stopped breathing. Alex was being careless with whatever secret he had. He wanted me to fear him and he wanted me to know that I had a reason to. Letting go of my face and pushing himself off of me, he walked away before I could find any words of rebuttal.

Standing in the silence of a threat that was ever escalating, I sucked in my lip, chewing on it carelessly. I squeezed my eyelids shut and opened them up again. I wanted to wake up. I wanted so badly to find out that it had all just been another crazy life-like dream. But as I stood there, watching Alex as he walked heavily through the parking lot, I knew that it had been real and that I had likely lost a friend because of it.

As I'd suspected, Tara had been a pawn all along, and I'd lead her right into Alex's trap. I blinked back tears and slid into the driver's seat of Trigger, unable to drive home just yet. Maybe I was just a pawn too.

Joel watched me. I knew that he wouldn't say that he'd told me not to go to school, but he was thinking it loud enough that he might as well have said it.

"Well?" I said, hoping to move past the *should haves* and *would haves* of the situation. I was safe; a little violated and down a friend but, considering the possible outcomes, I had been lucky. "Something is clearly not right here."

"It seems that he's formulated quite a few opinions about angels," Joel agreed. "The internet can't be ruled out. People assume that even the most paranormal concepts can be accurately answered by the click of a mouse. It might explain why he's been so cocky to throw out facts like he knows anything about my world."

"Yeah, maybe," I said chewing on my lip. "But what about hearing him when he's clearly not talking? He couldn't have learned to do *that* on the internet." Curious about the connection this all had with Joel, I added, "Can you do that?"

He took his thumb and index finger to my mouth, freeing my lip from my teeth. I blushed, wet my lips, and made a conscience effort to keep them in the pouted position.

"When I was still an angel I could have if I wanted to," he confirmed.

"Really?" My interest was immediately piqued. "Why didn't you?"

"I always felt that it was an invasion of privacy. When my kind, and well, different variations of my kind, are together, we don't speak aloud to one another, we communicate through mental projection."

"So he's talking to my *mind*?"

"Precisely. If that's what he is. Of course, the ability was never meant for intimidation. Beings that abuse their powers and have turned over to the dark side, however, don't really have the kind of moral code to respect that."

"You make it sound like we're in a *Star Wars* movie. Dark side? I mean…really? This is all beginning to sound very imaginary."

"The imagination of man is often sparked by what already exists, even if they're not consciously aware of it. Where I'm from…the world that used to be mine, it's not untouchable. How do you think demons and fallen angels can move from one to the other so fluidly?"

I shivered at the idea of it. Nightmares, horror films, and ghost stories, they were all fine and dandy right up until the point where it could all actually happen.

"Charlotte, please don't worry about any of this too much. It's very, *very* rare that the two worlds collide."

I looked up at him and blinked hard. Was he serious? *Don't worry about it?*

"Don't get me wrong, it would be a mistake to assume that he's simply using amateur tricks and misguided information to scare you. I honestly don't know what side effects occur when an angel falls or what a demon is even capable of. And the many other possibilities...I'm unfamiliar with all of it. I was a newly created angel when I was assigned to you. But the likelihood of an alternative, more supernatural cause is pretty small. Nearly impossible."

"Why do you say that?"

"It's not as if angels and demons walk around openly through the world as humans do." He brushed a strand of hair from my face and looked out the window, trying to form words of explanation. "It would be easiest to explain by saying that each of us is set to a different frequency. Whatever else is out there, and trust me...there are dozens of possibilities, I've never been in contact with any of them. Guardians; we don't exactly get together on weekends and barbeque. It's just not the way of my kind. My job, my purpose, was to be your guardian. There was never any need to communicate with others of my kind while on earth, so the option just wasn't there. In saying that, if Alex *is* out of this world, the question of why and how he chose you to target is presented."

"What do you mean?"

"Fallen angels, for example, fall for a reason. Be it greed or lust, they find something they want on earth and their thoughts become impure. That's what causes them to fall. Based on how he's been acting and given the evidence, out of all options, a fallen angel is the most likely case. But the point is still raised, why you? Out of millions of people in the world, I find it highly improbable that he would chose you. It's too coincidental if he were to actually be fallen. So while we'll keep that possibility in mind, it would be unwise to settle on it just yet."

"What, now I'm some kind of magnet to supernatural phenomenon?"

"That's the part of this equation that I can't quite sort out. There are people out there who are more susceptible to being possessed by demons. Something about their mind and their soul are weak enough to be possessed by them. But a person who attracts angels by nature? That's impossible. Angels are selfless protectors, they're of a different chemical makeup than demons entirely."

"But aren't demons really just fallen angels too?"

"It's a bit more complicated than that. They were the original fallen angels. The ones who followed Lucifer to hell. They are much more powerful and they're much, much older. A fallen angel, as far as I know, is a lot weaker and no more than a banished angel. Demons on the other hand are cursed and satanic souls. They performed the ultimate betrayal. Fallen angels are simply angels that lost their way. They're not completely unredeemable."

"Do you think that Alex could be a demon?" I felt my stomach coil as I pictured the possibility.

"Demons aren't physical creatures; that much I do know. The most realistic option in dealing with demons is that his human body has been possessed by one. But I'd say that's the least likely case."

"Oh, good." My tone was sarcastic at best. It seemed that worst case and best case scenario weren't far off from one another. What we didn't know could certainly hurt us.

"It's not important to know what he is. While it would help, it's not smart to try and search for answers we may not find in time. I know that it is all very frightening for you, but its best that we figure out how to protect you as best as we can before we start jumping to bold conclusions. Searching for answers will only put us both in further jeopardy."

When I heard a knock at my door, I jumped. Joel welcomed me into his arms but didn't seem to be on edge. He probably figured that, had it been Alex, there wouldn't have been a knock at all. Still, my heart couldn't find its way back to my ribcage. All this talk of demons and supernatural possibilities had gotten me dangerously on edge.

"Come in," I said, taking Joel's hand in mine.

Emily walked into the room and when she saw Joel, she turned her attention to me. "Can I talk to you for a minute?" she said, her voice unreadable. "Alone," she added.

"I'll be downstairs," Joel said, letting go of my hand and making his way from the room.

"Okay," I said weakly. When Joel was gone and I could hear his footsteps descending the stairs, I smiled nervously. "What's up?"

"What's up?" Emily repeated in question. "Tara just called me and asked if I could bring a bag of her clothes to her parent's house." She crossed her arms. "They live *two hours away*," she added as if to emphasize the magnitude of the situation. "When I finally got her to stop crying and explain, I could hardly believe it. Tell me what she saw was a mistake, or a misunderstanding. Something."

"Emily," I said calmly. "You need to understand something."

"Clearly. And Tara needs an apology."

"Listen," I said firmly. "Alex was the one who paid the bartender to drug me that night. He's using Tara to get to me."

I knew that I should have told my friends the truth sooner, that my last-minute attempt at setting the facts straight was poorly timed, but I had naively hoped that it would never come to this.

"So you made out with him?" Emily said, propping her hands on her hips.

"You think I'd *willingly* do that to Tara. That I'd do it to Joel?"

"You sounded willing enough from Tara's account. And you make a good point. One gorgeous guy isn't enough? I have been single for the larger percentage of my life. If I'd managed to snag a guy like Joel, I would do my best to appreciate him, not go out and see what kind of side dishes I could add to the mix."

"Are you serious?" I said, the volume of my voice escalating. "You aren't even listening to me."

"You know what? You've played off the whole I-don't-know-I'm-drop-dead-gorgeous charade pretty flawlessly since I met you, but clearly you're more than well aware of it now. You think that because all of these great looking guys are throwing themselves at your feet that you need to accept every invitation? I thought you were better than that, Charlotte."

"Why do you keep saying that I want this?" I was beginning to feel hopeless in trying to maintain my friend's respect. There seemed to be no hope in changing Emily's already tainted opinion of me.

"Well, you've got the house to yourself. I'm going to stay with my parents too for a while. You can have all the orgies you want now. Tara and I aren't going to sit by and watch you continue to make a mess of things."

Before I could continue fighting for our friendship or my innocence, Emily slammed the door behind her. I stood baffled by the absurd conversation that had just taken place. Was that really what my friends thought of me?

When Joel came back into my room, I was sitting on my bed in shock. "Normal just wasn't in the cards for today," I said, lowering my head into my hands.

Sitting beside me on the bed, Joel leaned forward and sighed. "If you'd like, I can get stupidly jealous about you having kissed another man then we can have passionate make-up sex and watch *American Idol* to round out the day."

I couldn't refrain from smiling, even with my greatest attempt. Sitting up, I leaned my head on Joel's shoulder. "Well, he got what he wanted. He's dismantled about everything he could, given the circumstances. I'm surprised he hasn't gotten me fired too."

"You think he's trying to isolate you?"

"If that's not the case, he's doing a great job of it anyway."

Joel rested his head against mine and rubbed my shoulder with his hand. "I don't want to baby you, Charlotte—"

"But?" I interrupted, knowing that he was already making plans just short of the witness protection program.

"But..." he said, smiling into my hair, "I think it would be best from now on that I take you to and from work and school. See you to the door, maybe lurk around campus like the secret service. I can't do the same at the bank of course or I'll be carted off to jail out of suspicion that I was casing the joint. But lucky for us, you work at a job that comes with maximum security."

I laughed at the idea of it. I considered how much work it would require, not to mention gas miles, but

Joel had a point. Alex seemed to know when I was alone and vulnerable, and he took full advantage of it. As much as I hated to admit it, the idea of being babysat by Joel nonstop was the first suggestion to bring me relief in quite some time.

"Okay," I said, kissing him on the cheek.

"Okay?" he repied with astonishment. "That's it? I won't lie, I'd expected a little more resistance."

"Had it been a different day, I might have put up a fight. But you're the last person I want to fight with right now. And in the end, I know it's what we have to do. It's all we *can* do at this point. Unless I start carrying a 45 in my purse."

"That's not happening," Joel replied sternly.

"Well then," I said with a laugh. "So as I said, it's our only option."

"Don't worry, Charlotte, I will do whatever it takes to keep you safe."

"That's what I'm afraid of," I replied, knowing that he stayed true to his word and that he was far from bulletproof.

Chapter

14

"I can't believe it took Charlotte this long to bring you by the house," my mom said, handing Joel a glass of iced tea. "Take a seat."

Joel sat down on the couch and placed his drink on the coaster in front of him. Taking the boyfriend home to meet the parents. I might have a chance at a little piece of normal after all.

In part, visiting my parents was my attempt at forgetting that I'd been living without Emily and Tara for the past few days. Of course, it had proven to be the time that I needed my friends the most. Since *meeting* Joel, we hadn't spent our usual amount of "girl time" together. But even the morning chats in front of the bathroom mirror and the quick breakfasts together before class began haunting me like ghosts in the house. Not only had I lost my friends but it was a clear indication of the rising threat that Alex posed.

"It's nice to finally meet you Mrs. Rush," Joel said with an honest smile.

"Please, call me Grace. Charlotte's father, Greg, will be home from work in a little while. I know that he's looking forward to meeting you as well."

"I look forward to meeting him also. I've heard only good things about you both."

My mom situated herself on the cushion and tucked one ankle delicately under the other. I could tell that she was a little nervous around Joel. The first man I'd brought home that she actually cared to impress. She was a good judge of character, I couldn't argue that.

"Charlotte wouldn't let us visit you at the hospital," my mom began. "She said she wanted us to meet you in person...you know, awake."

Joel laughed with understanding. "Yes, I'm much better company when I'm not drooling all over myself."

"You didn't drool," I defended.

He shrugged as if to say, *I might as well have been.* With a smile and subtle eye roll, I shook my head. I knew that Joel wasn't pleased with his new restrictions in a human body. He made the point regularly.

"Charlotte never mentioned how handsome you were," she added, making me blush against reason. Joel knew my mom, and he wouldn't leave me because of her flattering, but the blood in my cheeks didn't know that.

"Nor did she tell me how beautiful you were," Joel retorted with charming ease. "Now I know where Charlotte gets it."

It was the beginning of an average impress the parents speech. Joel had my mom giggling and it all seemed very by the book. Though I figured Joel had thought such things hundreds of times before. He knew my mom as well as I did if not better. And she really was beautiful. Inside and out.

Her hair was the same shade of brown as my own with a sprinkle of white throughout. She'd dyed her hair a few times in college but had decided long ago that natural suited her best. She made no effort to look younger than she was; she wore her own age well. Her eyes were a deep chocolate color and age couldn't touch them. Her body was slender but sturdy, any weight she'd welcomed over the years had fit neatly to her frame.

Knowing that Joel had been so close to my parents throughout my life, I sat back and absorbed her in a new light, the way I imagined that Joel saw her. As they talked, sharing small details of themselves with one another, I marveled at the fact that Joel knew just how fabulous my mom really was. She often gave herself less credit than she deserved. She and my dad were alike in that way.

Watching Joel sip his iced tea and listen to stories of my childhood, the ones my mom told at all of the family gatherings, I felt my heart warm. He'd been there too. And as she spoke in scattered memory, he was likely filling in the small details that had been lost and forgotten in time by everyone else.

"And she was always such a talented singer," my mom went on, pouring more tea into Joel's and my glasses. "She was very shy though, never up for trying out for the talent shows or chorus."

I had to remind myself not to be embarrassed. It wasn't a good practice to let my mom continue chattering on about my humiliating childhood without discouragement, but it was pointless to try and stop her. Joel was the last man I would ever introduce to my family, she could run through the memories of my disastrous potty training days and I'd have no sane reason to be upset about it.

"The tickets were sold out for her shower concerts though, I'm sure," Joel said, muffling a smile and winking at me with a knowing raise of his brow.

I shook my head and tried to prevent a smile from spreading across my own lips. Looking off towards the kitchen, I avoided his eyes and the escalating humiliation that had once again taken up residence in my insides.

"Oh, yes," my mom said with a smile.

"Better acoustics in the shower," I reasoned, getting up from my spot on the couch. "Does anyone want some cookies while I'm in the kitchen stuffing myself down the garbage disposal?"

"I'm good, honey," my mom replied, taking a sip of her iced tea.

"Joel?" I said, flashing him a witty grin.

"I'm fine too, thanks," he replied, sitting forward on the couch.

When I entered the kitchen, I placed my hands on either side of the sink, looking out through the kitchen window. The backyard stretched out for about an acre. The grass was short and snow matted but I knew that in the coming months it would be a brilliant green once again. Trees lined the property, still naked and awaiting their spring buds, sure to see a few more snow falls first. My old swing set sat off to the side in mint condition. My dad had made a real point to keep it in good shape for future grandkids.

Instinctively, I felt a lump form in my throat. I'd never much considered children before, being that I'd never met a man prior to Joel worth being intimate with. But now, looking through the window at the world that patiently awaited new life, my stomach knotted and I had to focus on not getting sick. Joel had said he couldn't have kids. There had been no reason to believe that anything had changed once he'd become human.

But my period was late. I'd never been late in my entire life. Part of me knew that that had been the real reason I'd wanted to go to my parents' house. I wanted to curl up in my dad's arms and cry. Ask my mom for advice I knew in reality I was too chicken to ask for. If I was pregnant then not only were Joel and I in danger, so was our unborn child. If there was ever a moment I wanted the comfort of my childhood home, this was it.

But I needed to remind myself that it had only been late a week. I wasn't feeling any different apart from some nausea and drowsiness that could just as easily be caused by stress, and I had no reason to panic just yet.

I had been under a lot of stress in the past few months. Anxiety had all kinds of crazy effects on the body. To assume that I was pregnant would be a very bold conclusion to arrive at after such a short time.

I'd once been told that as a woman you just knew these things. Once the chance was there, I was supposed to be able to tell if it was a false alarm or not. Well, that was crap. I couldn't tell anything. All I knew was that between my nerves and my newly reacquired lack of sleep, my stomach was in knots.

I put my hand to my stomach and looked down, smoothing my hand over the surface of my shirt, ,watching the flat surface of my abs as if in any minute it could blow out into a full-on pregnant bump. *I'm not pregnant*, I thought to myself.

"Hey," Joel said, walking through the kitchen door.

He looked me over and silently observed the hand that rested on my stomach. In an effort to deter him from jumping to any wildly lucky conclusions, I looked down and observed my shirt, picking up a small section of it between two fingers. I grabbed a damp sponge from the sink and dabbed the perfectly clean section of my shirt.

"I got some...chocolate on my shirt," I improvised.

For an instant too long, he just watched me as I soaked a large circle into my shirt. He looked suspicious, but probably only to my eye. He'd clearly decided not to question me about my strange behavior when a smile slid easily across his lips. He came up to me and kissed my forehead as I put the sponge back on the rim of the sink.

"Your mom is really nice," he said, kissing my neck tenderly.

"You already knew that," I said, trying to force my voice to sound normal.

"Are you okay?" he asked, turning me in his arms to meet my eyes.

"Yeah, I'm fine," I lied.

He looked at me warily, searching my face for truth. He either hadn't detected anything, which was unlikely, or he knew better than to pressure me for answers. "You coming?"

"Yeah, I'll be there in a minute."

As Joel walked away, I thought about everything he'd ever known about me. Which was...everything. He'd been with me through every embarrassing, humiliating, infuriating, and terrifying moment of my life. Was I really going to try and hide this from him? Even if it was no more than a late period. Didn't he have a right to know? Didn't I have the right to find comfort in not going about it alone?

"Wait!" I called after him.

Joel turned around in the doorway and smiled at me. "What is it?"

My mind raced and I wished that my heart could stop pounding so hard in my ears. It was making it impossible for me to think straight. How would Joel react to such news with his new emotions still not entirely reined in? Was it better to leave him in the dark until I knew for certain that I was pregnant or not? After all, it had only been about a week. That didn't necessarily mean anything.

"Charlotte?"

I looked up to see him walking toward me with worry in his eyes. Who was I kidding? I had to tell Joel. He was my best ally, my best friend.

"Can I talk to you outside for a minute?"

147

He turned his head in question and smiled. "You're not breaking up with me, are you?"

I laughed easily and felt the pressure of dread begin to drain from my muscles. Joel had an incredible way of knowing precisely when to be serious, and when to give me just enough humor to relax.

"If I ever try it, just commit me to a mental hospital, will you?"

I must have been giving off some kind of sign that said I needed a hug because before I could try and pretend like I was fine again, Joel had me in his arms. I pressed my face against his chest and let out a slow and shaky breath. I took the time to steady myself; thoughts and breathing included. Even without his magic angel touch, Joel had a way of taking a good amount of my stress away.

"Whatever it is," he began "We'll figure it out, and we'll be okay."

I didn't exactly doubt him, but I was hard-pressed to believe that it couldn't be that simple.

We walked over to the swing set without words. I sat down in one of the swings, knowing that it was going to be one of those conversations where I should be sitting down.

Joel followed my lead and sat down in the swing beside me. He remained quiet and allowed me to find the words I still wasn't sure I'd be able to say.

A corner of my brain was actually excited about the possibility. The corner of my brain that hadn't yet been informed that we were totally screwed, and this was far from the right time. But I still found myself looking forward to the fact that Joel might actually be able to have kids after all. When he'd first told me that he couldn't, I'd be lying if I said I hadn't been disappointed.

On the other hand, good old reason popped up its ugly head. Joel was an angel-turned-human with no proven identity and no way to get a job. I was a struggling college student with a car payment and college loans that would kick in right around the time the baby—if there was a baby—was born. Add to that a psychopathic-lovestruck-reckless-home-wrecker and I was off to a pretty hopeless start.

I sighed. Back to square one.

The same arguments had been eating away at my thoughts since I'd first expected my period and not gotten it. Precisely why I needed to buck up and tell Joel. I *needed* him to know, for nothing else but to salvage what remaining sanity I had left.

"I think," I forced out. "I might be pregnant," I said quietly. I couldn't meet his eyes when I let the words escape.

He leaned forward in the swing and dug his hands into his hair. Letting out a long breath, he said nothing for a precious minute. The silence hung fatally between us.

At the same time we turned to face one another. I raised my eyes to look into his. His expression was unreadable until a slow and sturdy smile made its way onto his lips.

"We're going to have a baby?" he asked, eyes lighting up.

"Well, we might not be...I mean, I don't know if we are. You're not mad?" I asked hesitantly.

"Mad?" he replied, shaking his head in disbelief. "Surprised. Shocked. Kind of terrified. But no, I'm not mad." He pulled my swing next to his and bound us together, wrapping his arm around my waist. "I'm happy," he said, pressing his lips to my forehead, letting the kiss linger in the cool breeze.

"What are we going to do if I am?" I asked, pushing myself to swing a little.

"Isn't *that* the million dollar question," Joel laughed, kicking his feet off the ground slightly to fall into rhythm with me. "We can't do anything but what we've already been doing. I'll continue driving Miss Daisy and you'll remain in my sights at all times."

I jabbed his side and laughed. "Miss Daisy's car wasn't nearly as cool as Trigger, thank you very much."

"And I'm no Morgan Freeman, but we can make do," he joked back.

Digging his feet into the ground below, Joel stopped his gentle swinging and leaned back thoughtfully, holding onto the chains of his swing. "Wow," he mused aloud. "A baby."

I pushed air through my lips. "Yeah."

Joel had obviously already invested himself in the idea that there *was* a baby. It was a reaction I'd already considered. I didn't have the heart to remind him that my poor eating habits and sleep cycle could be just as much to blame for the missed period. Joel, like my father, had been fashioned to have children. He had a certain rare quality about him that made him perfect for the role. But if I wasn't pregnant, and it was just the physical side effects of stress, then it probably remained true that Joel *couldn't* have children. A likely reality that I didn't care to mentioned just yet.

"I should just kill Alex and get it over with," he said wistfully.

"What?" I stopped my swing from pivoting, digging my heals into the woodchips. "Tell me you're not serious."

"The stakes could be a lot higher now, Charlotte. Give me a better solution and I'm all for it."

"You can't, Joel," I said weakly.

"And why is that?" he retorted.

"You just can't," I replied meekly.

Joel wasn't a killer. He was a protector. Though I was certain that nothing was off limits when it came to protecting his family. I just had to hope that it wouldn't come to that.

Chapter

15

When we got back inside, Charlotte's father was sitting at the table, looking through a stack of mail as her mother moved through the kitchen, getting ready to prepare dinner. As I closed the door behind us, Charlotte's father rose from his seat and extended his hand.

"Joel," he said, taking my hand in his and shaking it firmly, "so good to finally meet you. I'm Greg."

"Pleasure to meet you, sir," I replied.

Charlotte joined her mother in the kitchen, grabbing a knife to chop up the makings of a salad. Her father collected the mail from the table and lifted his briefcase from the floor.

"Joel, why don't you join me in the study? We can wind down and get to know one another before dinner."

"Of course," I replied, feeling unexpected nerves bubble up.

As her father led me to the privacy of his office, I could feel Charlotte's eyes following me until we were out of sight. We walked to the end of the hall and he led me into his study. A room that housed dozens of memories from Charlotte's childhood. A place I knew well.

"No need for us to get in their way," he began, placing his briefcase at the end of his desk.

"I'm sure you know your way around a kitchen just as well as your wife does."

"Every good man should be able to fend for himself, I suppose," he said with a smile.

It was astounding to see the difference between how Greg acted around Charlotte and how he acted when she wasn't around. Though he was always her father, there was a light in his eyes when she was in the room. But as he moved around his office, organizing his paperwork and unloading his briefcase after a long day of work, I saw a different side of him, one I'd rarely seen before. He was strong like an oak tree, every move he made was purposeful and he never made any attempt to intimidate me or make me feel unwelcomed. He acted as if I'd been in his office hundreds of times before, which I had, unbeknownst to him.

His clothes were dirty from a hard day's work spent on his knees, fixing this, installing that. He didn't apologize for his messy attire and I was happy for it. Greg was hard working; his strong build and his salt and peppered hair were proof of that. He'd never taken the easy way out in life and he did what was required of him to support his family.

"So tell me about yourself, Joel."

Greg made his way around his desk and took out a bottle of scotch I knew him to drink only on occasion. A bottle of scotch he'd shared with every man Charlotte had brought home. No matter how much I had been able to tell with a select few that he already didn't like them, he was generous and gave each man who'd caught his daughter's eye equal respect. A respect he was preparing to offer me as well.

He clanked two glasses onto the top of his desk and poured a small amount into each, sliding one over for me to have.

"Thank you," I said graciously.

"Have a seat," he offered, sitting down in the seat behind his desk.

I took the seat opposite him and swirled the liquor in my glass. "There's not much to tell," I said honestly. As a man, my record had very few marks on it as of yet. Though, I assumed that minimal answers accompanied by a dashing smile wouldn't win Charlotte's father over as easily as it had with her.

"You're either being modest or you're intimidated," he said with a laugh.

I smiled easily. "You'd have to be the judge of my modesty." I knew for certain by the tightness of my muscles and the adrenaline that seeped into them that I was nervous, and while I was sure he could detect it, I wasn't about to bring attention to it.

"How did you and Charlotte meet?" Though it was subtle, I could detect a prominent amount of respect in how he'd asked the question, different only slightly in how he'd asked her previous boyfriends. When asking the same question to other men Charlotte had brought home, Greg had referred to her as *his daughter*, not as *Charlotte*. Making it clear that he didn't acknowledge her as anything to them just yet. Once they'd proven their worth, which none of them had, then and only then would he refer to her as Charlotte.

"I had seen her for quite some time around campus." Still not a fan of lying, I did my best to fabricate an honest story that didn't venture too far from the truth. Which, to Greg, or any other sane man for that matter, would sound absurd. "I wasn't sure how to approach her at first. She had this air about her that said she wasn't like any woman I'd ever met before." Taking a sip of his drink, Greg listened with amusement.

153

"She was sure of herself. I could tell just in the way that she carried herself. When she walked the halls, she didn't need to be surrounded by her friends to laugh at her jokes or make her look a certain way. She just...was." I sipped my own drink and looked across the desk to meet Greg's eyes. "Was it like that when you first met your wife?"

"Very similar actually," he admitted. "They're a rare breed, but lucky for us, it seems to be genetic."

The mention of genetics quickened my heartbeat. Charlotte might be pregnant. I had to focus all of my attention momentarily on not letting the shock resurface on my face. "So, have you lived in this house long?" I asked in an attempt to draw my attention back on course.

"Grace and I moved in shortly after getting married. So, about thirty years now. I can't believe it's been that long."

I still couldn't seem to maintain focus. Kids. Marriage. A house. Supporting all of that. My mind was flooded with such normal and human concerns I could hardly stand it.

I placed my drink on the desk and looked Greg square in the eyes. "I know that you haven't known me for more than," I looked up at the clock "oh, ten minutes or so, but I need you to know that I love your daughter. And I will do anything for her."

"I think you've already proven that," he said inquisitively, taking a sip of his drink.

"A good father worries about his daughter and the man that she intends to spend her life with. How he'll support her. That he'll honor her. And I intend to prove myself in all of those aspects."

Greg leaned forward in his chair and met my eyes. "I can't say for certain what a *good* father would do," always a man of true modesty, "but I know a good man when I see one. You're a pretty-boy but I can forgive you for that."

Though I knew Greg just about as well as I did Charlotte, I had somehow managed to forget that he had a strong sense of things, and he trusted that sense. Charlotte was much like her father in that way. No matter what anyone else said or what the obvious answer might be, she followed what she knew to be right.

The constant flow of questions I'd expected based on the interrogation preceding Charlotte's first dates with Will Downey and Paul Phillips hadn't been necessary. Greg was a man who needed proof and not fancy words of promise. I, as it would seem, had already earned a full résumé where he was concerned simply by risking my own life for his daughter's. The questioning had been deemed unnecessary.

His worn smile was welcoming and I could already tell that he considered me part of the family. However, I needed a more concrete reassurance. I needed to do right by Charlotte. We hadn't exactly done much by the book as it was.

"There's something else isn't there?" Greg said knowingly. "You look nervous."

I had no idea what I was doing. I wasn't in my element at all and my facial expression was undoubtedly giving me away.

"I'd like to ask you for Charlotte's hand in marriage," I blurted out in a husky voice.

Greg smiled and laughed, understanding my nerves. I cleared my throat. Nervous. Well that was a new one. As the time between my question and his answer grew longer, I felt a knot form in my throat. He rose from his chair, stared at me long and hard, and extended his hand.

"You're the only man on earth that deserves her. Welcome to the family."

I shook his hand in gratitude and laughed at myself for being uncertain. It was as if I'd managed somehow to forget who Greg was. I couldn't help but question what everything felt like on this side of the looking glass. There was no outside perspective or ability to gauge the outcome of a situation based on the unspoken words in the air. I had nothing but nerves and human emotion to go by, both unfailingly distorting my view of the situation. They still proved to cause a distracting haze even when I'd managed to harness them as much as I had.

When we joined Charlotte and her mother at the table a while later, Greg and I shared a secret understanding. I would withdraw what little money I had to my name and purchase a ring. Charlotte deserved all of which I could provide. And once we took care of Alex, I would figure out the rest.

As Charlotte smiled over her water glass, sharing with me a secret of our own, I knew that in the short time I'd spent as a man, I was already living the dream. We were both uncertain of almost everything but it scarcely seemed to matter.

Though my body was twenty-five, my mind and nerves belonged to a seventeen-year-old adolescent. I was excited about everything and prepared for nothing. Love and love alone was carrying me from day to day. I shook myself internally, readying another forkful of Grace's meal, and shifted in my thinking. I needed to concentrate on the dangers that we faced no matter how much my heart wanted to dwell on the happiness that threatened to consume my focus.

I drew back in the conversation, trying my best to remain at least minimally present. Alex hadn't been hanging around for a few days. After he'd made his point in front of Tara, neither of us had seen him. Though at times, I could feel his presence nearby like a dark shadow. I had a feeling that he watched Charlotte from afar sometimes but I couldn't be sure of it. As long as we remained on the lookout and continued our new routine of my driving Charlotte to and from school and work, we were pretty safe. Based on his pattern of attacks in the past, it had always been when I wasn't around that Alex chose to make his move. I would see to it that she was never left alone.

I shook my head, angry that I'd even once considered that he had been a good man for Charlotte to marry. I'd passed the feeling along to her on a few occasions in the past but whenever she got close to giving into his subtle and at times, not so subtle advances, I urged her to pull away. Though I hadn't understood it at the time, I felt the suggestion of something, the feeling that I didn't want to see her with another man. A feeling it seemed that had saved her, for Alex knew as well as I did that love or even false love had the ability to make a person stay with someone who wasn't good for them.

But why had he been so secretive? It was as if he'd known that Charlotte was being watched every moment of every day. As if he needed to trick not only her but he needed to avoid me. It was a fact that might prove he was something more.

I wondered if maybe I'd begun to think a bit too much now that I was a man. Working at the facts until sense was mangled and manipulated into nonsense. I looked up from my plate to see Charlotte smiling nervously up at me. Not wanting to upset her, I took her hand in mine and left my questions to pick up another day.

I knew early on that Charlotte had needed to spend the night at her parents' house. Though I was never apart from her, I could still see the loneliness in her eyes. With the added possibility of a baby on the way, I could feel the relief that being home brought her.

"You seemed kind of lost in thought during dinner," Charlotte observed from across her childhood bedroom.

"There are a lot of thoughts to get lost in," I admitted.

She remained quiet, sat back on her bed and looked out the window into the darkness. "Are you having regrets?" I could tell that she was trying to be stronger than she had to be on her own. She placed her hand on her stomach briefly then moved both hands over the bed's surface to occupy them otherwise.

I crossed the room and knelt down in front of her, taking both hands in mine. "No, Charlotte, of course not." I waited a moment for her to pull her eyes from the window and look down into mine. "I love you, and if you are pregnant than that's the best news I've ever gotten."

"And if I'm not? If we can't ever have kids?"

"Charlotte, anything past being with you for the rest of my life will be a bonus. I am truly happy, please believe me when I say that."

The look on her face was gratified but I knew she was still daunted by everything that was piling up against us. I had every intention of doing right by her. A proper marriage, a safe home for our family whether it was getting bigger or not, and I would end our struggle with Alex. For good. Though time was not being rationed off generously, I still needed a bit more of it to figure out what to do. Alex was still a very large and dangerous question mark. The last thing I needed to do was to storm into a dark cave without knowing of the dangers inside.

"What did you and my dad talk about?" she asked, taking in a deep breath.

I smiled and looked down to avert my eyes. "Why don't you lie down for a little bit?"

The outside world was lit brightly by a nearly perfect moon. While the lamp on Charlotte's dresser was noble competition, the night sky could have easily lit the room on its own.

With a sigh, Charlotte kicked off her shoes and slid under the covers then let her eyes flutter closed.

"Well?" she said when her blanket was tucked neatly around her.

"Well, what?"

"What did you two talk about?"

I kissed her forehead and shook my head. "We talked about how poorly the Yankees have been playing this year," I joked.

Charlotte moaned into her pillow and forced herself to reply with a drowsy smile. "My dad hates baseball..." her voice was just above a whisper. "And so do you," she added.

"You got me," I replied, stroking her hair.

When she replied with no more than the gentle rise and fall of her chest, I got up from the side of her bed. Tired on so many levels, I hated knowing that I wouldn't be able to sleep. I rubbed my face and turned the lamp off to let the moon provide the only light in the room. I slipped my harmonica from my pocket and headed over to the window to look out over the yard. The shadows were thick and dark; making distinct and nearly solid structures across the yard. The earth was still, not a single gust of wind. The night was eerily quiet, but I knew that he was out there watching us. I was fighting with every ounce of restraint I'd managed to instill in myself not to race into the blue-grey night and call Alex out to finish it right there and then. The man in me, the animal, wanted to tear him limb from limb.

I put my harmonica to my lips and commanded my body to find calm as the music trailed through the air. I had managed to keep a certain amount of my old existence, my old form, with me. I hadn't forgotten who I once was and it was vital that I remain conscious of who I'd always been. Going mad and letting Alex manipulate my weaknesses into a self-destructive force was not part of the plan.

Chapter

16

By the time I'd gotten up the nerve to buy the pregnancy test, I learned that I didn't have it in me to actually take it. The infamous box sat nestled among my balled up socks in the top drawer of my dresser for days. It taunted me to the point that I'd made a few outfit choices that avoided the need for socks all together. But it remained in my drawer, pounding away at my anxieties like the telltale heart.

I'd been careful enough to purchase the test under Joel's radar. I couldn't stand to picture the look of disappointment on his face if it turned up negative. I knew how badly he already wanted a child. And if I was being honest with myself, I wasn't even sure yet what result I wanted to see. On one hand, a negative result would likely mean that we could never have kids, and while I wasn't exactly sure if I was ready now, that didn't mean I never wanted to have them. On the other hand, having a baby was a lot of responsibility, one that was big enough without the danger that we already faced. Either way, I wanted to shield Joel from my first reaction to the news. I would make the best of whatever came of it, but I couldn't stand the idea of hurting him with the relief or disappointment that I was sure to exude. Had I any indication of my reaction, I would have told him but the truth remained that I wouldn't know of my feelings on the subject until I saw the results of that test.

I'd avoided taking it for as long as I could but with the wind at my back and the race against time undoubtedly lost, I couldn't keep up my efforts to try and stop it any longer. I stared at the box in my drawer one last time like a loaded gun buried amongst my argyle knee-highs. Looking away for distraction, I took hold of it.

"Are you ready, Charlotte?" I heard Joel call from the stairs as he made his way towards my room.

I smuggled the pregnancy paraphernalia into my purse and clapped it shut as he pushed my bedroom door open. "Yup, all set," I replied, sure that I'd broken a sweat.

He swept me up into his arms and kissed my hair softly. "They say it's going to get pretty cold this evening, we might even get some snow."

"The proverbial 'they' let me down again," I joked.

I looked up into his eyes and thought unguardedly that our children would have looks to rival if they were fortunate enough to have even half of his features. Which, I mused, I guess they would. *Stop it*, I thought. I wasn't helping myself by imagining a life where Joel and I could have kids.

"Always thinking," he murmured as he took my hand, his other hand dug deeply into his jacket pocket.

"I thought you lost all of that sixth-sense-angel-stuff when you changed over to the homosapien side."

"You can't take back a lifetime of getting to know someone that easily."

Sitting down for a quick breakfast together, I could see the shadow of thought on Joel's face. Instead of asking me what I might want to do after work or telling me a story from my childhood, he sat quietly as he ate.

"And you say that I'm the one always thinking."

He tipped back the rest of his orange juice and watched me from across the table. He studied me curiously for a long moment before he spoke. "What do you make of dreams?" he asked.

"Aspiring dreams or sleeping dreams?" I got up from the table, taking our plates over to the sink.

"Sleeping dreams." Joel took our glasses and followed, crossing his arms over his chest.

"What do you mean, what do I make of them? They're okay, when they're good."

"Well, what I mean to say is, do you think that there's any truth to them?"

"Like do I think that dreams, the unconscious kind, can actually happen?"

"Yes."

I mulled the idea over in my head. I wasn't really sure. "I've dreamt that I lost something as a kid, like a toy, and a few days later I did. But that kind of thing is subconscious I think. If you think it'll happen, it will. Why, what did you have a dream about?"

"Nothing really, I was just curious what you thought about it. It's my first time experiencing dreams that's all. I'm still getting used to them I guess. Sometimes they feel so real."

"I've had a lot of realistic dreams. But usually dreams just reiterate what's on your mind before you go to sleep."

"Yeah, you're probably right."

Though he wouldn't tell me, I could tell that Joel had had a dream worth talking about. Not that I was in any position to force him to delve into it. I was keeping my own secrets after all.

As we drove to the bank, I took the opportunity to ask Joel a few more questions. Since he'd woken up in his new form, I hadn't really taken the time to find out what it was like to experience such dramatic changes. We'd spent most of our time just trying to deal with them. At the mention of dreams, he'd gotten me wondering what other differences he'd been experiencing and how he felt about all of them.

"I guess I don't really think about it most of the time," Joel went on. "I view everything I've been going through as such a distraction that I haven't had much time to view it as anything else."

"You even view dreams as a distraction?"

"Of course."

"But they happen when you're asleep. They're not real."

"So you're saying that you've never been affected by a dream before? A dream has never made you question something you did or fear something without an actual reason to?"

He had me there. I hadn't really thought about it much but Joel was right. Dreams, while formed out of imagination and not out of fact, where just as likely to get a person worked up as an actual event was if it was strong enough.

"Do you *like* anything about being human?"

"I like knowing that I can be with you and not have to worry about going back. And of course, there are other...benefits to being human."

I blushed, pretty sure I knew which *benefits* he was referring to.

"I'm not enjoying having to shave every morning though. And there are a lot of other things I have to do daily that I never did before. It's a lot to get used to."

"You don't have to shave every morning. Though I will admit, you've gotten pretty good at it."

"Something as simple as having facial hair is not what I'm used to," he admitted. "The more human I feel, the less confidence I have of being able to keep you safe."

"There are thousands of service men and women who would argue that you don't have to be an angel to be perfectly capable of keeping someone safe."

"Yeah, well, I feel like I do."

Stopped at a red light, I tried to imagine what it must feel like to be in Joel's shoes. He'd always had the job of protecting me. Apart from that, he didn't know any other way of life.

"If I wasn't in danger what would you do?" I asked.

The light turned green and he accelerated, pulling onto the road where the bank was located. "What do you mean?"

"I worry that you'll never be able to relax. That you'll always feel like you have to protect me." It was a concern that I hadn't really considered before. But mentioning it now made me wonder if being human and being less capable of helping me through life might lessen Joel's self-worth. That somewhere along the way he would begin longing for his old life.

"Charlotte, I've been doing this for a little over twenty three years. I was created for you. There are guardians out there who have been around for thousands of years, protecting and watching over hundreds of people or more. Yes, I'm always going to look out for your safety and wellbeing. I'll always worry when you come home late from work or when you wake up with a cold, but does that make me any different than any other man who loves a woman? I don't worry because it's my job; I worry because I love you. Sure, I'm not entirely pleased that I'm human, but I think most people would desire the eternal life that I'm used to over a mortal one. It was a lot less confusing, that's for sure. But that doesn't mean that I wish to go back to it."

Joel parked the car and I looked over at him. "I guess it's just still so hard to believe sometimes. I feel like you're going to be ripped away from me at any minute."

"Well, you need to start believing that this is all permanent. It's taken me a while too, don't get me wrong. It's strange. But I think I've gotten all the answers I need." He kissed me on the forehead. "I'm here to stay."

* * *

"I can't believe this," Heather said breathlessly.

"Shhh..." I whispered. Our words echoed in the small bathroom that connected to the break room. Even a whisper could be heard by the time it reached anyone on the other side of the door.

"When did you find out?" she asked with astonishment.

I sat huddled on the sanitarily questionable floor, staring at the white pen-shaped test that balanced on the bathroom sink. I shook my head then rested it on my knees. "I haven't yet."

"Does he know?"

"Of course he knows...that it's a possibility."

"Speaking of *possibilities*...how is *this* even possible? You know, considering what he is, or was."

"Trust me, this is happening because we didn't think it ever could."

Heather sat down beside me and rested her head on my shoulder in an attempt to bring me comfort. My heart was racing a mile a minute though and it seemed nothing could stop it.

We sat in silence, staring at the stick as if it could transform into a terrible monster at any moment. Was I excited? Afraid? I couldn't tell the difference between my own emotions. Did I want a baby? Was I ready?

Did it matter? My stomach turned with indecision, proving that whatever the outcome was, I was likely to vomit.

"Time's up," Heather said, noting the time lapsed on her phone.

We both took in a deep breath and rose from the floor, taking hesitant steps towards the sink. I took the stick in both hands and let out a breath. "Two lines," I said quietly. "That means I'm pregnant, right?"

I turned to Heather and she watched for my reaction, her hands to her mouth, muffling the obvious smile she couldn't completely banish.

My insides untangled and a single tear fell from my eye as an equally joyful smile spread across my lips. "I'm pregnant."

* * *

Dreams, I was finding, were wildly imaginative. Since possessing my new human body, I'd had plenty of them. Most of them I didn't remember, though I knew I'd had them, others I only remember parts of. Understandably, they all involved Charlotte and the dangers we faced or that I feared we would face some day. Taking that into account, I hadn't been nearly as disturbed by any dream as much the one I'd had the previous night.

I might have shared it with Charlotte when she'd asked had I not felt insane for actually considering it to be a window into the future. I'd heard of only one time where a dream had been more powerful than reality, it was a story any person of faith knew rather well. But I wasn't nearly that important. I couldn't have possibly been sent a message from heaven in my sleep. Could I?

In my dream, I'd been driving the Mustang. I'd pulled up to the same bank as the one Charlotte worked at but I'd soon realized that it was a different branch.

166

One I had remembered seeing about a mile from the university. I pulled the car into the lot and parked. When I walked up to the counter, I pulled out a small key and a driver's license I didn't actually possess and handed it to the woman behind the counter.

She took both and led me to the vault in the back of the lobby. We both slipped a key into the same safety deposit box, and when I pulled it out I woke up.

The dream had been so vivid, so real, and so out of place that when I woke up that morning I'd questioned momentarily if it had been a dream at all. To make things even stranger, when I'd reached into my pocket for the spare key to the Mustang that morning, I'd felt the jingle of another, much smaller key, and the slick surface of a card; very similar to that of a license.

Because Charlotte had been beside me at the time, I left the strangely out of place objects in my pocket and retrieved only the car key. After dropping her off at work, however, I reached into my pocket again to discover the same key and Michigan driver's license from my dream.

Now, I sat in the car looking through the windshield at the bank. A bank I'd never once stepped foot inside of before. The dream had meant something and there was no doubting it with the key in my hand. I was anxious to know what was in the box, hoping that it served as an answer to how we might deal with Alex.

Either way, I thought, I had intended to withdraw money to purchase Charlotte's ring regardless. It only made sense to do it at a bank she didn't work at. There was no harm in entertaining my curiosity about the dream and the mysterious license and key while I was at it.

After much hesitation, I got out of the car and entered the establishment. The bank was much bigger than the one that Charlotte worked out of but it was emptied of its customers and the interior was sparsely decorated. Apart from a few potted plants, dark wood desks to one side, and a neatly kept station to fill out deposits, the place looked uninhabited. Like a ghost town, I walked through the tremendous lobby with no more than the sound of my footsteps echoing off the walls.

Both tellers stood up from behind the teller line as I walked over and I chose to go to the woman closest to the safe.

I pulled the key and my driver's license from my pocket and slid them both across the counter, mirroring the scene that had played out in my dream. "May I please get into my safety deposit box?"

I was nervous again, a feeling I was far from comfortable with. I didn't want to be wrong. I didn't want to look crazy, I felt crazy enough on my own. As a human, I found myself much fuller of doubt than I'd ever been before.

"Sure," the woman behind the counter replied, trying to tame a smile.

I waited patiently as she checked all appropriate records and was surprised when she didn't look confused. She passed me back my license and the key and smiled again.

"Please follow me."

I hadn't expected that.

I followed her into the vault and the room felt abnormally tight. The way she kept looking over at me was making me uneasy, shrinking the room it seemed to half its actual size. "It seems to be warming up a bit out there, huh?"

"Just a little," I said with a nervous smile, trying to maintain a pleasant air about me. I knew that she was unaware of how desperate I was to know exactly what was in the safety deposit box. That she was simply trying to start up a friendly conversation, but I couldn't keep my thoughts still. I was still baffled by the fact that the box even existed at all.

She placed a small key, similar to the one I carried into the key hole of box number 913 and stepped back, but not enough for my liking.

"You can put your key in now, and then just turn it and you can take your box into the side room next to the vault."

I slipped into the small space between the girl and my box, feeling her pressed slightly against me. I turned the key and opened the door, backing up, forcing her to give me the proper space that I needed. I pulled the box out and tucked it under my arm.

"Thank you," I said, being sure not to lock eyes and give her an impression she was clearly looking to receive.

"Take all the time you need" she said, looking up through her lashes.

I forced a smile of gratitude onto my lips but it didn't stay there long. I found the door to the room she'd mentioned and closed it behind me. There was a table and two chairs in the center of it and I walked over and placed the box on top of the table. Without sitting down, I worked open the box and found myself perplexed.

As it would seem, God had officially granted me my humanity.

* * *

As Heather waited on a woman with her young daughter, I found myself looking on with an unprotected smile. The little girl stood at her mother's side, stroking her stuffed animal horse with a small brush. Her feet were pointed in with a stance of concentration. When her mother knelt down to hand her the sticker that Heather had passed over the counter for her, the little girl's eyes lit up. Her smile stretched from ear to ear and she showered Heather with gratitude. A sticker had done all that. Eager now to incorporate her new addition into her play, the girl tore the back of the sticker off, tucking the scraps neatly into her pocket. She stamped the sticker down on the horse's side delicately while being sure to apply enough pressure to make it stick. She held out the little brown horse to admire her work and seemed quite pleased.

The sound of a scratchy throat cleared and I was shaken from my trance. "Excuse me, miss, are you open?"

I looked up quickly, my face already flushed and my heart racing. I hadn't even noticed the little old man who stood patiently in front of my counter. "Oh my gosh, I'm so sorry, sir, I didn't see you there."

"Don't you worry about a thing, young lady, I'm in no rush." He slid his deposit over the counter and I started to decode his shaky chicken scratch. "They grow up so fast," he observed. "One day they're playing with a stuffed horse, the next day they're riding one, then before you know it they are managing a ranch of their own."

I smiled in reply, unsure of what to say.

So quickly my life had gone from revolving around the danger that seemed ever lurking to the new life I held inside of me.

As I locked up the doors for the night, I glanced outside and caught sight of Joel making his way to the sidewalk. His hands were stuffed into his pockets and he looked a bit more distracted than usual. A layer of shock or something of the like remained on the surface of his straight face. Once under the overhang of the strip-mall, he leaned against one of the support beams and glanced in. He pulled a hand from his jacket pocket and waved briefly in my direction. As if seeing him for the first time, butterflies filled my insides. I waved back and made no effort to mask my excitement, flashing a happy smile.

As he waited patiently outside with the setting sun casting his body in a masculine silhouette, I rushed through my duties and willed for Tim to do the same.

"I see lover boy's here right on time," Tim observed as he emerged from the vault.

"He's punctual, what can I say," I laughed.

"So when's the wedding?"

I blushed and laughed weakly. "We only met a few months ago." It was a lame excuse but...technically true.

"It hardly seems like it. I mean, I'm about his age and I'm nowhere near ready to settle down, but man, he's definitely ready. By the way he looks at you...he's hooked."

"Hooked, huh?" I laughed. At the rate that Joel and I were going, with the crazy directions, and the obstacles that we faced on a regular basis, I'd hardly even considered marriage. I hadn't really been given the chance to.

Fabulous. One more thing to keep me up at night.

Tim was out of the door first and I followed quickly behind. "Hey, how's it goin'?" he said as he passed Joel, who now stood up to receive me in a hug.

"I'm good, thanks. And yourself?" He held me in to his arms and kissed my forehead.

"I'm off work, couldn't get any better than that," Tim replied with a smile and a wave. "See you guys later."

"Good night," I called out.

"Drive safe," Joel added.

When Tim was nearly to his car, Joel and I looked at one another. He had a smile smuggled somewhere under his lips but I couldn't keep mine from showing on my face. He tilted his head in question, knowing that I was excited about something in that way he knew everything before I actually said it.

"What?" he asked, letting a smile creep up onto his lips. He seemed almost suspicious.

"Well…" I began, taking his hands in mine. "It's official." I paused for theatrics. "I'm pregnant."

"That's great news." His smile was pure and though I sensed worry just below the surface, I knew that we would be okay, that this was a *good* thing. "We should go out to dinner to celebrate."

"It's so tempting, but I have a lot of homework to catch up on. Can we do it on Friday maybe? A nice way to end the week?"

"Sure, whatever you want to do."

I squinted with suspicion at his reply. There was something about his tone, about the way he avoided my eyes more than usual, that brought on an excited suspicion. Joel was a warrior if I'd ever seen one. He was very serious and very direct when a threat was near. But this…this was excited, nervous, and secretive Joel. Don't ask me how I'd managed to arrive at such a bold conclusion, but I had a feeling that he was doing his best to conceal a secret. Some body language and no obvious signs otherwise wasn't fuel enough for such an accusation normally. Joel though, he hadn't really managed to recognize *all* of his emotions, especially the ones that registered on his face. I found myself amused by the fact that he seemed convinced that he'd kept his frustration of lust in check when meanwhile I was reading his feelings loud and clear on his face.

I pushed my lips to one side in suspicion and took his face in my hand to make him look me in the eye. "What are you up to?" I asked with a tilt of my head.

His eyes grew wider just long enough for me to notice before his face took on the form of a solemn gaze. "I'm not up to anything," he replied easily.

"Yeah, okay."

Though I fought the feeling hard, I could sense that everything was falling into place again. The gun-shy part of my brain repelled the idea like the plague. Past experience had proven that happiness was always short lived. That the waters of life were only ever calm for short spurts before the current picked up again. But mostly I knew that it was all just part of life, a theory I'd managed to gain a great deal of support for in the past few months. But no matter what I might be faced with down the line, I knew that in the end I would be okay, because guardian or not, Joel was the best thing that had ever happened to me.

Chapter

17

"Have a good day at work," Joel said.

Fridays were always my most dreaded work day, add to that the morning sickness that had waited until that morning to act up at full swing, and I was set. With no stomach for breakfast, I'd bypassed the whole idea of eating, though it hardly seemed to matter. I was nauseous anyway.

"Not likely," I argued, smiling up at him.

Leaning against Trigger in the bank parking lot, we kissed one last time before I pulled away to head inside. "Don't forget about dinner tonight," he said, pressing my lips in another soft kiss. "We're going to celebrate and we're both going to relax, really relax." He looked to the ground then met my eyes again. "Let me take care of everything. You only have one thing to worry about right now. Okay?"

"I'll try," I managed. "Relaxation has never been my strong suit, you know that."

Sadly I couldn't see enjoying a meal in my near future either but I decided it was best not to mention that. In spite of a body that seemed to be backfiring more with every passing day, I was looking forward to a real-live date night with my guardian-angel-turned-boyfriend-turned-baby-daddy.

Joel smiled and pulled me in for a final hug. "I'll see you later."

"I love you," I whispered.

"I love you too, Charlotte."

With one final attempt at taming my weak stomach, I made my way into the bank. I could feel Joel's eyes following me as he watched me enter the building. Once I was safely inside, he got in the car and headed back to the house. At the end of the day he would pick me up as he'd done dozens of times before. It had become so routine at this point that it hardly seemed to be a precaution anymore, rather a way to spend every second we could together. Alex hadn't been around for a while and I'd let myself appreciate the new schedule as something else entirely. It was that mentality that kept me sane most days.

"Hey, Charlotte," Claire greeted from her desk.

"Hey," I replied, placing my purse at my station. "How's it been today? Busy?"

"Busy for one teller to be working alone," Heather piped in. "I've been waiting to pee for an hour now. Hurry up and get your station set up," she added in desperation.

I laughed and, as requested, tried my best not to drag my feet in getting myself situated behind the teller line.

When Heather sprinted off to the bathroom I discreetly flipped open the *Motherhood* magazine that I'd picked up during my lunch break the day before. I scanned the pages; littered with ads for breast pumps, prenatal vitamins, and organic bathing products. I skipped over everything that made me uncomfortable, which left me with very few pages to scan through.

As I turned my head in curiosity at the spread of prenatal yoga poses, Claire called over from her desk.

"It looks like Joel has been taking you to work a lot lately," she said observantly. "Is everything okay?"

I looked up from my magazine and tried not to fidget in my seat. I slipped it back into my purse and sat up straighter in my char. Sometimes it felt like everyone knew all of my secrets like they were written all over my face.

"No, why do you ask?" I said, trying to keep my voice steady.

"I just..." she stopped as if to consider her next words. "I dated a guy once who requested things like driving me everywhere. It started off very small. The signs were so subtle at times that I hardly noticed or connected them. Not until..." She closed her eyes as if to fight back a past that threatened to suck her in. I swallowed hard, knowing what she was about to say next. "Until he hit me," she finally said.

"Oh, Claire."

"I left him the first time," she assured me. "I just can't help but notice the signs when I see them. And I wouldn't want for you to go through what I did."

Part of me wanted to tell Claire everything, for the sake of clearing her of her worries...if not just to be able to open up to someone about it all. I hadn't even told Heather about Alex; the one person I could trust and that knew about Joel. The problem with keeping information so secretive was that it became harder and harder to actually tell anyone the longer you kept it from them.

I figured it was probably best to meet her halfway. I took in a big breath and let it out slowly. "To be honest..." The words were sticking in my throat. "Someone's been stalking me," I began, feeling instant relief with the admission. "Joel and I have no idea what to do about it. We can't prove it and there's nothing concrete to hold against the guy. It's one of those things where pressing charges might actually put me in more danger." I paused, fanning a pad of post-it notes between my fingers as a distraction. "I've already seen what that can do, and I hate to be afraid," I admitted. "I hate that Joel has to stop everything to babysit me, but I'm scared." My throat grew tight and I couldn't stop the tears from burning my eyes.

"Oh, honey," she said, getting up from her desk and making her way over to me. Once she was behind the line, she pulled me in for a hug. "I'm so sorry."

"And my friends," I sniffled, the floodgates bursting open, "won't talk to me because they don't believe me. They avoid me at school..." I took in a breath and rubbed my face. I needed to be strong, relaxed, and conscious of the fact that I was putting stress on our baby. *Our baby*, I thought. I shook my head in disbelief of my own life.

"It's okay, let it all out," Claire said, stroking my hair.

Choking back the remainder of my tears, I found an unexpected comfort in knowing that I'd told someone other than Heather about what had been going on. While I had still left the big details out, I was relieved that I no longer had the burden to bear on my own anymore. Why I hadn't talked to Claire sooner or why I still had yet to talk to my parents was a curious thing. It seemed that Joel and I were similar in that way. We both felt that we had to face our struggles alone.

"I'm alright," I said with a new bout of confidence.

I was done hiding everything from the people that cared about me. It was that lack of confidence in my friends that had driven Emily and Tara away in the first place.

Claire pulled back and looked me in the eye, seeing a confirmation of my words. She let go of my arms and smiled with a mother-like pride. "You're a strong woman, Charlotte. You've been taking on the world in your personal life but I never even caught a glimpse of it at work. Here I was worrying about you."

I'd be lying if I said I didn't often worry about myself, but she was right.

The important thing was to stay strong. To know what I had the ability to do, and to do it. Past that, I had to let everything else go. Most importantly, I had to keep reminding myself that I had support.

Heather came back out into the lobby as Claire returned to her desk. When she settled back into her station, I tried to figure out an easy way of telling her the one detail I knew she'd have the hardest time believing.

"Heather, if I tell you something, will you try really hard to believe me?" I said past the divider that separated us.

"That's a strange thing to ask," she said with a laugh.

"I know."

"Of course I would trust you, Charlotte. You have no reason to lie to me."

"Well, you know that Emily and Tara have stopped talking to me," I added cautiously.

"Is that what this is about?"

"Sort of. They didn't believe me so I *really* need for you to."

"I'm all ears," Heather replied, rolling her seat closer to me.

"It's about Alex. He's not who you think he is. He's not…a good person."

Heather's expression instantly changed. I could tell that she was hoping that I was wrong, though she seemed inclined to think that I wasn't. "Where's this coming from? I thought that—he always seemed…okay."

"I know. Trust me, half the time *I* don't believe it. I guess that's why it's taken me so long to tell you."

"Tell me what? What did he do?" Her eyes grew wide.

"He's been following me. And I don't just mean recently. He's been following me for *years*. Before I worked at the bank, even before I was in college. I know it sounds crazy but it's true. And the reason Tara and Emily are ignoring me is because Alex kissed me in front on Tara."

Heather put her hand over her mouth in shock. "But he knows who Joel is. He knows that you love him. Why would he do that? And how the hell does he know you from before working at the bank?"

"Both very good questions, sadly I don't have an answer for either of them. Want to know the best part?"

Heather was unmoving.

"He was the one who drugged me that night at the club."

Heather blinked repeatedly, at a loss for words.

"I overheard him admit to it the night that Joel was shot. I don't know why he's so desperate all of a sudden, but I feel like it's getting worse. And now..." I lowered my voice. "With a baby, I can't be any kind of reckless. Joel's human so he can't do much of anything either."

I could read empathy across Heather's face. She took my hands in hers and squeezed them tightly. "Whatever it takes, I'm here to help you. You've been through enough and it's about time that you stop feeling like you have to constantly look over your shoulder."

I smiled gratefully and choked back a lump in my throat. "Thank you."

"I don't want you to ever feel like you have to worry about coming to me again, alright? I'm here for you, truly."

"I'm sorry I didn't tell you sooner. I guess I was just scared."

"Don't be sorry, I get it. I just worry that you take too much onto yourself sometimes. There's no need for you to tackle this alone."

By the time we got back to waiting on customers during the evening rush, I was feeling a hundred pounds lighter. My stomach had settled and I felt a ray of hope shine through the smog that seemed to be ever present around me.

When Heather and Claire left for the day, I was sad to see them go. Claire hugged me again before passing her shift over to Linda and Heather slipped me a note across the counter scribbled onto a deposit slip.

"Have a good night, hon," she said before leaving the bank.

I smiled with gratitude then looked down at the folded up deposit slip. I opened it up and read the short message scribbled in red ink.

If you need ANYTHING text me, okay?

Folding up the note and slipping it into my pocket, I smiled up at Linda who was pulling out files to begin her shift. While she seemed nice enough, her predecessor had made it rather hard for me to warm up to her. She kept to herself and didn't ask for or offer much personal information. In no real mood to talk myself, I was content to open up my magazine again and cringe past the ads for things I didn't want to think about just yet.

As the day wound down, I found myself looking forward to my dinner date with Joel. For the most part, we spent most of our time at home, stopping by my parents' house once now and then to change things up. I was definitely looking forward to the change of scenery.

Peering out the window, I watched for Trigger. It was a quarter to seven and Joel was usually in the parking lot by now. The sun was nearly below the horizon, leaving a soft orange and purple glow in its wake. It was already nearly dark outside but he was still nowhere to be seen.

Making my rounds, closing everything up, my stomach turned uneasily. Fifteen minutes later Joel still hadn't shown up. I peered out of the large storefront window, and as Linda switched the lights off, I felt panic sink in.

"Ready?" she asked, grabbing her coat and purse.

"Yeah," I answered with hesitation. My stomach knotted as I grabbed my belongings and waited for Linda to set the alarm.

We made our way into the cold evening air and parted ways. "Good night," I called out trying to control the trembling of my voice.

"Night," she called back, heading to her car.

I stood out front for a moment longer, trying to see the Mustang parked in the lot when it clearly wasn't. Momentarily, I wondered if Joel had planned a surprise to add a bit of romance to our dinner date. Maybe he would pop up out of nowhere with a dozen roses. Make it two dozen. I smiled at the possibility. But as I scanned the lot again with no sign of Joel or the car, I began to feel uneasy again. I hadn't known Joel to be the kind of guy who popped out of dark alleys in an effort to be romantic. He'd always been a pretty straight forward guy. Besides, this was hardly the time to try and thrill me with romantics.

I shivered just thinking about it. It was pitch-dark now and most of the stores on the stretch were closed, lights out, no longer illuminating the concrete walkway. It was frighteningly quiet and I felt a shiver crawl up my spine as the seconds standing out in the darkness stretched on to feel like hours. Everything disappeared out in front of the dimly lit sidewalk. The small amount of light that remained was enough to shift shadows and cloak corners, making me wish even more that Joel had showed up on time.

I dug my hands into my pockets to fight the cold and made my way down the strip towards the well-lit and heated McDonald's at the end. Walking briskly, I sensed what felt like a sharp breath against my neck and turned around with fright. There was no one there. My heart was racing and I had to remind myself to stay calm. I was psyching myself out. Joel was just late. He wasn't perfect and he was human...traffic, a flat tire, whatever it was; he'd be here.

Halfway across the strip mall now, I felt relief as I got closer to refuge. I was clearly not in my element in the dark. It played tricks with my mind and set my nerves off like aged and fragile dynamite.

Just as I'd managed to sooth my anxiety, I felt a hand reach out and grab me, cupping over my mouth to prevent me from screaming. I shuttered when I felt strong arms hold me to a firm and steady frame. I thrashed and resisted but it was no use. He held me firmly in one place, easily taking control.

As I looked on with fear, his chest pressed against my back, my vision began to blur. He dragged me back easily, ignoring my attempts at digging my heels into the concrete to get away. Losing both of my shoes and shredding my pantyhose in the process, he pulled me into complete darkness. I gasped heavily, too late to realize that he'd placed a cloth over my mouth. It carried with it a strange and sweet smell that made me weak and drained my body of the ability to continue resisting. Falling limp in his arms, my body surrendered to the odor soaked cloth and the world around me disappeared.

Chapter

18

I could hear the muffled sound of logs crackling in front of me. The smell of burning wood and warm heat on my face. My head was throbbing. As I forced my eyes open, I felt a clear sense of déjà vu. But this time the room was rather well lit, largely illuminated by the fireplace in the center of it. A cool blue glow poured in from outside, reflecting off of the snow.

In a daze, I considered the fact that it hadn't snowed for weeks in Dearborn. Where was I? I readjusted myself and tried to stand up, realizing with a knot in my stomach that I was tied to a chair.

I had been waiting for Joel to pick me up from work. The last thing I remembered was being grabbed from behind, a damp cloth, smelling overly sweet, had been placed over my mouth. As reality slowly took place of the fog I'd been in, I felt panic take over once again. My eyes darted around the small room with fear. It was minimally furnished and covered in a generous layer of dust. Someone, Alex no doubt, had taken me to absolute isolation.

Through my all too familiar haze, I tried to concentrate on freeing myself without success. I pulled at the ropes around my wrist, trying to grab them with my loose fingers. I moved my legs the little distance they would budge and tried to find a flaw in the bindings. I couldn't. The ropes were too tight and my feet tingled from constricted circulation. I stopped the useless struggle, knowing that it was no use to waste my energy.

Joel, usually in the parking lot a good fifteen to twenty minutes early, had been nowhere to be seen. Also probably Alex's doing. Where was he? Was he okay? I didn't have the sense to worry about myself as long as I was unsure of his safety. For the moment, I was alive.

When I looked down, I saw that was I still fully clothed, something I was becoming far too familiar with checking. Though it did serve as some relief. Alex wanted compliance, but in order to get it, he needed to separate me from everything else that mattered.

A cold chill entered the room and I flinched, sensing that he was behind me. Steady and firm steps rounded the chair I was forcibly sitting in. His cold hand trailed through my hair and caught my chin before falling to his side.

"You're awake," he observed, lowering to a crouch in front of me. He looked up into my eyes, still a bit blurry in my vision.

I said nothing and looked out through the window, determined not to make eye contact. He stood up and laughed to himself, finding pleasure in my weakness. A man entertained by forcible obedience in my eyes was no man at all.

"He's not coming," he said, throwing another log onto the fire. "It's just you and me now, the way it was always supposed to be."

I resisted the urge to scream or cry or both and pulled hard at the ropes around my ankles and hands again before I let myself go limp in the chair. "What do you want from me?" I asked.

This was what he'd wanted the night that Joel had intervened. A very distinct parallel was being drawn as he used my every weakness to his greatest advantage. His slick smile, his dominant and steady walk, a swagger that suggested victory. But Joel, Joel had been equally weakened by the drug that Alex had given me. A fact he might very well have been counting on.

He leaned on the mantel of the fireplace, lighting the candles that stood in a row. "What do I want..." he trailed off. Turning to face me he looked me up and down like a savage beast. "What do I want from you?" he repeating, strutting lazily over to me, leaning down to put his face level with mine. "Everything."

I tried to swallow the knot in my throat but I couldn't get it down. He was only inches from my face, forcing me to stare into his soulless black eyes. Closing my eyes to deflect him in the only way I knew how, a tear trailed down my cheek betraying my defenses.

Taking a thumb to my face, he swiped it away with his rough cold hand. "Shhh," he whispered insincerely. "I'm not going to hurt you." He got up and walked back to the fireplace. "Yet."

Chapter

19

The muffled sound of cars passing by, somewhere off in the distance, was the first sound to register in my ears. My chin was tilted back, heavily weighted by gravity. I breathed out in slow breaths, my lungs feeling deflated with every pass of air through them. I coughed but I felt no pain, I felt nothing but the suggestion of a cold chill against my face.

I pushed my eyelids open to find that my vision was blurred, everything seeming be move dizzily around me. I couldn't focus on anything. As my eyes finally began to adjust, I noticed the bright crimson of blood splattered across the white surface in front of me. Confused, I squinted and tried to remember what had happened and where I was.

I wasn't afraid and my body was still numbly in denial of pain. *Blood*, I thought. *Why was there blood?*

As consciousness came back to me in slow spurts so did the pain. The evening air was sharp and cold on my face now. My eyes struggled to stay open and I was quickly fighting pain from all sides. My body and muscles were tight and my head was throbbing.

As I blinked hard in an effort to encourage my eyes to stay open, I noticed the shattered windshield of Charlotte's Mustang. Through the cracked glass, I could see the front end wrapped around the side of a tree. With blood rushing to my head, causing me to feel a sense of vertigo, I realized as I looked at the grass covered sky that the car had flipped over.

I was in the Mustang...

It hurt to think almost as much as it hurt to breath. I'd been going to pick her up at work.

I moaned in agony as the seatbelt constricted my chest. My forearm was raw from the sting of the airbag that was now deflated and coated in my blood. I put my hand up to the cool spot of liquid that dripped from my forehead onto the interior of the roof. I had a large and painful gash above my eye. I drew my hand back and watched as fresh blood soaked my fingertips.

It was all coming back to me now.

Time had slowed and I couldn't distinguish up from down as the world blurred in front of me. After jumping the curb at a dangerous speed, the car had done summersaults the entire way to the base of the thick and sturdy tree. Then everything had gone black.

Fear. With a thick and sturdy force, I felt absolute terror wash over my body. Charlotte. Something was wrong. I needed to get to her.

Taking a quick inventory of my injuries, I flexed my toes and fingers. I rotated my neck and arched my back. It all hurt, but none of it was broken. I pushed the deflated airbag to the side and examined myself further. No shards of metal or slivers of glass were protruding from my legs. Either would make mobility a lot harder.

The cold of the harsh night air had settled deep into my muscles and began its way to my bones. I didn't know how long I'd been unconscious, but it had been long enough to suck any and all warmth from the vehicle and my body.

Groaning, I reached for my seatbelt while simultaneously bracing my hand against the roof. Breathing in once more, I clicked the button to release the latch and dropped the short distance to the ground, landing in a mess of blood and broken glass. Crushed against it now, I maneuvered myself, ignoring my aches as best as I could, and shifted my weight before leading my body out of the car.

As I crawled through the shattered driver's side window, I recalled the gut wrenching feeling of pressing the brake pedal and receiving no response. The car continued to pick up speed, heading into the turn and the wheel had locked, sending the car straight for the wooded side of the road, missing the edge of the drop off by only a few merciless feet.

Clenching my teeth against more relentless pain, I propped myself up to rest on my hands and knees. *Useless, useless body*, I thought.

Charlotte and our child were in danger and I was assumed to be taken out of the equation. I bit my lip with hatred so pure I nearly punctured the surface. I steadied myself and pushed off of the ground to stand, stumbling to the side as my body attempted to regain its center. I began to walk steadily toward the road, the darkness of nightfall shutting out the rest of the world. There were no street lights or houses for miles.

The ideal place to kill a man.

But it was Alex who had made the fatal misstep, not me. He hadn't finished the job. I wouldn't make the same mistake.

Chapter

20

When I reached the outskirts of town, I kept going. I pushed past the pain and avoided the stares I received from people as I passed them on the street. The cold night air was numbing but I hadn't the will to stop. Knowing I was within a mile of the bank, I picked up speed. Shifting from a brisk walk to a quick jog and finally to a frantic run, I closed the distance between myself and Charlotte's workplace.

It had taken me two hours to get to town, sprinting when I could cringe past the pain, and slowing back down to a brisk walk when it caught up with me again. But now I ran with vengeance. I ran so fast my feet hardly hit the pavement. I couldn't even be sure that I was taking in breaths at all. Adrenaline powered through me, refueling quickly whenever it seemed to be running out, supplied by my drive to get to Charlotte. I'd paced myself before but I ran myself into the ground as I approached the bank. The clock propped on the top of the strip mall sign read 10:21. A dangerous amount of time had passed since the car had crashed.

Rounding the corner, I slowed to a stop. Most of the stores on the strip were closed apart from the McDonald's and a local car rental place at the far end. The bank was lit by nothing more than security lights in the rear of the expansive lobby. The parking spots were vacant at the bank's end of the lot. Like the deserted back road, the location had been ideal for Alex's obvious plan for abduction.

I jogged up the sidewalk, taking the time to observe my surroundings. If I knew Charlotte, which I did, she wouldn't step off of the sidewalk into the poorly lit parking lot when she hadn't seen me waiting for her . And if too much time had lapsed, she would have called her parents or Heather to come pick her up. I doubted, however, that she'd received a ride home.

I continued on the path I was sure she had taken to the well lit end of the establishment. Jogging up the walk, I came to a sudden halt at the sight of her abandoned shoes. I lowered to the ground and took one in each hand, observing the coarse scratches on each heel. I closed my eyes in anger. Every one of my worst fears was unraveling before me.

She'd been taken.

I stuffed each shoe into either jacket pocket and paced in front of the building. I knew the danger. I knew the threat and who was behind it all. But where was he? Where had Alex taken her? I needed to be thorough and well calculated as he had been. He could have taken Charlotte anywhere.

I opened up my inner jacket pocket and dug deep to retrieve the small *Littman Jeweler's* box I'd tucked away for our dinner that night. Flipping it open, I watched as the dim light from the streetlights glistened over the two carat solitaire. The platinum band sparkled and reflected the shine from the diamond that sat perched in the middle.

I wanted to do right by Charlotte. We'd gone about most things backwards and far from how I'd have done them had I seen any of it coming. I was coming to find that was a side effect of being human. I couldn't plan for things as I'd done before. And with a pit in my stomach, closing the box and placing it back in my pocket, I wondered if maybe I couldn't protect her either.

I hadn't discussed it with Charlotte yet but my visit to the bank a few days earlier had confirmed that I had officially been granted my humanity. That we could begin our lives together once and for all. In the safety deposit I'd found everything I needed to exist in the world as a man; a valid passport, birth certificate, and social security card.

In addition, my bank account, one that had been created as a way to be closer to Charlotte, had grown to nearly thirty million dollars. Severance pay, I assumed. I had discovered the money when I'd gone to the ATM to withdraw cash for the engagement ring. Originally, I had a mere two thousand in the account that I hadn't intended on touching as Charlotte's guardian. It had been a front, another way to seem tangible and real to her while I performed my job. I had no other need for it past that.

As an angel, money had made no difference to me, even as a human it was worthless in my eyes, but I knew what kind of life it would allow me to give Charlotte and our baby.

I closed my eyes in remorse. This was all information I'd planned on sharing with Charlotte over dinner. She would never have to worry about another thing in her life. But as it seemed was customary, as everything began to fall into place, the ground opened up and hell was only one long fall from being my reality.

I made my way somberly to the other end of the lot and walked into the late night rental place. I stood at the front desk, waiting for the return of the clerk. I could hear him rustling around in the back and tapped the service bell to let him know that I was there.

A few moments later a man in his late thirties filled the empty space behind the help desk. "Sorry 'bout that," he said. "What can I do for ya?" He glanced up briefly at the clock, suggesting that the doors would be closing shortly.

"I'd like to rent a car," I replied, opening up my wallet. "It doesn't matter what kind, I'll take whichever one is parked the closest."

"You got it." Realizing that he and I were on the same timeline, the man began typing away at his keyboard. He glanced up and studied the gash above my left eye and the blood that had hardened where I hadn't managed to wipe it away. "You look like shit, if you don't mind me sayin' so," he pointed out, still pecking away at the keyboard. "You should drive this car right on over to the hospital," he added.

"I'm fine," I reassured him.

He didn't believe me but he didn't argue either. After scanning my license and running my card, he handed me a set of keys.

"Follow me," he instructing, being sure to flip the *open* sign to *closed* as he walked through the door. "Here ya go," he said, pointing to a black Toyota Camry. "It's all yours. Just be sure to fill it up with half a tank before you return it."

"Will do," I said, opening the door and slipping inside.

Sitting in the car, engine running, I sighed. "Where are you?" I said to no one in particular.

Alex could have taken her anywhere. The obvious places like Charlotte's house were out of the question. Given the past, a hotel room lacked class, even for a man who might actually enjoy the irony in it. Not to mention it was too obvious.

While he had made a mistake in leaving me for dead, Alex wasn't stupid. He wouldn't have taken her somewhere well populated. Nor would he take her to a place that he would have to check in and out of. He wanted to be cut off from the world. It was what he'd been preparing for in separating Charlotte from her friends and from me. But where would he take her?

I rested my head on the steering wheel, grabbing at what leads I might have, hoping that I could figure it out in time. I was racing the clock. It wasn't the time to fall short on being right. Racking my brain for memories that might lead me in the right direction, I sifted through what might be useful information. I had taken Charlotte to a hotel because it was close by, easy to get to, and safe. Alex was sure to do the opposite. He would take her to a place hard to access, far away, and forgotten about.

Lifting my head and looking through the windshield, paralyzed by my own worst fears, I realized with a start where he'd taken her. It was a risk...and a far drive to be wrong, but I was surer than I'd ever been of anything in my entire life.

The perfect place to escape from the world.

Chapter

21

"I have to use the bathroom," I protested.

Alex had spent nearly thirty minutes just staring at me with a satisfied smile on his face. He was clearly pleased with himself. I did my best to look away but there was only so much I could look at. Staring at the fire made my eyelids heavy and looking out the window served no purpose. It only made me think of how terrified and alone I really was. The cold snow outside made for an impossible getaway. I couldn't run without leading Alex right to me. Not to mention my lack of shoes. Maybe that had been an unintended bonus, or he'd planned everything perfectly. It made me wonder if his plan involving Joel's "disposal" had been equally well executed. A knot formed in my throat once again.

"Be my guest," he said with a smirk.

I had no time or patience to play his games. If Joel was gone...really gone, I had to choke back on the tears that wanted to escape. I had to do what was needed to protect our baby.

"I'm not going to try and escape," I said, running my tongue over my teeth in an effort to bite back the words I wanted so badly to say. "I just have to pee."

Alex watched me carefully then pushed himself up from his chair. He crossed the room in a few long strides and tilted his head venomously. Leaning in, he whispered poison into my ear. "If you try to run, I will make you sorry that you're not already dead."

I fought a chill that wanted to paralyze my entire body with fear. Without words, I nodded obediently.

Taking my face in his hands, he ravaged my lips in a kiss that exuded pure dominance. I forced my eyes shut and did my best to repel the kiss. I was teetering on the edge of consciousness. If my body couldn't escape, my mind would most certainly try. He let go of my face—I was sure he'd left a bruise—and went around to the back of the chair to loosen the ropes.

Before letting my hands free, he pressed his lips against my ear. "Next time I kiss you," he growled, "you're going to kiss me back."

My hands were shaking and I had to focus to slow my breathing. As I went to shut the bathroom door behind me, it stopped in its tracks. I turned around to see Alex's hand propping the door open.

"I don't think so," he said, leaning on the door frame.

"I can't have a little privacy?" I argued.

"See that window?" He gestured to the window above the bathtub. "Yeah, so do I. So go now or not at all."

Biting down on my lip to stifle the slew of curses that I wanted to say, I turned toward the toilet, grabbing a towel on my way over. Placing it over my work slacks as a shield and reaching over to turn the faucet on full blast, I pulled down my pants and sat down. I shot him a look that dared him to oppose any of my preparations. He laughed with good humor and didn't make any objections.

When Alex had me strapped back to the chair, he took a place at the window, taking in the scenery as if he had a lifetime to break me. "Excuse me if my patience has run out," he said, turning to look at me. The blue glow of the moon lit the side of his face. "I've been waiting a long time to have you," he continued.

"Two years isn't that long," I argued as a test.

He laughed incredulously. "So angel boy never figured it out huh?" He made his way over and my heart began to race again. "I guess he was too busy failing to protect you."

Every word that seeped out of Alex's mouth was hateful and had obviously been stored up for some time. It was impossible not to feel the sharpness in his words, like razorblades on my heart.

"What are you?" I asked, sure I would get the answers I'd been looking for.

He walked over to me at a slow and methodical pace. Centering himself between the light of the fire and the light of the moon. When he pulled his shirt up, I turned my face away and closed my eyes. My thoughts were immediately submerged in the darkest of possibilities.

"Look at me!" he barked.

I flinched at the abrasiveness in his voice and opened my eyes, tears burning at the corners of them. Raising my eyes slowly, I gasped at the sight of Alex's ribcage. Illuminated by an orange glow on one side and a blue radiance on the other, his body was wickedly twisted. He was sculpted much like Joel but where script tattoos trailed over Joel's ribs, Alex wore jagged scars. They pulled at his skin like acid had burned away his flesh, his oath to God had been painfully removed from his side.

He had been an angel. Our suspicions were right.

"Pretty isn't it?" he said, glaring at me, holding his t-shirt off to the side.

He turned around in mocked display to reveal even more devastating scars that raced down the length of his back, starting at his shoulder blades. It looked as if he'd been dragged over the burning embers of hell itself, removing his wings in the process. Turning again to face me, he made his way closer. His coal colored eyes seemed blank and lacking of all emotion.

"This was all for you," he said bitterly. "I became everything you could ever want in a man. Who doesn't love a funny and compassionate doctor right?" He placed his hands on either armrest, looking down at me, a position of dominance he seemed to favor. "I waited for years in this worthless body for you to come around. But no...you had placed me so easily in the friend zone. You'd condemned me to sit and watch you date one loser after another. Lucky for me they were all so easily swayed. Some even went through the trouble of making a show of it. Pretending that you'd been nothing but a mistress all along."

I fought hard against the rage that began to course through me. Alex had sabotaged my entire love life. I couldn't find the words to accuse him. All I could do was to listen as he unraveled every truth I'd so easily missed.

"But angel boy...he was a hard one. He had no home address, no phone number, nothing. There was no way of locating him to easily persuade him out of your life. I thought it was strange at first." He rose from the chair and paced in front of the fireplace, the light dancing across the surface of his scarred flesh.

"The only time I ever saw him was when he was with you. I considered the possibilities, don't think I didn't." He walked over to the window and looked outside. "But then he appeared out of nowhere to take that bullet for you and confirmed it. The bastard had taken you from me again!" He pounded his fist against the wall beside the window, making me flinch, his hateful words echoing in the small room.

"Again?" I asked, confused.

"Right," he said with false entertainment. "He probably didn't even know. Why would you?" I ached as he spoke of Joel in past tense.

"Know what?"

Alex turned around to face me. "*I* was supposed to be your guardian." He paused for a moment to let his words sink in. "Yeah, that's right," he continued. "I was all lined up for the job, and then the decision was made to send lover boy in my place. They'd told me that a *special* guardian was meant for you. That the conditions had changed. I didn't even get a chance to defend my shot. I'd been waiting around for over *a hundred years* for a job like that one. Then they passed me up for some new guy. At first I was just angry that I'd lost my chance to go down to earth."

Though Joel and I had suspected that Alex was a fallen angel, I couldn't help but feel surprised by it as I watched Alex, still in shock from all that he'd said. His scars were still exposed, a reminder of what he'd given up...*for me*.

"I looked in on your life whenever I could," he continued. "As you grew up, your beauty became harder for me to resist. I decided that this replacement could have my spot for all I cared. I would have you in a way that he couldn't...as my lover. So I fell. I would bid my time until you were old enough for me to insert myself into your life, until I could make you fall in love with me."

I forced breaths in and out of my lungs. "That night at the club," I said, looking away as he slipped his shirt back on. I closed my eyes and a tear escaped. "You knew that Joel was there, that he'd be affected by the drug too."

"*I* was supposed to save you," He said through clenched teeth. "*I* was supposed to be the hero. Then out of nowhere I see this guy scoop you up. I couldn't let you know I was there unless I was the one who'd rescued you. Otherwise you might figure out that I'd been the one to drug you in the first place. I didn't know who the guy was, if he meant you harm or not but I couldn't act suspicious..." he trailed off and shook his head in agitation.

Throughout my entire life, Alex had been trying his hardest to be exactly what Joel was without even knowing it. But for Joel, it all came so effortlessly. He did everything without a thought of himself. Alex understood loosely what I needed or might want, but he didn't want to give me those things for my own sake. He was a selfish creature making his best attempt to pull strings and make me into his little puppet.

"You're disgusting," I hissed. "What would have happened to us had I taken the bait, huh? Your walls of deceit would slowly but surely crumble. Then what? You'd make me into the woman you want me to be? A slave?"

"You know what?" Alex whipped around. "You're a spoiled little brat. You think you're so perfect, like no one's good enough for you. You didn't drink until you were twenty-two. Never picked up a cigarette or touched a drug. You don't party. You get good grades. It's sickening. Do you know how incredibly boring you are? You'd be *lucky* to have me. No one will ever be able to keep you on that pretty little pedestal you've been propped up on your whole life."

Tears burned at my eyes and I swallowed hard. His words, despite my better judgment, hurt like knives.

"He will," I said with a strength I thought I'd lost.

"Angel boy's dead, sweetheart. You better get good and used to that. Denial isn't a flattering trait on you." He walked heavily through the room and into the kitchen.

My body jerked and shook and tears flowed down my face. I tried to force air through my gasped breath and sobbed against the part of me that struggled to remain strong. Had Alex seen him die? Could he be telling the truth? As much as I wanted to believe otherwise, Joel hadn't come to the bank. It wasn't safe to hold onto the hope that he was alive. I had to focus on what was still in danger. I had to focus on the good things. I had to maintain a reason to survive this.

No matter what happened, I had been with the most amazing man on earth, the love of my life. And inside of me I carried a piece of him, a child I would raise to know of their father's bravery. As far as I knew, my parents were unharmed. It would have to be enough to get me through this.

My eyes dried quickly from the radiant heat of the fire and I took back control of my body, fighting against the desire to cry again.

"That's it, huh?" Alex walked back into the room with a beer bottle in his hand. His expression was amused and his smirk made my skin crawl. "Have you given up?"

"Never."

Chapter

22

Before I drove the four hours or so it would take to get to the cabin I suspected Alex had taken Charlotte to, I needed to drive by her parents' house to be sure that they were okay. I hoped that Alex hadn't gone through the trouble of cutting *all* ties from Charlotte, but with her friends strategically out of the picture and me assumed to be, I had to make sure.

When I pulled up to her parents' driveway, I got out of the rental and made my way quietly over to the scarcely lit house. I could feel the threat of snow in the air and I was sure that I would meet it head-on as I made my way north to find Charlotte. Another obstacle I wished not to have to face.

Staying close to the tree line, I crept up to the living room window where a blue glow from the television flashed against the yard. I was relieved to see Charlotte's mother and father sitting quietly in one another's arms as they watched a movie. Neither looked alarmed, both unaware of what was going on.

While I hadn't seen any reason for Alex to target Charlotte's family, I still found myself in need of confirmation. I had stupidly miscalculated Alex's urgency and his desperation to eliminate me from the picture.

It was becoming very clear that there wasn't anything that either of us could have done to stop him. As angry as I still was at myself, Alex had been planning this for too long to have ever given up without a fight. It was obvious now. All I could do was race to the ends of the earth to stop him from following through with his plans.

As I drove, the weather got progressively worse. Snow was accumulating as I headed north and the temperature was falling rapidly. I drove fast and I didn't stop, making only minor alterations when faced with poor road conditions. The gash on my forehead had stopped bleeding but the pain had vastly increased, but it wasn't enough to stop me.

* * *

Alex leaned against the window that still emitted a blue saturation from the snow outside. The moon's glow was brilliant and by any other standards it was a beautiful night, complete with thick and lazily falling snowflakes. But his silence was deafening, his stare paralyzing. He had nearly rendered my restraints unnecessary. Not forgetting the fact that Joel was gone...really gone. A fact that the wide knot in my throat refused to let me forget for even a second.

"If it had been me that had saved you that night," he began, pushing himself away from the window, "how do you think this might have played out differently?"

Every time Alex spoke my stomach knotted. From the moment I'd woken up in this forsaken cabin, I had remained jumpy whenever he addressed me. It was a hard reaction to fight taking everything into consideration.

All I could think was that maybe…if I'd just ended up with Alex, even if I was miserable for it, at least Joel would still be alive. While I might never have known him, of his part in my life, his love, I would never have had to lose him either. I shook my head and swallowed hard to clear my throat to speak.

"Alex." I shook my head. "If it had been you that had saved me then, yes, maybe it would have made me look at you differently. But the truth remains that you *drugged* me to manipulate me into seeing you that way."

Alex edged closer, so close that I could feel his breath on my cheek, something he seemed to enjoy doing, and caught my eyes with his own. The strong angles of his face were cast in the orange glow of the fire again; drastic shadows concealed the rest, giving him the appearance of being two-faced.

"Don't worry, sweetheart." He took my face firmly in his hands. "I've been doing penance for twenty-three years in preparation for what I was prepared to do to claim you as my own."

The way he talked about me was unsettling. Like gaining a piece of property. He seemed to have no emotional connection to me at all. The coldness that he portrayed seem to go much deeper than skin.

Boldly, I jerked my face from his hand. "I don't see the point," I said, ignoring the flashing red sign that said, *Don't go there!* He retracted to absorb my next words. "You can't feel anything anyway. What's the point of having something if you're not meant to have it? If it can't bring you pleasure. You *will never* feel the warmth of a woman."

The corner of my mind that clung to self-preservation shuttered with disbelief of my flippant tongue. The silence that followed my words was thick and choked my ability to breath.

Instant regret.

Alex's eyes formed sharp slits like razor blades, dicing through the thickness that I had only so recently begun to fear but immediately wished back. But it was too late, he was zeroed in and I could tell by the look in his eyes that he was determined to get his point across for the final time.

I sat in the chair unmoving, all courage flushed from my body. I resisted the urge to shiver and wanted nothing more than to get it over with. Alex had a rage in him that shone brightly through his nearly colorless eyes. But his lack of immediate action was becoming more frightening than anything he'd done or said in the past.

Ripping his eyes from mine, he left the room without a single word. Not even the floor boards dared to creak as he left me to sit in a mixture of relief and a terror that threatened to unarm me.

My eyes fluttered closed and I let out a shaky breath. Why was I so stubborn and pigheaded? How had I been able to forget what mattered most in a fit of human emotion gone dangerously out of control? As it would seem, without Joel, not only had my intuition gone out the window, but so had my will to live.

Chapter

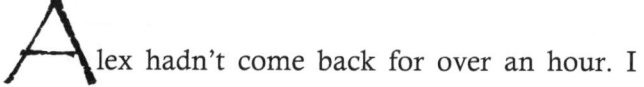

23

Alex hadn't come back for over an hour. I didn't know where he was in the house or even if he was in the house at all. It was a risk but I needed to at least try and escape. Looking around one last time as far as I could, I determined that the coast was clear. As quietly as I could manage, I pulled up on my arms and worked at trying to free my hands from behind my back. The ropes that tied them were strong and tight. I could tell that I was losing the struggle and only damaging the skin on my wrists with the efforts. I moved on to try and free my feet. I pushed, pulled, and jerked my legs with little to no success.

Frustration and fear escalated and I began to see for the first time how very much at his mercy I really was. Being tied up; spitting in his face every chance I had wasn't going to save me and my baby...Joel's and my baby. It was only going to put us both in greater danger. Something else I'd stubbornly ignored up until that point. Taking a deep breath, I knew that my first goal had to be getting out of this perfect isolation. Whatever it took...I needed to start the process of singlehandedly freeing myself and ridding myself of Alex for once and for all.

"I'm surprised to see your chair still upright," I heard him say with amusement from behind me. "With the attitude you've been giving off, I was sure you'd try and escape in my absence."

I ran my tongue over my teeth and took in a silent deep breath. *Survival*, I reminded myself. This was all for my survival, something that Joel would...and had given his life for.

As he approached from behind me, I sent a very controlled shutter through my body. I backed away ever so slightly and hoped that he'd noticed both. It would be a tedious job but I needed to pull him in and convince him that he'd finally won.

As Alex walked up beside me, I lowered my head and turned away. "You're afraid of me," he said victoriously. "It seems like you've finally smartened up."

He took my face in his hand and guided me to meet his gaze, though I made sure to keep my eyes to the floor. With his thumb, he traced my jaw line and my bottom lip.

"Say something, my delicate little flower."

I pulled my eyes up slowly and rested them just below his eyes to confirm my fear. "Why were you never like this before?" I asked just above a whisper.

"Like what?" he asked, almost puzzled.

"Fierce...strong," I brought my eyes up to meet his and whispered the last word with deliberation. "Sexy."

I had clearly thrown him off with those three very powerful words. He backed up only a single inch, but it was inch enough to mark the beginning of my success. "Sexy?" He sounded confused and satisfied all at once. "What are you talking about?"

I pulled my eyes down and sucked my lip in. "Before...for the past two years, you never made a move. I thought…I thought you weren't interested in me. You were my supervisor and I was afraid to lose my job so I never made my true feelings known…" I stopped myself and suggested with my retraction that I'd said too much.

"What?" Alex was thrown off by this admission. "You're messing with me," he accused.

"Messing with you?" I looked up and furrowed my brow. "Seriously, Alex? Do you know how long I ignored my feelings…how hard it was for me…" I trailed off.

He leaned in and placed his hand dangerously on my leg. "What? No, don't stop. I'm sorry. What were you going to say?"

Begging. Right where I wanted him.

"You wouldn't understand."

"Try me."

I looked up and rubbed my lips together in preparation to deliver the best and most artfully crafted lie I would probably ever tell in my life.

"When I met you…I knew that you were different than any other man I'd ever met. Something was hidden behind that good-guy exterior you donned so well. But after two years, I started to lose hope that that was true. You were nice, polite, hell you even gave me advice about my love life on a few occasions. And I'll admit…it was that same mystery that I saw in Joel that attracted me to him. When I found out that he was an angel it made him that much more appealing to me. I didn't want Joel…I wanted you. But you just let me go, I figured, hey, maybe this is best. But now," I paused for effect. "Now you're the mysterious and sexy one again, and you've shown me that you will do whatever it takes to have me. What took you so long?"

Silenced by surprise, Alex rose to stand in front of me. He crossed his arms and studied me. I looked down and blanketed my face with an expression that exuded shock and embarrassment.

"I am such an idiot," I mumbled to myself. "Why did I say that," I added in a whisper.

"No, no," Alex said, lowering himself to look into my eyes again. "I'm just surprised, that's all. I never knew you felt that way."

"I shouldn't have said anything," I chastised myself.

"No, no, tell me what you're thinking," he said reassuringly.

"Why did it have to come to this?" I raised my eyes and did my best to give him a soul-deep stare. "Why couldn't I have just told you how I felt? I've been so hurt and jealous these past few weeks. Especially with you dating Tara...but I couldn't." I paused again for theatrics. "I couldn't hurt her. I couldn't just take you away from her. So when you kissed me...I panicked. It's all so confusing."

Alex got up and paced the room. He seemed to have planned for every defense but this one. His stance changed and I could tell that he had to work hard at keeping on his stern front. It was a good sign.

"Forgive me," I whispered pleadingly.

Tilting his head with satisfied confusion, Alex walked slowly toward me, similar to that of a wolf, making sure that his pray had truly surrendered. I resisted the urge to faint, scream, or throw up. Either sign would surely give me away. Instead, I kept my eyes on him and let my lips rise to one side in a contented smirk.

The closer he got to me, the faster my heart beat and the fuller of regret I found myself. He took my face gently in his hand again, bringing my eyes up to his. He looked on with curiosity and I was sure that he'd managed to see right through my poorly executed plan.

But as I watched him studying me, I knew that his desperation had left a very large and vital part of him vulnerable, his ego. I was showing him the affection that he'd wanted for so long. A need too great flashed across his eyes, leaving him oblivious to the most discernible of warning signs; my bad acting skills.

Alex knelt down so that our faces were parallel and I was sure that my heart would stop. His eyes softened and he looked at me through his lashes. "Say it," he said with a sexy lilt. "Say that I have you."

My lungs grew tight and every muscle in my body stiffened. When he wanted to be, Alex was the sexy and charming man I'd once known him to be. His words, though carrying a very dominant meaning, remained inviting and seemingly optional. Though it was an choice he made nearly impossible to decline. But the Alex that had once tricked me for so long now held no power over my naiveté. I could see right through his charm and to the black core that lay beneath his surface.

"You have me," I answered with a subtle pout of my lips. He was good, but I needed to be better. Deception seemed to be the only likely way out of this horrible nightmare.

I could see the escalating retraction in his approach and knew that my plan was slowly but surely working. Whether he realized it or not, I was disarming him.

"I'm not going to run, you know." I cursed the words that would follow. "I know that I'm meant to be with you, that Joel...he was just in the way." The promise of angry tears threatened to expose my true feelings.

A sleek smile crept onto Alex's lips and I knew that he was falling more and more mercilessly into my trap. I choked down my disgust and pushed on, knowing that I had no other choice.

"I want to apologize..." I cooed. "A *real* apology."

Alex reached over and took hold of the ropes around my wrists. As he worked them apart, he put his lips to my ear and whispered lightly. "You do know that this will not end well for you if you *do* run...right?"

His warning was an afterthought, it was clear that he'd already managed to lose focus with my promises of compliance. And though I knew his threat was real, more so now that he was getting what he'd always wanted, his words remained sultry and sweet. He had this way; I must give him credit, of using his voice like a beautifully spun web to capture his prey. He had even managed to make a threat sound romantic, a skill I was sure he'd practiced to perfection over the years.

I nodded my head gently, being sure to graze his cheek with mine as he pulled his face away.

When my hands were free I left them to rest at my sides. Sudden movement was probably best to avoid. Alex took a hand and brushed it through my hair, taking his sweet time as he unwrapped me, like a gift on Christmas morning. Little did he know that nothing more than the ropes would be coming off. He brought his hand down, grazing my leg as he lowered himself to untie the bindings around my feet.

Sickness stung the back of my throat and I could sense my ability to keep pretending being tested as the minutes lapsed. When my feet were free, I had to focus most of my attention on not trying to make a fast and very clumsy attempt at escape. Alex stood up and crossed his arms, waiting for me to get up.

I put my hands in my lap and rubbed the tender spots around my wrists in an effort to bring life back to the skin that had been strangled by the tight ropes that had bound them. Looking up through my lashes, I waited for a reaction or any indication as to what he was thinking. I needed to manage a bit of mind reading from this point on if I hoped to keep him under my thumb. There was a lust in his eyes that seemed uncontrolled enough to use to my advantage.

"You play hard to get," he said, walking over to the fireplace. "Don't tell me that you're still afraid of me."

Though it was probably wise to be...I wasn't. I had been once, but now I knew that fear would be a worse enemy to me now than Alex was in this very fragile situation. "No," I replied, lifting slowly from the chair. "Well..." I said smoothly. "Maybe a little. But not enough to stay away."

Thinking about Claire and her previous boyfriend, I tried to pull together what I knew about men like Alex. Men that wanted control. He wanted me to fear him but he wanted me to find him sexy too.

I stepped out of the ropes that lay like limp nooses around my feet and walked toward him. I closed my eyes briefly and asked that God and Joel forgive me for giving Alex even an ounce of satisfaction in order to claim my freedom. When I lifted my eyes, I looked over at Alex who was now leaning on the mantel, the heat of the fire cast as a backdrop behind him.

Cringing, I came up behind him and slid my arms around his waist. I pressed myself up against him and said as convincingly as I could, "How could I be afraid of you? You've done all of this just to show me how much you care about me."

Alex placed his hand over my arms that were wrapped around his torso. Though we were only a few feet from the blazing fire, his hand was still ice cold. I held back the urge to shiver and bit my lip before I could say something that might blow my cover. He turned in my arms and moved me gently so that the fire's light fell over both of our faces. He drew up his hands and rested them on my hips and looked deep into my eyes. I wanted desperately to look away and break the trance that he was creating but I knew it would only put me in danger.

"Tell me what you want," he said.

I was learning that Alex didn't do romantic or chivalrous. He knew only one thing: greed. I could tell that in order to keep him pleased, to keep him believing in my act, I would have to give him what *he* wanted.

Not that I intended to give him much. Just enough to keep him weakened and at my disposal. I cringed inside and took in a slow breath.

Inside, I was screaming but as I raised myself up to meet his lips, I knew that I was going in the right direction to embrace freedom. Closing his eyes, Alex lowered his lips to mine and met them in a rough and power-hungry kiss. I knew that he couldn't feel it, not in the way that he wanted to and it was obvious by the way that he tried with desperation to get more from it. Sensations aside, Alex was delighted at my advance. He smiled into my lips and kissed me again. For me, the kiss was lifeless as long as it came from anyone other than Joel. And at that thought, tears threatened once again to fall from my eyes.

Alex pulled away and looked down at me with gratification. He bent down again and kissed my neck tenderly. As he trailed kisses down my neck, he brought his hands to the back of my shirt and began to draw it up. I knew that unless I started to direct him elsewhere this plan was going to end very badly. I needed to buy time.

"Mmmm," I moaned, "first, do you think we can eat something? I'm *starving*."

Truth be told, I really was. It had been hours since Alex had kidnapped me and nearly twenty-four hours since I'd eaten. Reluctantly, Alex let his hands drop and held me out in front of him.

"You sure do know how to make a man suffer, don't you, Charlotte."

Before waiting for a reply, he walked through the small living room into an even smaller kitchen. I figured it was probably best to follow him to reinforce the idea that he could trust me even though every muscle in my body wanted to take advantage of his turned back and run.

As I walked through the small cabin, I noticed that it was in a lot better shape than I might have expected.

Though I didn't know exactly where we were or how long Alex had lived there, I could tell that it had taken some work to clean it up as much as he had. Dust was still very thick on most of the surfaces and as we got further away from the fire, I could tell that it was the only heat source in the house.

"Is this where you live?" I asked wistfully.

"No," Alex chuckled. "I found this place for us. I figured it was an isolated and safe place for us to...get to know one another."

I entered the small kitchen where he was prepping a small portable grill to light. I sat down at the small table that looked out over the snow-covered landscape. I couldn't make out a single thing about it. Where the hell were we?

"Where are we?" I asked, hoping that he was caught up enough by his progress to overlook the fact that he would be delving out valuable information in answering my question.

"I would tell you," he replied. Great. "But, then this whole date would lose its romantic and mysterious appeal."

Without blatantly saying that he still didn't trust me, Alex hadn't given me any room to budge. As much of his well-thought out plan as I had already infiltrated, there were still miles and miles left to go before I could break free from him. In truth, the possibility remained that I may never manage it.

"Oh, is that so," I replied. I knew it wasn't safe to push him for answers, it would only give me away faster.

"I hope you're in the mood for eggs and bacon. It's the easiest thing to make on one of these things."

"It's perfect."

Alex set a griddle on top of the lit grill and made his way to a cooler that I hadn't noticed before. From it, he retrieved four eggs and a package of bacon. He pulled a spatula from one of the drawers in the kitchen and cracked the eggs onto the griddle. It was difficult at times like this to grasp that the Alex I'd thought I had known had been nothing but a show.

"So, were you faking it the whole time?" I asked boldly.

He turned around to face me as the eggs and bacon sizzled behind him. "Faking it?"

"When you worked at the bank. How much of that was real?"

"All of it, Charlotte."He turned back to the griddle and flipped the bacon. "I may have been a bit crazy lately, but please don't mistake that for my mask coming off.

"I'm not sure how much you know about me and my kind, but because I fell for you, it's like I have this thirst that I just can't quench. I'd paid Matt to drug you out of desperation…and I'm sorry for it. I'm sorry for so many reasons. Then, when angel boy showed up, I figured, great, another guy who's fallen victim to your beauty. Of course, in the beginning, I'd worried that he meant you harm. Without a way of tracking him, it was a conclusion that kept haunting me.

"After a while you seemed so happy and I knew that he wasn't a danger…not to you anyway. But once I found out what he was…it was like a switch was flipped and I couldn't control myself anymore."

Alex put an even portion of eggs and bacon onto two plates and brought them over to the table. He grabbed two glasses and some orange juice from the cooler and brought them over too.

"Lust, Charlotte, is a force to be reckoned with. When I started out as an angel, I was warned of its dangerous powers and the life it would doom me to. I had believed that I was immune to lust. That I would never know how it felt to experience it. But when I was passed over and the job as your guardian was *stolen* from me, something sparked inside of me. As I watched you grow into your beauty, I realized that you could only be mine if I gave into lust completely. So I did."

Did I believe that the Alex I'd once called a friend was the *real* Alex? It was a hard thing to convince myself of, especially after all he'd done. The fact was, no matter whom Alex claimed to be and no matter who he really was, he'd killed Joel. And for that, I had to escape as quickly as possible. And though I didn't know what would happen afterwards, I wasn't fearful in not knowing. An unstable and unpredictable future was something I'd become all too familiar with.

We ate the rest of our food in companionable silence. Alex watched me from time to time and seemed pleased. I was happy to know that whatever it was I was doing was actually managing to keep up my façade.

"What time is it?" I asked.

Alex referred to his watch and smiled. "It's early morning. The sun should be coming up soon. I guess bacon and eggs was an appropriate meal to serve."

I smiled in reply, faking amusement.

Morning? Time seemed to be slipping away. I'd gotten off of work at seven. After that I couldn't be sure how many hours had past but as time separated me from when I'd last seen Joel alive…from when I'd last felt safe, I grew more numb and lifeless inside.

As if to confirm the time, I could see a light orange and pink haze wash over the landscape outside. It was still nearly pitch-dark and impossible to see, but the sun was surely making its way up in the sky. And with the spread of light from over the horizon, I felt an equally spreading doubt that I would ever escape Alex for good.

Chapter

24

I'd driven through the night in a blizzard that must have picked up its tailwinds in hell itself. The car pulled to either side of the road and a ride that would have taken me four hours on a good day, managed to take me several hours more. I was angered as the minutes passed and Charlotte's life remained in peril. I'd even begun to question my bold decision to assume that Alex had taken her to the small abandoned cabin we had seen weeks before while snowboarding. He and I had been the only two to see it. It was my best guess to assume that he'd take her there with no one else to suspect the location.

Alex hadn't been around for a week or more. I hadn't even picked up any inkling that he'd been stalking Charlotte in recent days. He must have been readying the cabin for her capture. That, or I'd let my eagerness and desperation put her in even greater danger. Either way, it was too late to turn back now.

I pulled into the empty ski lodge parking lot as the sky welcomed the orange and pink hues of morning. The sun was beginning its ascent into the sky, By the time I could make my way up to the cabin, it would surely be light out.

The snow had stopped falling but a thick fresh layer of it covered the surface of the ground. Alex must have made several trips back and forth to the cabin prior to capturing Charlotte and his path to bring her up to it must still be somewhat traceable. All I needed to do was find the path he had taken to get there.

I pulled my jacket snug and brought my hood up over my head. The air had easily dipped below freezing over night and my trek through the wintery terrain would only add to its bitterness. I headed in the direction that I remembered the small shack being. Lit only by the bright reflective snow and the subtle suggestion of sunrise, I started up the mountain, hoping that I wasn't already too late.

As I trudged through the snow that was over a foot deep, I came up alongside a small barn. The carriage that sat nestled up to one of the walls looked familiar. It was covered in snow and would require a great deal of time and work to uncover. Still, I drew more curious and felt a ray of hope surrounding me as I made my way over to it. My feet were nearly frozen already as I reached the large sleigh. I brushed off a layer of snow with my bare hand, regretting it almost instantly. I rubbed my hands together briskly and dug them deep into my pockets.

It was the same sleigh we'd ridden the day we had gone snowboarding. Sadly, it wasn't even close to something I could use. With no way of utilizing the sleigh to get to Charlotte any faster, there was no point in hanging around any longer. It would only delay in her rescue and increased the effects of what the cold had already begun to have on me.

I moved around the side of the sleigh, making my way back up the mountain and heard the muffled sound of heavy breathing. I was startled at first, not having expected the sound. As I made my way closer to the entrance of the barn, I heard a gentle stomp and a light whinny from inside.

"Horses," I thought aloud. They must have been the same ones from our sleigh ride.

With the rough winter conditions already taking their toll, I knew how difficult my journey would be on foot. There was no time to weigh my options or the moral standards that I might be compromising in *borrowing* a horse. I closed the space between myself and the door and unlatched it. I opened it just enough to slip inside and found myself looking upon the same two beautiful black English shires that had pulled our sleigh weeks before. Their coats gleamed and heat rose from their backs in small clouds.

The one closest to me nickered and raised his nose to my hand. I petted him softly, running my fingers over the white patch on the bridge of his nose and brought my other hand up to his broad neck.

"Do you mind helping me out for a little while?" I whispered.

The horse nuzzled my hand and didn't seem to oppose the idea. With no more approval required, I turned around and spotted a wall of equipment hung on thick iron hooks. Most of it seemed to be for attaching the horses to the sleigh but I narrowed in quickly on a horse blanket and a leather saddle for riding.

With as much precision and timeliness as I could manage, I set the saddle on top of the gigantic horse's back and fastened it into place. With no more time to waste, I unhooked him from his stall and lead him out into the cold morning air. With a shake of his head, he welcomed the much cooler temperatures and allowed me to hoist myself up onto his back without protest.

"Good boy," I said, running my fingers through his coarse mane.

I slipped my feet into the stirrups and softly tapped them to his side. With a start, he moved forward and I urged him to pick up speed. I didn't want to run him into the ground but there was no more time to spare.

I needed to get to Charlotte, and fast.

* * *

Alex cleared the dishes from the table and placed them in the sink with what seemed to be no intention of washing them. I was sure that when this was all over he would pack me up and leave the cabin just as we'd left it. Dirty dishes and all.

"Join me in the living room?" he cooed.

My stomach turned and I couldn't be sure if it was due the pregnancy or disgust. Maybe a combination of both. Instead of answering him with a giggle or words that would likely get stuck in my throat, I smiled coyly and followed him into the living room.

As we walked toward the couch, I started to fantasize that maybe I hadn't lost Joel forever. He'd been an angel once and there had to be some type of cycling process. Didn't there? He had proven himself worthy of the role as a guardian once before. Maybe he'd been granted the job again once he'd...I couldn't even form the words in my mind. Maybe he was my guardian angel again and he was with me now. The idea that, at the very least, he was watching over me was something I could hold onto.

"So what now?" I asked boldly.

"What do you mean, what now?" Alex's voice was smooth and sweet, suggesting that there was no need to rush. He sat down on the sofa and watched me with amusement.

"I just wasn't sure if you had plans for once I admitted my feelings for you." More like, admitted insanity.

"I forgot the champagne in the car," he joked. "Forgive me."

I shifted on the couch to face him and smiled. "You didn't think I'd give in, did you?" In part, I was actually entertained by this possibility. Alex had been pretty cocky since Joel had been shot. He had seemed so sure of himself and his abilities to win me over.

He looked away and chuckled but the sound lacked humor. "No, I didn't," he admitted. Shrugging, he brought his eyes back to me. "You seemed hopelessly devoted to angel boy." *He has a name. Had a name...*"I just figured you'd have taken all of this a lot harder. It felt like you would rather die than be with me." He actually seemed wounded by the idea. I might have felt bad had he not killed the love of my life. *Might have.* But he was right, if it wasn't just my life I was fighting for, I would rather die before giving Alex what he wanted.

"You don't give yourself enough credit." It was more likely that he gave himself too much. "I mean, it's your determination, your passionate pursuit, that made me realize how much I need you."

"Need me?" He was clearly honored by my word choice.

"Of course." I slid over on the couch and sat closer to him, leaning in slightly to increase the intimacy between us. "I need to feel wanted, not protected. You were right when you said that I was on a pedestal, and while I'm not proud of it, I need to be admired. I need you to find me attractive." I had to stop myself from gagging. "Joel, all he cared about was protecting me. He made me feel like some kind of job. I don't want to feel like a job, I want to feel like a goddess."

Alex leaned back in triumph. "Is that so?"

My stomach turned and I closed my eyes for a moment to try and set the room back on its axis. When I opened my eyes, I nodded and tried to mask the queasiness that bubbled up in my throat. Oh please no. Not now.

I shifted on the couch and leaned forward, hoping that the warmth of the fire would settle my escalating nausea.

"Are you okay?" Alex sat up and placed a hand absently on my back. "Are you feeling alright?"

"I'm just a little...queasy, that's all." I tried to brush off my increasing desire to vomit.

"There was nothing in the food I gave you. I promise. I trust you now, Charlotte."

How comforting. my fallen-angel-homicidal-self-declared-boyfriend, was ensuring me that he hadn't drugged me. *Again.* And he was the one who had abandoned *his* trust issues? Unbelievable.

Alex rubbed my back in small circles and surprisingly made the feeling worse. Not that I'd admit it. There seemed to be no way of soothing or deterring my body's decision to get sick.

"Can I get you anything? Water maybe? You don't look well."

I closed my eyes and rolled them in undetectable circles. Ridiculous. I was finally making some progress and now my own body was going to betray me. "Yes, please," I croaked.

Alex shot up and jogged over to the kitchen. He popped open the cooler and yanked out two bottles of water before heading back.

"Here," he said, opening a bottle and putting it to my lips.

I took a few small sips but could feel it already beginning to work its way back up. "I'm going to be sick," I warned.

With no working plumbing to speak of, Alex helped me up to head out through the side door. He stood by the door and gave me some space as I threw up over the side of the mountain. When I was done saying goodbye to the only real nutrients I'd seen in nearly twenty-four hours, I put some fresh snow in my mouth and sloshed it around before spitting it out.

"Okay," I sighed with a shiver. "I think the show's over."

Alex ushered me inside and shut the door behind us. When we got back into the living room, I was shivering uncontrollably from the short time I'd spent in the cold without a coat or shoes. He walked over and stood by the fire watching the flames dance.

"Thank you," I said through chattering teeth.

I stood beside him and raised my hands to warm them by the fire. He said nothing and I figured it was probably best to wait for him to speak. Without warning he grabbed my hand and pulled me into him.

"Why are you sick?" he demanded.

"I-I don't know," I stuttered. "I must have caught something."

"You weren't sick before," he argued.

"That doesn't mean anything," I tried not to sound scared or angry. "I think it's reasonable to assume that my body's just been through a lot."

Alex looked down at me as if to consider what I'd said. "Yeah, you're probably right." He rubbed his neck anxiously and I could tell that he was still leery. "You did eat that breakfast pretty fast," he reasoned.

"It was good and I was starving," I laughed, hoping that my voice had come off as well-humored and not terrified.

I breathed in and out, trying to tame what nausea still remained and the fear that wanted to push tears from my eyes. I was so close. Close enough to touch freedom. I could feel it.

Alex turned on a pivot and took my shoulders in his hands in a flash of movement. "How can I trust you?" he asked, his voice low and threatening.

I sucked in air and tried to maintain my previous ability to keep deceiving him. "Are you doubting my feelings for you?" I tried to sound hurt by the accusation.

He shook his head and loosened his grip slightly. "No," his reply wasn't convincing. He was confused, forced to choose between what he wanted to hear and what made more sense for me to feel. "It's just, it seems too simple. I didn't think it would be this easy."

Easy? Was I a prize that he was trying to win? "Why not?" I said, biting my tongue.

He let go of my arms and turned back to the fire. Be it morning sickness or relief, my stomach turned again. I tried to focus my attention on the mantle and the flickering candles that sat on top of them, leaving pools of wax at their base. Before my eyes, the flames began to blur and move in unnatural swirls. I put my hand to my head and blinked hard. Lightheaded now, I felt my body sway and I stumbled to the side.

Alex caught my arm and propped me back up, studying at me again. I put my hand to my chest and felt my body want to purge for a second time but I resisted, mostly because I had nothing left in my stomach to get rid of.

When I righted myself, Alex was still staring at me. His eyes became daggers and I let out a few long wavering breathes as he watched me try and collect myself. He radiated with doubt and distrust.

My nerves betrayed me, sending a shiver over my skin. He yanked me closer. "What was that?"

"What was what?" I breathed.

"You shivered."

"You're scaring me."

Alex tilted his head and his eyes formed dangerous slits. He pushed me away and as I stumbled back I heard the familiar *bing* of my cell phone, indicating that I had a text message. My eyes shot over to my purse. I swallowed hard as his eyes followed mine.

"Who could that be?" he asked dangerously.

As he walked over to my purse, I couldn't breathe. I hoped that it was Joel, or my mom, anyone but

Heather. If she'd texted me about Alex then it was all over.

He propped open my purse and jerked his head in my direction fiercely. Not good. Something was terribly wrong. He reached into my bag and unearthed the *Motherhood* magazine I'd been reading at work. I stood motionless as he held it in his hands, eyes fixed on me.

He stood up slowly, gripping the magazine in his hand. Walking over lazily, he pitched it into the fire. From the corner of my eyes, I watched as the pages caught and the blaze began to consume the magazine, blue flames licking at the edges.

"You're pregnant," he offered boldly. "Angel boy got you pregnant...didn't he?"

Chapter

25

"Alex," I pleaded. "Please, Alex, don't."

"Don't what?" he said menacingly to my thoughts. *"Don't kill you?"*

I couldn't breathe. I could hardly even will myself to move. With great effort, I inched away from him, unsure of what good it would do.

With a grin so terrifying and reckless, Alex crept closer as I moved away. He didn't lunge at me as I'd assumed he would, he simply continued to stalk my every move. Matching me inch for inch.

"Alex, it's not what you think. That magazine's not mine." It was a feeble attempt at covering up the truth but I had to at least try.

"Then why is your hand on your stomach?" His voice was alarmingly calm; as if he'd just pointed out that I still had my coat on after coming in from outside.

I looked down. Damn. I hadn't even meant to but somehow my body was hell-bent on betraying my cover, with or without my consent. I dug both of my hands deep into my pockets to restrain them from doing it again.

"I feel sick, that's all. You saw me. Why wouldn't I put my hand to my stomach?" I said with challenge.

Still, he moved closer. "You're sick," he said with another tilt of his head. "And lightheaded. I'm not familiar with any virus or disease that has those two symptoms. None except for bearing a child that is. And I don't buy for a second that the magazine isn't yours."

I concealed my fear as best as I could. "I don't know what you're talking about."

"You were never a very good liar, Charlotte." He was getting closer and my options were running out. I needed to distract him. I needed to bring his focus away from the baby.

"I love you, Joel," I blathered out, hoping to redeem myself with an admission of love.

"*What did you call me?*" His words were like shards of glass in my mind.

Oh crap.

"I-I mean…" I stammered. But I couldn't make myself say it. I couldn't combine the words "love" and "Alex" into the same sentence.

With a speed that shattered reason, Alex closed the space between us and held me up by my neck, my toes barely touching the floor. I gasped and I gagged, clawing at his hands in an effort to escape him.

"*What now my little goddess?*"

The room and everything in it began to blur. I could feel the air from my lungs being choked out as my last breaths tried to break through Alex's strong grip on my windpipe. With words and struggle no longer at my disposal, I could feel myself accepting that this was it. I'd failed at trying to save our baby.

Lead by the thunderous slam of the front door, I felt the unforgiving winter air burst into the small cabin. Alex's focus was immediately distracted and he dropped me without even a thought.

"You have *got* to be kidding me," I heard him say as I gasped and choked on the floor, bent over in front of the fire.

I squinted hard and coughed around my seemingly collapsed airway. When I caught my breath enough to look up, I saw Alex standing perfectly still. He was staring at the open door like it had transformed into something more than a simple board with a weak latch and rusty hinges. I looked over with curiosity and my body instantly began to shake.

Joel stood in the doorway with the light of the rising sun casting a long shadow out in front of him. Had I been right? Had he become my guardian again? Soft sobs erupted from inside of me. It was bittersweet to see him standing in the doorway, the mirage of a man I'd lost faith in ever seeing again.

For the longest moment I'd ever witnessed, they both just stood in silence and watched one another.

"You're like a freakin' cockroach," Alex hissed. "Just die already."

Joel strode closer into the center of the cabin. "What can I say, you're not good at much of anything."

He hadn't died? Joel *wasn't* an angel again? I found myself confused and equally relieved. It wasn't until then that I noticed the large gash above his eye, blood hardened onto his face. Whatever Alex had done to try and kill Joel had clearly made its mark.

In spite of the open door, I could feel the escalating temperature in the air. Alex moved around the room to circle Joel. This had clearly become something much bigger than lust. It wasn't about me anymore. It was about revenge.

"You think you've won, don't you," Alex said through clenched teeth.

By now Alex and Joel had swapped places. Alex stood in front of the open door and I found myself comforted by the fact that Joel now stood between him and I.

"I think we can learn to be civil with one another." I could hear the resentment in Joel's voice.

I tried to convince myself that this was real, that I hadn't imagined all of it. Reckless tears still streamed down my face. Seeing Joel, feeling him around me again, it had accessed very real and very pure emotions that were considerably difficult to rein-in. I wasn't even fully able to concentrate on the fact that something bad was undoubtedly going to happen, and soon. My mind latched onto only one thing. Joel was alive.

"Civil?" Alex said mockingly. "So in other words, you two lovebirds carry on with your lives and I crawl into a hole in the ground and pretend like you haven't taken everything from me?"

Joel didn't answer. I could tell that he was still trying to figure out who and what Alex was, though I was sure that he'd more-or-less figured it out. But I could see it in his eyes, no matter what Alex had planned next, he would do whatever it took to keep us safe.

"Oh, that's right," Alex chuckled. "You never figured it out, did you?" He lifted up his shirt to expose the burn that spanned the length of his side and a devious smile crept onto his lips. "You took my job, *brother*."

Joel didn't speak, his eyes never left Alex's and he seemed uninterested in his little presentation.

Standing perfectly still, Joel tilted his chin up. "It makes no difference to me what you are or what you think I stole. Charlotte and I are leaving and you will *never* come near her again."

Alex laughed again and crossed his arms, like a man that had nothing to lose. And he didn't. "I'm going to kill your precious *girlfriend*," he said with deliberation. Like I was nothing more than a chess piece. He looked past Joel to me and then back at Joel again. "And your baby."

Any restraint that Joel had so effortlessly managed to hold onto before went right out the window. With a speed and a force that drew the breathe from my lungs, he charged forward and plowed Alex over, the two of them tumbling out the door into the cold white snow.

From where I sat, shocked on the floor, I could see Joel pull his arm up and send his fist into the center of Alex's face.

"Charlotte!" he called back to me. "*Stay inside!*"

Chapter

26

I pressed Alex deeper into the snow as a cold-blooded rage coursed through my body. My grip on his shirt was locked and I raised my fist to punch him again. His face absorbed the blow but not without leaving a mark. His lip was bloody from my first punch and now he had a cut below his left eye. Even with the uppercuts to his face, he wore a twisted smile. He looked as if he'd hardly noticed he'd been hit at all.

"What are you going to do?" he laughed. "Kill me?"

Alex wiped the blood from his lip and spit even more blood from his mouth and onto the snow next to him.

"Don't tempt me," I replied. "I'm going to offer you peace only once more." While I didn't actually believe in the likelihood of peace, I needed to remain true to myself. I needed to remain true to the man that God wanted me to be.

Within only one single beat of my heart, Alex had thrust his knee up into my stomach, knocking the wind out of me. He pushed me off of him, scrambling to his feet. Gasping for air, I translated that as a no. With the possibility of a treaty now gone, I knew that it had to end here. I hadn't expected otherwise but part of me had still hoped that he would meet me somewhere in the middle. I didn't want it to come to this.

From my peripheral, I caught sight of Alex drawing back his leg. In the instant before his foot was about to connect with my face, I grabbed it and pulled him to the ground, landing him on the flat of his back for the second time.

He coughed from the impact and it took a few long moments for the air to reach his lungs again. When we both got up from the ground, snow covering a large percentage of our bodies, we circled one another. In a poorly practiced dance around each other, I tried to gauge where I could hit him that would do the most damage. I wasn't trained in fighting, I didn't even consider myself to be very good at it or likely to win, based only on man-to-man combat skills.

Being a fallen angel gave Alex the upper hand. He wasn't as strong as an angel that remained under God's graces but he wasn't human either. And while he wasn't indestructible, he would be hard to beat. I was merely human, a fact I found myself cursing more often than not. Besides giving me a way to be with Charlotte, it hadn't done much else but cause me aggravation.

"Just give up, angel boy," he growled. "You know you're going to lose."

And maybe if physical strength and fighting skills were all that mattered, he would be right. But they weren't. Alex was missing a very vital weapon: love. While all emotions, lust included, were strong, love was the strongest. And being fallen meant that Alex was in fact incapable of feeling love. And it was love that would ensure that I didn't lose this fight. Because above all other things, above even my own life and desires, I had to ensure that Charlotte and our baby were safe.

My hands were numb from the cold. Or maybe from the impact to Alex's face. I didn't know. But where the cold left off, threatening to weaken me, adrenaline took over. It pumped through my veins and urged me to charge at him again.

We ran at one another, both determined to gain the best angle. We grappled in place for a few long seconds before Alex had managed to push me away. I lost my balance, caught my foot on a protruding branch, and began to tumble down the mountain for a few yards before I was able to plant my feet and stop myself.

I heard the impressions in the snow as Alex made his way over to where I'd landed. As his steps grew closer, I looked up, too late to gain any advantage. Alex had the collar of my jacket in his hand before I had a chance to shuffle out of his reach then he sent me back into the nearly foot-deep snow with a direct punch to my nose and cheek. The pain was sharp and split through my face like an ax. The agony from my already injured skull was no longer drawing the majority of my attention where pain was concerned. The combination of past and present injuries were nearly enough to render me unconscious.

I dabbed the stream of blood that trickled from my nose with the sleeve of my jacket and looked up at Alex. He was a few feet away now and wore a smile that said he'd gained the advantage. I knew that whatever came of this fight, he'd merely won a battle, not the war.

I braced my hands on my knees and pushed myself up from the snow again.

"Don't worry, I'm not going to kill you," he said through tight lips. "You're going to watch while I kill your precious little family." His pause was spiteful. *"Then I'll kill you,"* he spoke to my thoughts.

I charged him then, utilizing every muscle in my body, propelling myself forward. Though he'd anticipated it, he still hadn't been able to dodge me. I took him to the ground at full force, knocking the air from his lungs for the second time, causing him to double over. With the angled mountain under our feet, we fell down the slope in a tangled heap. As we tumbled down the mountain, we separated and I knew that it was imperative that I try and stop myself from sliding any further.

When I got to my feet, shivering and cold, I looked around to place Alex in the landscape. I brushed the snow from my jacket and pants as best as I could. As I searched around me, I didn't see him anywhere and that fact worried me. If his goal was to kill Charlotte, then he could be making his way back up to the cabin.

I worked my way through the snow as best as I could, fighting gravity that pulled at my back and cold that covered my body in pin-pricks and bitterness. Walking past where we'd begun to tumble down the mountain, I noticed a fresh set of tracks that lead into the woods and immediately followed them. I ran through the woods with determination. Was Alex really running away? I had factored in conniving trickery but cowardliness I hadn't considered.

When the tracks broke into a small opening, I slowed down. I followed them around a turn, realizing with surprise that they lead to the end of a drop-off that not even a fallen angel could survive. I stepped closer, being sure to keep my footing sturdy and peered over to look for Alex's mangled body. Nothing.

Then, clearly timed with my arrival at the location, I heard hard foot steps behind me. I calculated their timing and distance as best as I could and side stepped just as Alex's hand grazed my arm in an attempted push. But instead, he was the one careening toward the base of the cliff. As if in slow motion, I watched as he lost his footing and ran out of earth below his feet. He grappled for the roots that stuck out like lifelines from the overhang and I heard the abrupt smack of his body against the wall of the cliff as he managed to grab one. With a low moan, I could hear him over the lip of the cliff, making his way up again.

I walked to the edge and noticed that he was having a hard time getting up. His grip was weak from sending his fist into my face and his body was equally weakened. He looked up at me and said nothing, turning to look away again and try and manage a way up from his vulnerable position. But the rock protruded at the top of the cliff, leaving a concave mountain side and no way for him to use it to his advantage.

I couldn't watch him struggle and die without offering a chance at redemption. It wasn't in me to let a man die. I got down to the ground and pressed my body to the snow, giving myself leverage and anchoring myself to the mountain.

"Give me your hand," I called down.

Alex looked up in shock. Blood trailed down his face and snow soaked his clothes. He looked defeated and I couldn't help but pity him. I didn't know what he had been through. I was unfamiliar with the mentality he'd adopted that made it so easy for him to hurt others in order to obtain what he wanted. But I knew the look in his eyes. The look of failure and remorse.

"Why would you help me?" he choked. "If you let me fall then all will be right with the world."

"It's not in me to let you die," I said outright.

"Hell is just a short drop away." I could hear the sacrifice in his voice. "It's what I deserve."

"You don't have to be the man that fell from heaven." I could see in his eyes that Alex fought internally over who he was and what he'd done. Feelings he'd been propelled by. Feelings I knew personally to have strength enough to weaken a man.

"If I get up, if I live through this, I *will* kill you. I will take Charlotte as my own and I will do whatever it takes to keep her." I could actually detect remorse in his tone, it was the only reason I didn't let him drop once he'd said the words.

Alex clenched his teeth against pain. "I don't deserve her. I know I don't. But I've given up everything I had for her. That will never change. I can't live in her world and be a better man."

I was surprised by the honesty in his voice, the sorrow, and the self-loathing that coated his every word.

"Good-bye, brother. You deserve her." And without another word he let go and disappeared into the fog covered canyon of rocks below.

I moved away from the edge slowly. Propped up in a squat, I remained motionless and replayed the scene in my head again and again. Had he really sacrificed himself? I couldn't comprehend it. Sacrifice wasn't a sign of lust but love.

Part of me hoped that his change of heart had earned him a better future than that of one spent in an eternity of purgatory.

Chapter

27

From the moment that Joel had ordered me to stay inside, I'd been fighting the urge to follow him anyway. In the end, I'd stayed inside, avoiding the windows and the sounds that came from just beyond the glass. Had I gone out after them, I would have only acted as a distraction. I would render Joel vulnerable while simultaneously offering myself up as a tool to bargain with. Neither was something I wanted to be responsible for.

I had paced the room at least a hundred times since they'd left the cabin. In my hands I held the poker from the fireplace. I was trembling with fear but I needed to try and keep myself still. If Alex was the one to breech the doorway then I needed to be ready for him.

Tears had tracked in thick lines down my face and my heart beat a mile a minute. Every noise, every suggestion of life outside of the cabin, made me jump. I'd tested many angles of where to stand or hide. I'd even considered running for it but I found myself in the center of the room again. The warmth of the fire set me at ease and it seemed that with Alex, hiding wouldn't be in my best interest anyway. The last thing I wanted was to be cornered.

Seeing Alex walk through the door had sadly been the outcome I was inclined to prepare myself for. I had no idea what he was capable of as a fallen angel. Could he die? Was his strength unmatched? Were his powers of deception greater than what I'd experienced? I had no idea. All I knew was that I'd already lost Joel too many times to satisfy myself with the idea that it might finally be over. That we were actually safe.

When I heard the doorknob to the front door turn, a shiver coursed through me. I lifted the fire poker up with both hands, pointing it at the entrance. My legs were braced to prevent myself from toppling over, they just couldn't seem to stop shaking.

The door opened slowly and Joel drug himself inside on exhausted legs. I immediately dropped the iron rod and ran over to him, wrapping my arms around his neck. He groaned slightly but hugged me past his pain. He rested his tired head on my shoulder and inhaled my scent as if to confirm that we were really together again.

He moved us slowly into the cabin and shut the door behind him. Wordlessly, we made our way closer to the stoked fire. I wanted to fuss over his bruised and battered face but I resisted. His knuckles were raw and red, his clothes soaked to the bone. I found myself thankful that I hadn't decided to be stubborn and follow him outside. What had happened to him, how the fight had ended, they were all details I was happy I wouldn't have to see flash across my eyelids at night.

"Is…" I whispered into his ear, unable to finish the question out loud. I helped him shrug off his jacket and he slipped out of his soaked shoes.

"It's over," he said in confirmation.

I swallowed hard and couldn't believe that we'd seen the last of this seemingly endless threat. Part of me wanted to know what exactly had happened to Alex. I wanted to know how close Joel had come to being the one to say good-bye forever. But by the hollow look in his eyes, I could tell that he was fighting with something inside himself. He didn't want to talk about what had happened. I knew in time he would eventually tell me everything, that I would know the truth, but for now I was content in knowing that he was safe and in my arms.

We stayed in the cabin for an hour or so more. Joel dried his clothes by the fire and we sat huddled together beneath a quilt I'd found in the small bedroom. With a long trek down the mountain and an even longer drive ahead of us, neither of us was too eager to get back just yet.

"I don't think he deserves to go to hell," I heard him say after a nearly endless bout of silence.

"*What?*" I would have argued his statement further but I was more interested on why he'd said it. After everything Alex had done, why did Joel think he deserved anything less than an eternity in hell?

"Before..." he paused. "There was something in his eyes. I could see that he was struggling to do the right thing. That he was fighting to be a better man against everything he'd done."

"Well, clearly he wasn't a better man," I argued with a tone of bitterness. "Otherwise you wouldn't have killed him."

"I didn't kill him," Joel replied.

My heart raced. "What do you *mean* you didn't kill him?" I turned to look at him. "So he's still out there? Plotting his next move?"

"He killed himself," he replied solemnly, eyes fixed on the crackling logs of the fire.

Oh.

My heart sank. Alex killed himself? The concept brinked on insanity. He'd been so determined, so dedicated, and so unrelenting that giving up that way seemed unreal. It was an outcome I hadn't expected. Now I could see where Joel was coming from. I hadn't wanted for Alex to die. All I'd wanted was for this living nightmare to be over. And in the end, he'd been the one to grant me that wish.

"Everything he's done has brought us together," I said with astonishment. "Brought us to this moment."

I hadn't considered it before but it was true. If it hadn't been for Alex having drugged me at the bar. If it hadn't been for the case against Matt, even the gun shot that sent Joel into a coma. All of it had granted us a life together that we wouldn't have had otherwise.

Joel kissed my forehead wordlessly and I could tell that he was feeling the same gratitude that I was. After everything that had transpired, no matter what happened next, we had been granted the one thing we truly cared about: our love, without restraints or limitations.

When Joel's clothes were finally dry and we'd both summoned enough strength to get up off of the floor, we made our way through the cabin. After putting out the fire, he took his coat and draped it over my shoulders.

"Won't you be cold?" I protested as he reached for the door knob.

"I'll be fine," he insisted.

In one quick motion, Joel had me cradled in his arms and walked us out into the cold mid-day air. The sun was warm on our faces but the temperature was still dangerously low.

"You can't possibly carry me the whole way down the mountain." But Joel kept walking.

He walked through old tracks, the ones I imagined he'd left on his way to the cabin. Then from what sounded like a very close distance, I heard heavy breathing and scrambled up into Joel's arms. My heartbeat quickened and I tugged on his shirt.

"Joel, there's something out there." Unwavering, he kept walking.

I ducked my head into his neck and peered up through the collar of his shirt as the strange sounds got closer. As we walked around a large pile of stacked wood and a thick tree line, I saw a big and beautiful black horse tied to one of the tree trunks.

"You rode *that* up here?" I said in bewilderment. "I guess you're growing rather fond of mustangs of all varieties," I joked.

Joel hoisted me up onto the horse's broad back. "About the Mustang," he said, hooking a foot into the stirrup and hoisting himself up behind me. "I think that Trigger's seen his final days."

"Oh no," I breathed. The gash above Joel's eye. Alex's plan to get rid of him. "You crashed the Mustang?"

He took the reins and edged the horse forward. "Don't worry, I'll make good on my deal."

"What deal?"

"One Chevy Camaro named Joel, comin' right up."

I had forgotten about my threat the first time Joel had driven Trigger. On our way to go back to the club to find out more about Matt, I'd told him that if anything happened to the Mustang while he was driving it, he would have to replace it with a Camaro. He had smartly retorted that he would only do so if I named the car Joel.

"Very funny," I replied. That was one deal neither of us could afford to pay up on.

* * *

I shouldn't have been shocked. I should have known that this dream sequence that had taken up residence in my reality had only just started to work its magic. But my jaw remained dropped as Joel ducked out of the jet black Camaro he'd parked in Trigger's old spot.

"It's a rental," I insisted.

"If you want to loan it out to your friends that's up to you," he said, tossing me the keys.

I caught them in my hand and smiled at the wing charm attached to the key ring. *Joel* was engraved on the back.

"Pretentious aren't we?"

"It was part of the deal," he argued, flashing an easy smile.

I walked over to the car with the heavy weight of the keys in my hand. I ran my hand over the hood and smiled at the sleek black paint. As I took the door handle in my hand I looked up. "How can you afford this?"

He shrugged and a smile washed over his face. "I want to take you somewhere," he said, reaching his hand out. "Do you mind if I drive?"

As eager as I was to drive *my new car,* I was even more excited at the idea of what else Joel had up his sleeve. I tossed the keys his way and made my way around to the passenger's side. "What are you up to?"

"I'd like to make up for missing out on our dinner date."

A few weeks had passed since the night at the cabin and I had completely forgotten that we'd even had plans. The last few weeks had been hectic with doctor's appointments and finally managing to sit Tara down and explain things to her. Lucky for me, Joel had been by my side for the whole thing and, though I could tell that she was still hurt, I knew it wasn't because of me anymore but Alex. She said that she'd suspected that he'd been stringing her along but she'd avoided all of the signs. I couldn't blame her. I had avoided the signs too.

We hardly had time to reschedule our dinner date, in fact, it seemed silly to even try now. We were so busy with other things.

As Joel drove, I realized that we weren't going towards town but away from it. "Where are you taking me?" I asked, sure I wouldn't get a straight answer. "Aren't we going to dinner?"

"Have we really ever been the couple that goes out to dinner, Charlotte?" he said with a laugh.

"You've got a point there. So where are we going then?"

"You'll see soon enough." He placed a warm hand over mine and brought it to his lips for a kiss. While he was playing everything rather smoothly, I could actually detect a bit of nervousness in the way that he kept his eyes forward. It made me even more curious as to where we were headed.

A few minutes later, Joel pulled up along the side of the road next to the park we'd walked through the first day of the case, before I knew what he was. It felt like years ago now.

He put the car in park and got out. "Why don't you wait on one of the benches," he prompted. "I'm going to go pick out a dog to walk."

"Wow, this brings back memories," I beamed. "Pick one that looks especially lonely," I added, knowing that he would anyway.

As Joel walked towards the shelter, I made my way through the entrance of the park. The snow had cleared, leaving surprisingly green grass to either side of the path. The aged blue benches didn't stand out as much with the white carpet of snow gone but they still held their own in the beautiful surroundings. I sat down on the closest bench and crossed my legs at the ankle. I breathed in the scent of spring and welcomed the feel of the warm sun on my face. In only a few weeks, the weather had undergone a drastic change and I was certain we had seen the last snow for the season.

"You look picturesque," I heard Joel say a few minutes later.

I looked up and smiled. "Drover, it's always a pleasure." I got up from the bench and knelt down to greet the friendly brindle mastiff we'd walked the first time we'd been to the shelter. "I can't believe he's still here." I ruffed up his ears and looked up at Joel when I noticed a bright red bow amongst the dog's wrinkled fur. "What's this?"

"I busted him out for good," he said with a proud smile.

"You *adopted* him?"

"Seeing as how we're both allergic to cats, and neither of us has had a dog before, I figured he would be a nice addition to the family."

I sat back on the bench and pressed my face into Drovers fur and couldn't help but agree. As I hugged his neck, I felt a hard box slide beneath my fingers, attached to the ribbon around his neck.

"What is this?"

As I met his eyes, Joel was lowering to rest on one knee and my heart caught in my throat.

"Charlotte, I'd once considered myself lucky for having the honor of serving as your guardian. It was a job that I performed with great pride and I cherished every minute that I got to watch you grow into the beautiful, fearless, and intelligent woman you are today. A woman that stands for something…a woman that I fell deeply and madly in love with."

My eyes burned with happy tears and I swiped them away as he continued.

"I know that our life together has been dangerously unplanned and crazy from the moment we first met in the club that night." He took a ring from the box around Drover's neck and presented it to me. "The question is, do you want to live a crazy life with me?"

I couldn't find words. All I could manage was an enthusiastic nod. I smiled and cried again as he slipped the beautifully flawless ring onto my finger. He stood up and lifted me into his arms, swinging me around in a small circle.

When he let me down, I ran a hand over my tear clad cheek again. I looked over to the car and back to Joel. "How are we going to get Drover home in that?" I laughed.

He made an expression that said that he hadn't planned that far ahead.

Epilogue

I fell back into the freshly fallen snow and began to wave my arms and legs. "Like this," I said, pushing the snow further out around me.

Joel lay down beside me and did the same, the hands of our snow angels touched as if to hold hands.

"I wanna twy!" Chloe said, plopping down beside Joel. "Daddy, can I twy?" Her bright green eyes glowed brightly with excitement and her dark hair fell down in ringlets around her face.

"Of course you can," he replied with a smile.

I sat up in the imprint of my snow angel and watched as Chloe flapped her arms and legs from side to side. Joel sat up in his own indent and watched her with a smile so wide nothing on earth could rival its majesty. As he watched her, he lit up in a way I still hadn't managed to get used to.

After all we'd been through together, we could finally take comfort in knowing that life would be much simpler from here on out. As if to confirm the idea, Drover plodded over and licked Chloe's face gently. She giggled and squirmed in an effort to escape his slobbery kisses, knocking into the edges of her angel as she did so.

"Come, Drover," Joel called out.

Drover complied and trotted over to Joel who slipped a treat from his pocket and threw it a few feet away. Drover pounced after the treat, digging his muzzle into the soft snow to uncover his reward.

"Daddy," Chloe protested. "Dover made me weck my snow angew."

"It's okay," he replied with a smile. "Look over there, there's a nice fresh patch of snow for you to make another one."

Chloe steadied herself, thickly insolated by her winter coat and pants, making movement very difficult, and stood up in her imprint then made her way delicately over to the section of unmarked snow. As she trucked through the snow, I got up and moved to sit beside Joel. I leaned into his side and took his hand in mine. I admired the wedding band wrapped around his ring finger and the charmed bracelet that poked out of his jacket sleeve on the same hand. No matter how many times I pinched myself or how many times I closed my eyes to fall asleep at night, expecting to wake up to a different life, this was my reality. I had actually managed to reach out and grab too-good-to-be-true.

I looked up at Joel, who was now smiling warmly down at me. I couldn't help but smile too. His face was coated in a six o'clock shadow he'd willingly embraced in recent years but apart from that he hadn't changed a bit.

"What?" he asked before kissing my forehead. "You look deep in thought again." Reading my expressions regularly, a skill he would seemingly never give up.

"I was just wondering what we should do for Chloe's third birthday. It's kind of a big deal for her, don't you think?"

He tilted his head and suggested that he doubted that it was actually what I'd been thinking. But in truth, I had been wondering about it at one point in the day. Maybe it was brief but it *had* happened.

"It's the first one she might actually have a chance of remembering," I added, emphasizing my point.

"She's turning three; kids barely remember anything before the age of five," he argued.

"I beg to differ," I said, poking him in the chest. He knew as well as I did that what he'd said had been proven wrong years ago by yours truly. "Besides—"

"Mommy, Daddy, come hewp!" We both looked up to see Chloe propping herself up in her snow angel. "I don't wanna mess it up, can you get me out?"

We both got up from sitting in the thick snow and made our way to her. Joel headed over and took hold of her little snow boots while I took a firm grip on her mitten clad hands.

"Ready?" Joel asked?

"Ready," I replied.

"One…" he began. "Two…three."

On three, we both lifted and moved carefully away from the imprint with our daughter laughing and wiggling, spread out between our hands. When we were a safe distance from the angel, Joel eased her feet into the snow and when she had her footing, I let go of her hands as well.

Like a full-grown adult, Chloe walked to the edge of her imprint with her hands propped up on her hips to observe the final product of her hard work. I had to cover my mouth with my hand to keep from laughing. Sometimes she took herself so seriously it was like looking in the mirror.

"What do you girls say to some hot chocolate?"

Chloe turned around wearing a wide smile. "With candy canes and marshmewows?"

Joel laughed easily. "If you'd like."

She clapped her hands with excitement. "Yes pwease!"

I made my way over and took her hand in mine and Joel wrangled up Drover to head back into the house. They both caught up quickly to Chloe and I, and we walked through the yard together. Joel looped a hand behind my back and kissed my forehead.

As we made our way into the house Chloe turned around and crossed her arms over her chest. Looking off in the direction of her imprint she said, "Come on, Awex!"

My breath caught in my throat and I thought, *it couldn't possibly be*...I turned to Joel and he wore a similar look of shock on his face. Chloe was quickly at our side again, dancing and flapping her arms in the air like wings.

Acknowledgements

First, I would like to thank my husband, David…for coming home safely! I'm happy to say that this book was only *started* during his deployment. Thanks to all of the help, brutal honesty, and support he gave along the way. When it would have been easier to tell me what I wanted to hear, he told me what I *needed* to hear and really helped me create a better story. And also for putting up with the craziness that was *me* during the first few editing stages of both *Volition* and *Severance*.

To Erika, my twinster, for the endless support and shared excitement about this series. She expressed so much pride during my writing and never stopped believing in my ability to write a good story. Even with her own crazy life, she expected to receive an e-mail of every chapter as I wrote it, giving her feedback and praise along the way. And I hope that she knows I intend to do the same with her and her writing.

To my parents, for their support and guidance. I don't know who I would be without them. Throughout my life, I've felt honored by their pride and encouragement to follow my heart and reach for the stars, something I would like to think I'll never stop doing. With all the bitterness that the world has to offer, my parents have guided me through it, pointing me in the direction of success and happiness.

A special thanks in particular to my amazing mom. She agreed to have me send the proof of *Severance* to her for editing. With limited resources while living in Germany for the past two years, I've turned to my mom and sister for a great deal of support. They have both been amazing, giving insight and editing the series. I received an edited copy of my proof in the mail thanks to my mom's tedious efforts. And for that, I am truly blessed. Between her grammatical help and Erika's help with the storyline, I contribute a great deal of this story's success to them.

Thank you also to Isha Greene for tackling *Severance* with the same excitement she did with *Volition*. I don't know what I would have done without her enthusiasm for this story. Without her questions and curiosity, *Severance* would probably have fallen very short of the book that it is today.

And to Tori Gruber, my BEEF, for the endless support, even in distance. It was hard saying goodbye, but alas, that's what the military life is all about. But I know that I have made a friend for life who supports me and my dreams in a way I could never have asked for.

And to all of my great friends who have supported my writing and helped with spreading the word and encouraging others to check out my novels. Without the endless support of my friends, those I know well and those I wish I knew better, I might never have had the confidence to continue writing this series or the novels that followed.

About the Author

Shawn Maravel is a devoted Army wife who makes her home wherever the Army sends her husband. She has lived overseas in Germany and is currently stationed in Upstate New York and looks forward to seeing where the tide will take them next.

A New Jersey native, she enjoys spending her summers on the beach and curling up with a good book.

Shawn's other works include: *Volition, The Wanderer, and Shifting Gears.*

15702935R00146

Made in the USA
Charleston, SC
16 November 2012